PENGUIN BOOKS

Sole Survivor

Maurice Gee is a New Zealander who lives in Nelson with his wife and two daughters. He writes adult fiction, children's fiction, and television scripts. *Sole Survivor* is the third and final novel in the 'Plumb' sequence; this began with *Plumb* (1978), which won the New Zealand Fiction Award, the Buckland Award, the Wattie Book of the Year Award, and the James Tait Black Memorial Prize, and was followed by *Meg* (1981; Penguin, 1983), which won the New Zealand Book Award for Fiction. He has also published *The Big Season*, *A Special Flower*, *In My Father's Den* and *Games of Choice*.

MAURICE GEE
Sole Survivor

PENGUIN BOOKS

Penguin Books Ltd, Harmondsworth, Middlesex, England
Penguin Books, 40 West 23rd Street, New York, New York 10010, U.S.A.
Penguin Books Australia Ltd, Ringwood, Victoria, Australia
Penguin Books Canada Ltd, 2801 John Street, Markham, Ontario, Canada L3R 1B4
Penguin Books (N.Z.) Ltd, 182–190 Wairau Road, Auckland 10, New Zealand

First published by Faber and Faber Ltd, 1983 in association with Penguin (N.Z.) Ltd
Published in Penguin Books 1984

Copyright © Maurice Gee, 1983
All rights reserved

Filmset in Plantin (Linotron 202) by
Rowland Phototypesetting Ltd,
Bury St Edmunds, Suffolk
Made and printed in Great Britain by
Cox & Wyman Ltd, Reading

Except in the United States of America, this book is sold subject
to the condition that it shall not, by way of trade or otherwise, be lent,
re-sold, hired out, or otherwise circulated without the
publisher's prior consent in any form of binding or cover other than
that in which it is published and without a similar condition
including this condition being imposed on the subsequent purchaser

I

This morning I watched my niece and her cousin making love in the river. I was walking on a track by the Aorere in Golden Bay and they were in the shallows of a pool that plunged down in mid-river thirty feet, drowning blocks of stone as large as houses. It was getting on for noon. I was sweating from my walk and needed a breather. But I would have stopped even if I'd been running to catch a train. That is not a confession to be ashamed of. I can't imagine anyone walking on. I'm careful with the word but I say without hesitation that Jilly and Hank were beautiful.

And I had come from my talk with John Jolly, Jolly John. I needed something to take my mind off that. John had found me with a telegram. My face throbbed as I read it, I swelled with anger. *Ha gotcher. Ring me soonest. Clink clink. J. J.* Clink clink meant there was money in it for me. I did not need money. I did not need work or Wellington or telegrams that threatened while pretending cheeriness. Soonest! I let him stew two days. Then I took Sharon's shopping list and a sack of returnable tonic water bottles and set off for Collingwood. I turned into the loop path and stopped at the Gypsy Trailer to see if Jilly and Hank wanted anything. Jilly, as usual, ignored me. 'No thanks, Uncle Ray,' Hank sang in his Yankee falsetto. He was tacking opened-out plastic bags over the windows of their saucer. *Golden Grain Fibre Bread* said the sheet he was fixing. I wondered what the Venusians would make of that. Jilly painted *Gilgamesh* on the prow. Neat little letters. She was a neat little girl.

'Would you like me to bring a bottle of fizz for the launching?'

She must have murmured her opinion of me to Hank for he patted her and gave his squeaky laugh. They were, I thought, marvellous to look at; in their surfaces and joints; but a disappointment in most other ways. They had, though, purpose and certainty. One can only laugh at them for a while. I went off defeated down the track.

In Collingwood the tide was in. I drove up the narrow road by the fishing boats and rickety jetties and stood outside the pub admiring the town. It has a hick-town seediness, the kind of distillation of minimized aims – and, I imagined, crooked desires. It belongs more to its rednecks than the commune and craft and simple-life folk who have come in lately. I feel threatened in its main street and listen for rumours of incest and of lynchings.

Talking to Jolly John blew that away: city air. He demanded a profile of Douglas Plumb. 'One of your clever pieces. Bography-cum-hatchet job. In a velvet glove. In view of what's happening.'

'What's happening?'

'Come on Raymie, don't play games. All that country air has made you dull.'

'I like dull. I haven't read a paper in three weeks. Or heard a radio.'

'Stop being boastful. The TV news –'

'We don't have TV. So what's with Duggie? Someone assassinated him?'

'Would that they had. No, he's making his move. He's let it be known etcetera. Willing to serve. In the interests of the party. No personal ambitions, mind.'

'Did he talk about the fall of the Roman Empire?'

'The fall of Singapore.'

'Ha!'

'Is that all you can say?'

'That and no. I'm out of the bography business. And the Duggie Plumb business. How did you find me?'

'No one knows him like you, Raymie.'

'Don't call me that.'

'Sorry. Raymong.'

'Or Raymong.'

'If you do this for me R. Sole I'll call you Ray for ever.'

Jolly John going down with his guns all firing. We argued away, and I had the last word: no.

'How did you find me?'

'Your cretin brother phoned. I told him Raymond Sole doesn't work here any more. His guess was you'd be at your daughter's place.'

'What did he want?'

'His runaway little girl. His good-kid-really-in-spite-of-everything. Thought you might put your ear to the ground. He's coming to see you.'

I drove ten miles down the Aorere, sweated across the paddocks with my sack of groceries, and came on Bobby's little girl making love with her cousin in the river. Her second cousin, let me get that straight. But I'm an old ex-puritan and ex-family-freak. I caught a brimstone whiff and mounted on my toes to thunderbolt them. Then I saw that what they made was beautiful. My aesthetic sense is not always in good order. On this occasion it saved me from foolishness. I watched, admiring, breathless. They were like figures on a vase. Behind them pool, translucent; blocks of stone tumbled in green water. He stood thigh-deep and she was locked on him. She was slick as a seal, seal-head gleaming. Her sodden hair lay spade-shaped on her back. Their bodies glistened. His bony Pilgrim-father hands were cupped under her buttocks, pulling her in. He rocked a little, bounced with a water-supported finesse, providing their motion. Soon it was not enough. Jilly unlocked her arms. They joined hands, hooked their bones, and began a good old-fashioned in and out, working with tensed arms and elbows concertina'd. Jilly arched her back. Her hair went splash splash splash in leaden lumps. The crown of her head dipped in the water. Hank was solid, a post. She worked against him. Still I did not feel like a voyeur. She gave a cry when she came, like a child at the top of a Ferris wheel.

He let her float a moment, then drew her up and hugged her. They kissed long. Then she backed off him with a school-gymnasium jump and knelt up to her armpits in the water. To me his penis seemed out of proportion, not unnatural so much as extravagant. I was surprised to see Jilly so familiar with it. She changed its angle to suit her and took it in her mouth.

Now I was more than admiring, so it was time to go. I did not want to but I was ashamed. My vision, if I can call it that, was over. This was what Duggie Plumb called going down town for lunch. Hank had his hands on Jilly's head, making her go faster. Greedy devil, I thought, full of envy. But when he saw me I winked encouragement. I swung my sack on my shoulders and trudged on up the path.

Sharon was digging in her garden, bare to the waist. She put her T-shirt on when she saw me coming. Carlo had made a road for his truck up the side of a tomato row. 'Brmm, brmm,' he said.

I put down the groceries and pulled my fingers straight. 'I'm not fit.'

'Grab a spade,' Sharon said.

'I'll take these up. I got everything.'

'Did you see Hank and Jilly? They were heading for town.'

'They're in the river.'

'What doing?' She looked at me sharply. 'They'd do it up trees if they could.'

I crossed the garden – 'Grandpa, you trod on my bridge,' Carlo wailed – let myself through the possum fence and climbed the bush path to the house. Sharon worries me. She claims to be happy but she is not happy. She claims to have got her life all sorted out, but is full of badly-hidden discontents. Hostilities make her tongue an iron spike. She whacks her tomahawk into a pumpkin, splits it like a head. But later her face seems to bloom, she breathes in deeply, slows all her movements down – and though she does not say so I know that *now* she's happy. It's almost as if she has taken a shot of some drug; but it isn't that, she leaves that to Hank and Jilly. She knows some secret but cannot always find it when she wants. I do not try to help. That's not my role. A parent can only keep on loving; be around when he's wanted, make himself scarce when he's not.

Instead of going back to help her I set the table for lunch. She meant to pass the rest of her life in this place, drawing her benefit, growing food in her garden. Desi, her man, was booted out. 'I couldn't stand him any longer. Boohooing round the place. One kid's enough.' She let him get the compost privy finished, then sent him down the road. 'He's not Carlo's father anyway.' She doesn't only worry me, she scares me. She's one of this new breed of women that cuts the balls off rapists; or rapes men. And I bred her, with a little help from Glenda. Sharon, the pre-schooler who had wanted to marry Daddy: now she would let me stay a while, as long as I didn't get under her feet.

I went outside and sat in the sun. Knuckles of hill stood behind me, bushed up to the skyline. South were Mount Olympus and Lead Hills, reddish-brown. The Heaphy Track started round to the right: three days walking to the Tasman Sea. I had sunned myself like this for several weeks, through Jan. into Feb. and my hairy paunch had a yellow patina. Lovely sun, I thought, lovely silence; and wondered why I was half-hearted about them. Not just those children in the river, those golden ninnies. I grew randy thinking of them, and told myself, Come on, you're fifty. And fifty was the age of Douglas Plumb.

Yes, Douglas Plumb. In spite of my claim to be finished with him Duggie sat squarely in my mind – always had, always will. Cousin Duggie. How could I hope to ignore his 'move'? He was like a wart on my palm or flea in my crotch.

So I drank two cans of beer and made myself sleepy. A helicopter flew by with a policeman hanging out of the door looking for marijuana gardens. I waved at him. Soon I fell into a doze. 'You lazy old bugger,' Sharon said, clunking down her spade. I jumped up guiltily. An empty can rolled off my chest and she belted it, killed it stone dead. That seemed to make her happy.

'Get my tonic water?'
'Yes. I set the table.'
'Good for you. Your phone call go all right?'
'He wants me to write a profile on Douglas Plumb.'
'That pig.'
'He's trying for Muldoon's job.'
'Another pig. Are you going to do it?'
'No.'
'What are you going to do?'
'Stay here a while. Dig in your garden.'
'Huh!'
'John told me Bobby's coming down. Your uncle Bob.'
'Pig number three. What does he want?'
'He thinks I might know where to find Jilly.'
'In the river. Did that upset you?'
'It made me envious. We didn't do things like that when I was young. "Sexual intercourse began in nineteen sixty-three." That's a quote.'

'Don't you start. Desi kept on Hesseing me and this lot keeps Von Danikin away and God knows what. Think some thoughts of your own.'

This lot, Hank and Jilly, joined us for lunch. Jilly's hair was plastered on her skull, bunned on her neck. She was like a weasel and would have loved a free bite at my throat. Beautiful in the river, ugly now. I turned that about and found no answer.

'Speak up, Jilly.'

She tore a crust instead. Her nose was white with anger, a little icy peak in her brown face.

'I was on a public path.'

'You didn't have to stop.' Her teeth made an ugly wound in a tomato and I heard her mutter, 'Dirty old pervert.'

'Wrong three times, my dear. I wash a lot. I'm very clean. And I'm only middle-aged. I don't expect young people to know the difference. And what I am is curious not perverted. I thought you were beautiful in the river. I went away when it got too interesting.'

Sharon giggled. I make these locutions to amuse her and am pleased that I can still succeed with them. But our exchange made Jilly angrier. 'I'm not going to be old. I'll kill myself when I'm twenty-five.'

'It used to be twenty. But of course, you're getting close. And Hank's twenty-two.' I smiled at her. 'Things will be better on Venus.'

'Everyone over twenty-five is dead.'

'I'm over twenty-five,' Sharon said.

'Jilly's a bit spaced out,' Hank said.

We exchanged sly grins. Masculine stuff. But what a child he is, this New England boy. There's puppy fat on his face; and an incredible innocence in his voice, though he's as amoral as a rabbit and foxy in his dealings with his elders. He's the grandson of my mother's sister Agnes, who fled the crazy Plumbs to San Francisco and married an engineer, Gerry Lerhke. Their son went east, lost himself on the teeming seaboard, and thirty years later Hank Lerhke stood on my brother's doorstep: bare feet and beads, rucksack and guitar. Bobby asked him in, there was no way round it.

Jilly's tomato squirted on my wrist. That pleased her. She's no child, though young enough to be at school. Sharon, in one of those intimacies that break me up by the ease with which they subsume our past, took my hand and licked off the seeds.

'You two are in trouble.'

'Why?'

'Your father's on his way. He's probably got his shotgun in the car.'

Jilly went pale with fright. Then she was beautiful, with eyes gone mad and tilted chin. She was my mother. 'How did he find out? You rang him, Ray. By God – by God –'

'Jilly,' Hank cried. He was too late. She threw her tomato at me. It struck me on the cheek. Modern times are too much for me. I felt like crying. Associations are too much. I had seen my mother, saw her still.

Sharon handed me a cloth. 'You two can clear out of the trailer. I need it for Dad.'

'Ah, Sharon,' Hank began.

'Stuff it, Hank. Don't crawl to them. We're going anyway. And not coming back. So fuck my father.' She ran out.

'Jilly cross,' Carlo said.

'I'll say.' Sharon stroked his hair.

'We were going to leave,' Hank said. He made a little bow in his New World way and thanked Sharon for having them so long.

'Flying out in your saucer?' I asked.

His clear-eyed look made me feel ashamed. 'It's been swell knowing you, Uncle Ray.' I thought his whistling sad as he went to the trailer, but soon the bush made it indifferent.

Sharon washed the dishes and I dried. 'I'll be pleased to see the back of them,' she said.

'Are they really going to fly? In that thing?'

'They're on a grid intersection. It makes a force field. That's what they fly in.'

'Are we allowed to watch?'

'Might as well. It's something to do.' She was sour again. She put Carlo down for his nap and lay on her bed. 'Close that door.'

'Yes, dear.' It was like being married. I pottered round the kitchen and the shed. I had not been lonely here but now I was lonely. Sharon and Carlo were sleeping. Hank and Jilly were in the trailer, smoking pot and sniffing amyl nitrite. And here I was, Raymong Sole, wondering how to fill the afternoon.

After a while I fetched my exercise book: the one I'd bought in Collingwood after talking to Jolly John.

2

Sharon and I crept out in the dusk to watch Hank and Jilly fly away. We each had a glass of her boysenberry wine, made drinkable with tonic water, and we sat in the bush by the saucer, whispering back and forth. She was happy again; slowed down, rounded out. She leaned on my shoulder. I put my arm around her.

'What do you do when you lock yourself in the bedroom?'

'Meditate.'

'Ah. Here's to the Maharishi.'

'I don't need him.'

'It does more for you than pot does for Hank and Jilly.'

'I don't need that either. I'm glad they're going.'

'Did you mean it when you said I could have the trailer?'

'If you want it.'

'I do.'

'I might have someone coming into the house.'

'A new man?'

I felt her smiling on my shoulder. 'Good old Dad. Interested. Do you think you'll ever get yourself a new woman?'

'One day. One day I might.'

She yawned and dozed a while until wine spilled on her leg. 'I'd better get back. Carlo wakes sometimes.'

'Here they come.'

Hank and Jilly walked hand in hand out from the trailer. They had not dressed for travel. As far as I could make out Hank was in his overalls and Jilly in one of her wrap-around 'ethnic' skirts. She had plaited her hair. He helped her into *Gilgamesh* in a gentlemanly way. Its timbers creaked.

'Fuck,' Jilly said. 'I've torn my dress.'

Hank pulled the cardboard hatches down. Then a bush silence fell. Insect hummings grew in it and faded out of hearing. Sharon went to sleep. I heard my stomach rumble. I was feeling foolish and wanted to shout derisively; but remembered that I'd been around and nothing got me worked up any more. A match flared behind the plastic bags. They were smoking Golden Bay green in there, waiting for power to concentrate and lift them away.

Sharon woke and gave a sigh. 'I dreamed they were floating like one of Mum's mobiles.' She pecked my cheek. 'Come in quietly.'

I sat in the bush and sipped my wine; felt my blood coursing silkily; and felt a dread grow on me until I had an arterial thump in my joints and prickle in my fingertips. I seemed to hear a humming from deep space. The night was velvety and the stars were bright. Mount Haidinger, up north, crouched like a cat. Forces were in the air, invisible. I felt them lapping round my face like water. And surely in the clearing was a dreadful hole in nature – Hank and Jilly sucked up into nothing.

The bush can make a man believe anything. I got to my feet and crashed around like a boar. 'Jilly. Hank. Are you in there?'

The hatch sprang up against the sky. Jilly arched out and spat at me. Hank squeezed up in front of her. His voice seemed to come from her belly. 'Uncle Ray, they won't come while you're here.'

'Oh,' I said, 'I'll get to bed then. Bon voyage.' I trudged back to the house and got into my sleeping bag. I stayed awake for a while, my heart knocking, but heard no humming, saw no brilliant lights. In the morning Hank and Jilly were gone. A stubbed-out joint lay on the nursery stool that served as a pilot's seat in *Gilgamesh*. Jilly's clothes, Hank's guitar and book or two were missing from the trailer. I walked down to the river and looked over the paddocks. Their van was gone.

'Good riddance,' Sharon said.

We worked among her beans and gooseberries. In the afternoon I cleaned out the trailer. It has yellow wheels and green sides and an overhanging roof with an iron chimney. There's a double bunk inside, a Tilley lamp, a small pot-bellied stove, a table and chair, crockery, cutlery, a pot, a pan, an enamel basin for washing up. I saw I would be happy there. No water. But I would fetch that in a bucket from Sharon's tank. I would grow a beard, bathe in the river, and be a little dirty in the winter. As for calls of nature, I had peed in preserving jars before. And Desi had dug a long-drop in the bush.

I swept the floor. I cleaned the stove. I carried Jilly's love-stained sheets round to Sharon's for washing. There Bobby found us; panting up from his rental car, with a king-sized bottle of *Wilson's* held like a club.

'Ah, Bobby. John told me you'd be coming.'

'Stuffed. Rooted. 'Scuse, Sharon. Let me get my breath.' He collapsed on the divan. 'Places people live. Jilly here? I'm looking for my girl.' Beetroot red. I thought he might have a stroke.

'Beer?' I got him a can from the fridge.

'Thanks.' He guzzled it. 'Saved my life. Is Jilly here?'

'She was, Uncle Bobby, but she's gone,' Sharon said.

I told him all about it and Bobby began to cry. He made deep gulping noises, oop, oop; then said, 'Sorry, sorry. I'm like a bloody girl.'

Sharon got a cloth and washed his face. Bobby is a tough guy but when he gives in to things he really gives in. I went outside while she helped him get together. I carried Carlo round the paths on my shoulders. Bobby and I are opposites. Where I'm inclined to be mild he's all bull's-roar. I'm likely to feel quickly, soften up, but soon I have to fight against cynicism. Bobby will sneer, he'll wisecrack, talk about bleeding hearts, say the only thing that counts is money and the only friend you've got is number one; but in the end tears start in his eyes. You never know where you are with Bobby. The children at his school must love and hate him.

He came out and joined me, thrusting out his chin like Mussolini. I put Carlo down and he ran in to his mother.

'Well, Bobby –'

'I'm going after that Yankee prick. I'll have him in the courts for carnal knowledge.'

'Jilly's over sixteen.'

'She wasn't when they met. He was into her the day he got in my house.'

'Can you prove it?'

'I'll prove it. Walk down to the car with me.'

'Relax, Bobby. They're through the Lewis Pass. Or down the Coast. Come and see where they lived.'

He cried again when he saw the double bunk. 'He'll be teaching her that ninety-six. Oop, oop. The day he came my little girl was in her school uniform.' And she looked round her father's shoulder, saw this barefoot freak, and turned her nose up. Bobby didn't

14

understand. It wasn't Hank's beads and guitar that did for Jilly, it was his saucers. His faith was what seduced her. Jilly wanted above everything else to fly away. From all sorts of things, not least of them Bobby.

I looked at the roll of fat on his neck. He had been a beefy boy and I had spent half the day trailing along with him in an armbar. When I cried he felt a rush of love. It was terrifying. Now his meat and muscles had turned to lard. And I felt something like love for him.

'She'll get sick of him. Give her time.'

'Maybe. I went to see Duggie Plumb last night.'

'Why Duggie?'

'He's my MP. He's Minister of Police. Do you know what he said?'

'I can guess.'

'Screwing never did a girl any harm. To me. Her father. Doesn't he know I vote for him? Not any bloody more.'

'Duggie chucks a vote away now and then. It makes me feel good.'

'He kicked me out. Said he was busy. He'll need to be. Muldoon will eat the prick.'

'I wouldn't be too sure.'

I took him outside to look at the saucer. He kicked holes in its sides. 'What's happened to kids? They've gone all soft. This Zing stuff. Zang. Whatever it is. I liked them better when they were screaming murder.'

'She'll come home.'

'Sharon too, with a tarpot kid.'

For what was left of the afternoon we drank his whisky. At tea we got sentimental and talked about our mother.

'That's not a table topic.'

'Who made an odour?'

Sharon put Carlo to bed. She stayed in her room to meditate, while Bobby and I played our family like cards. We trumped each other: Grandpa in his study, while the world rolled by: Auntie Esther, with her purple plonk: Willis chasing ladies in his orchard: Emerson, the Sundowner of the Skies, beating up Peacehaven in his Gypsy Moth. There were others too: mad old Wendy weeping as she packed her car with books: mad old Merle and Graydon, naked as skinned rabbits on their lawn. We grew drunk on memories as much as whisky.

I helped Bobby into the sleeping bag and wrapped myself in blankets in the trailer. I could not sleep but that did not bother me. Possums coughed in the night. I believed I would be happy.

In the morning I took him swimming to cure his hangover. We porpoised in the river, yelling like boys. 'Ow, Googie Withers.' He dived and came up purple. 'Touched the bottom. Your turn.'

'I get scared down there.'

'Yeller-belly.' Down he went again. I saw him in the green water, breaking into cubes.

'You'll kill yourself.'

'Still a bit of a pansy, ain't yer? I thought old Uncle Alf was going to get you for a while. He fancied me.'

'Did he?'

'Liked me muscles. Jesus, I scared the little bugger. I went into one of those underground dunnies in town. And there he was in a corner, chatting up some kid. "Gidday, Uncle Alf," I yelled. You should've seen the little sod. He almost went through the roof. Then he was up those stairs like a rat up a drain pipe. Last time I ever saw him.'

We towelled ourselves on Hank and Jilly's sand. I came on schoolgirl footprints in a corner and trod them out.

'How long are you going to stay here, Ray?'

'Through the winter.'

'Doing what?'

'I thought I might get on to my book on Mickey Savage.'

'Go back to the *Sunday Post*. That's where you belong, boy. Reckon you'll ever get married again?'

'Who knows? If I meet the right woman.' I do not believe in right woman. Or right anything much. Right beginnings, right ends. Even right circumstances.

'That Glenda really sucked you dry. Bit of the old knuckle needed there.'

'Come on Bobby, save the act for someone you can impress.'

'No act. It proves you love 'em. Oh my God, look, look. That's Jilly's footprint. And that one must be his. *In between*. Oh Jesus, my little girl.'

So I took him to the house and fed him beer. After lunch I put him in his car. He smiled at me and blinked his eyes, ready to work up some feeling.

'You'll miss your plane, Bobby.' He had worn me out. I watched him as far as the corner, then walked across the paddocks to Barlow's cow-shed and dipped a billy of milk from one of the vats. I whistled as I walked back to the river. The Bobby thing, the Jilly thing, was over. I swung the billy in a giant wheel without spilling a drop. Then I saw Bobby's car coming back up the road. It was slewing in the metal, pouring dust. He skidded a quarter-circle on the grass and burst his door open. The scream of steel guitars came over the paddock. He climbed on to the bottom wire of the fence. 'Duggie Plumb's been shot.'

I put the billy down and lumbered through the cow pats.

'I got the end of a special bulletin. They've taken him to Auckland hospital.'

'Who?' I said. Duggie made a collage: face upright, diagonal, lying on its cheek. Splashes of blood coloured him.

'They don't know how serious it is. You've gone all white.'

'Who did it?'

'There's a man in custody. Stand up, son. You don't like the bugger that much.'

I let the fence-wire go and started to run.

'They said there'd be more bulletins,' Bobby yelled. 'Get your radio on. I've got to go or I'll miss my plane.'

I picked the billy up and ran slopping milk down to the river. Through the trees I saw dust smoking in the hedges as Bobby drove away. Sharon was in her garden. I yelled the news to her as I went by. She followed me to the house and we tried to thump her radio alive but got only threads of a voice.

'I'll listen in my car.' I hurried to the road and sat spinning knobs. Music: pop here, Sunday there. I lay on the seat a moment. Running had made me dizzy. Heart beating away, whacking my ribs. I felt blood running in my wrists and ankles. How comical it would be if Duggie and I, born within a day or two of each other, should die on the same day. The Corsican brothers: I felt his wounds in my chest. Comical because I hated the bastard. 'Don't die, Duggie. You're going to be Prime Minister.'

Soon I climbed up behind the wheel. I felt old, slack-muscled, full of broken tissues, and felt it unjust that I should be forced into action like a boy. Then my head began to clear, the noises stopped, I was rational and fifty. I drove fast and safe to Collingwood.

'I thought you wouldn't be long,' John Jolly said.

'John, can you give me the news? What's the latest?'

'For people who won't write for me, no news.'

'I'll write for you.'

'Next Sunday? A nice long piece?'

'Anything you want. Just how is he?'

'Hang on. There's someone coming on the other line.'

I heard clicks and a distant voice that only grunted.

'Well now, Raymie,' John came back. 'This isn't timed right for us. Yesterday would've been spot on. We'll have to let the dailies do the news. But what's it matter when we've got Raymond Sole?'

'For Christ's sake, John.'

'I want all that dirt you've been sitting on. You can't slander the dead.'

'Dead?' I heard my voice smack like a rolled-up newspaper on the walls of the booth, and I kept safe by imagining an existence for myself outside attachments and concerns.

'Dead on arrival. Ray, you there?' John's happy voice was suddenly careful. 'Why don't you sleep on it, eh? Then get yourself weaving.'

'Who did it?'

'Some old bastard. No names yet. I've got Tom Farquhar fishing. Blew a hole in his chest with a German pistol. War souvenir, Tom thinks.'

I saw the old man with his pared-down face, vestigial face; and saw the gun – a Walther P38 – lying unused since the war in a strong-box in that little house in Parnell. And I thought, it happens that way. You can't just pretend you're empty in there.

'Ray?'

It comes and gets you. You can't just walk off in another direction.

'You know who this old guy is?'

'No,' I said.

'OK. Now look, you can do this job better in the office.'

'I'm not coming.'

'You're doing this for me. You gave your word.'

'I'm sorry, John.' I put the phone down and walked out into the main street of Collingwood. Duggie was dead. I tried to imagine that the empty street lay outside time.

3

Duggie said he came from humble beginnings. It's a common boast of public men. They also claim their honours make them humble. Duggie never did that. And he spoke of his beginnings only once. He was helping out in a Labour marginal at election time and hoped that he might sneak a few votes over. He went on to say what hard times his parents had seen, and confessed they voted Labour in the thirties. But those times were gone, good times were here, and his parents – 'my old Mum and Dad' – had switched their vote to National before they died. That was a lie but nobody could catch him out in it. Willis Plumb learned to hate Tories at his mother's knee. He was all over the place in his other opinions but never budged an inch in politics. As for Aunt Mirth, nothing mattered to her but 'my man', whoever he might be. He was mostly Willis. I heard her say once that she'd never voted.

Duggie did not have humble beginnings either. Mirth and Willis were poor but never meek. They were flamboyant and tricky. They were life-lovers. Everything that pleased them they devoured. Duggie could not be sure of anything. Perhaps, though, he was sure of me.

I lived in the Loomis valley, west of Auckland. Peacehaven was my grandfather's house. Duggie lived four miles up the road on a citrus orchard hacked out of scrub at the foot of the ranges. A mile of Loomis creek 'belonged' to us. It started over the road from Peacehaven and ran in a shallow gorge past the back of town and ended at the tidal pool above Moa Park. The Peacehaven orchard also belonged, with the swamp and paddocks at the back. The swamp drained into a stream flowing under a toy-town bridge and through a culvert under Millbrook road. It joined the creek in a small waterfall. Peacehaven stood on a hillside looking over the lawns and summer-house at Wendy Philson's cottage, hidden in wattles, and Merle and Graydon Butters' turretted house. Uncle Robert looked after the garden. He kept a house cow and a dozen sheep. Grandpa Plumb, dressed always in a grey suit and tennis shoes, dozed in the summer-house or scribbled in his study. The Butterses crossed the bridge two or three times a week to visit him. Wendy came up daily. Later Bluey Considine lived in the cottage with a cripple called Sutton. I catalogue these names and map the place to hold them still.

The war was on and walls had ears. For Duggie and me it was the time of Beautiful Olga and Schimmler, the Serpent of Berlin. They might be sitting by you on the bus. They might ask if your father was fighting and where his unit was stationed, and Olga would smile and breathe sexy things in her German voice. We would not be fooled, we would gather evidence and report them to the army. But we never found anyone beautiful or even sinister. No one said 'Donner und blitzen' by mistake. So we spied on Wendy Philson and Merle Butters instead.

Wendy was lovesick. She stood on her side of the creek, watching our grandfather on his lawn. Tears ran down her face and she licked them from the corners of her mouth. Down the bank by the water Duggie and I practised our self-increasing art. We heard her groan and saw her work her fingers in her ribs. It was my first acquaintance with adult passion. I was panting with a kind of sickness and greed. I wanted more of Wendy but wanted to run and hide. 'She wants to have a go with him,' Duggie said. All I could see was that she was in pain. I thought she might be poisoned. She bent almost double, folding her hands inside. Her mouth was black and her eyes were messy. 'Oh George, love me,' she groaned.

'See,' Duggie grinned. He felt around for a stone. I was a better spy than Duggie. All I wanted was to take it down and creep away. That's probably why I'm a journalist. Duggie wanted to be part of the action. He wanted to add his bit. He lobbed the stone at the pool by the culvert, where it plopped like a frog. Wendy jumped to her feet and backed away. Her face was blunted with fright. She tried to push something off with her hands. Then she turned and lumbered through the bean-rows to her cottage.

'Jesus,' Duggie breathed. He was delighted.

'That's the pool she tried to drown herself in. It's true,' I said. 'Uncle Bob had to pull her out.'

'Who told you that?'

'Mum.' She had also made me promise never to tell. 'They had to stick her in the wow.' I threw a stone at the pool. 'She must have thought something was coming to get her.'

It pleased me that Duggie looked alarmed. We went to the bridge and crossed the lawn, which brought us up on Grandpa Plumb. He was deaf and that made him easy. One of Duggie's pleasures was to stand behind him and fart. Grandpa was sleeping in the summer-house. He had his handkerchief on his face. It blew like a flag when he breathed out, then dented in his mouth neat as a spoon. Before long it slid off and settled on his chest.

Duggie said, 'My turn.' I did not like the way he had made a game of this. Grandpa was a sacred being to me. When I put his handkerchief back I was purified. And when I failed and his eyes sprang open – eyes of a fighter ace – I felt shrunken and unclean. My sitting with him then and my grinning chatter was a kind of prayer for renewal.

Duggie took the handkerchief by the corners. He raised it and let it fall in place. My grandfather's fingers twitched. The handkerchief started fluttering. Duggie grinned. He put his hands together and made a Japanese bow. I pulled him out of the summer-house by his arm. I was confused. Duggie freed me but he put me in danger.

Who came next? My mother in her kitchen. She saw our heads popping up at the window and gave us lumps of *zwieback* – horrible crusts of twice-baked bread – and sent us away. We went down through the garden, where Uncle Bob was digging. He wore a handkerchief too, knotted at the corners, on his head. Although he was only thirty he was bald. He was adenoidal and breathed through his mouth. I got on well with Uncle Bob, but Duggie had a way of making him not there.

We crossed the bridge and wriggled under a barbed wire fence into the Butterses' place. And this was the greatest of our days, for Merle and Graydon were lying on the lawn without any clothes on. They were worshipping the sun. Bobby had told me about it but this was the first time I had seen. They lay supine, outspread. I'm not sure whether they embraced the sun or were crucified. Merle's face had a look of ecstasy. When I had wondered at her other parts I lay cheek down to see it better. Its purity of line – her forehead, nose and mouth – was startling to me. I knew that Merle and Graydon were in a kind of madness; but not a kind that made me want to laugh. They were untouchable. I do not know even now whether theirs was a triumph of faith or art.

Duggie was wriggling. 'Look at the size of . . . Look at her . . .'

I had seen. It was the first I had known that women had hair between their legs and pink knobs like lollies on their breasts. I had not known men grew penises so big. But it was their faces that intrigued me, especially Merle's. I became outraged. Some trick was being played against everything I knew. My anger made me want to go away.

I started to crawl backwards through the hydrangeas. But seeing was never enough for Duggie. A garden hose ran snaking down the lawn to Merle and Graydon. He crept round to the tap on the wall of the house and turned it on. The end of the hose reared up like a cobra and sent a jet of water over Merle. She screamed. Graydon rose on his arms, his head went round like a periscope. He ran towards the house, where Duggie was slipping into the shrubbery.

'Do go away, you silly little boys,' Merle cried in her la-de-da voice. Then Graydon started to laugh. He galloped back down the slope with penis jigging and seized the hose and charged among the hydrangeas, flashing it like a scimitar. I saw him coming, maniacal, bright-eyed. His hairless chest wobbled like a lady's. He wet me from the back of my neck to my heels. Then he made hunting cries and went after Duggie. But the hose had reached its full length and though he put his thumb on it to make it squirt further Duggie scrambled off without a wetting.

We stopped at the curve in the gravel drive. Graydon was hosing Merle and she was squealing. They ran up to the house hand in hand and left the hose writhing on the lawn. Their white rumps flashed as they passed inside.

'Loonies,' Duggie said. 'Did you see . . . ?'

Yes, I had seen. More than he had seen. And taken it all down. And he had made them jump for him. So both of us were happy. I had the worry though of what my mother would do when she found out. As well as being naughty I had sinned against purity. I knew that I should have to pretend that all I had seen was bottoms.

I am distorting him. There was more to Duggie than this. What I cannot get away from is his dominance of me. It came from his ease and knowingness in places where I was guilty, out of my depth, plain ignorant. I should have been boss. I was bigger and stronger. He dominated me through knowledge; but if I had been equal would have managed it through will.

Wendy packed her car with books and drove away to live somewhere else. Bluey and Sutton came to live in the cottage. The police called for Uncle Bob and though Mum insisted he was as brave as any soldier Duggie and I kept quiet about him. No one had to tell us conshies were cowards. Soon we heard of Pearl Harbour and we set about making buck teeth and Japanese fingers in tobacco tins. Auckland filled up with Americans. We collected cigarette packets – Camels and Chesterfields and green Luckies and white – and hung around Auntie Esther's Yanks until they fished gum from their pockets and told us, 'Get lost, kid.'

They liked Duggie though. His bold talk made their cheeks turn pink and they gave their hee-haw laugh and said to their girls, 'You hear that, honey?' The girls looked on Duggie with horror. They nodded with prim satisfaction when Esther came up on him quietly and slapped his behind so hard sparrows scattered from the summer-house roof. 'Go home and tell your mother she wants you.' Tears of humiliation streamed on his cheeks. 'Go on, or you'll get another one.' She had no liking and no pity for him. When she looked at him after that he slunk away.

To get his revenge he told stories about her. She stopped her car on Millbrook Road and passed a note to a man. 'Heil Hitler,' she said, and drove away. She left her kitchen light on for Japanese bombers to see. And once in the drive at Peacehaven with Marine Sergeant Cuchiella – 'my Brooklyn boy' – she reached through his legs from behind and grabbed his tool as though she was picking grapes. 'Yeah,' Duggie told me twenty years later, 'that one was true. The poor bugger looked as if he'd swallowed a golf ball.'

The Americans enriched our lives in a number of ways. We even saw one die. It was on a Saturday afternoon. We paddled down Loomis creek in canoes made from roofing iron and sealed with pitch. Duggie led. Beak Wyatt, a stringy boy with a blade of a nose, came in the middle. The black pools made him jumpy. He always spoke rapidly on the creek and laughed a lot in a screechy way. I came last because I thought the middle place unworthy. I gave myself the task of guarding the rear. Like Beak Wyatt I was nervous on the creek. We broke into a darkness, we killed quiet. Mum praised me for imagination so trying hard became natural to me. The creek was also Nature. Brought up without religion, I had been told to worship there. Duggie was the only one who was free. He shot his canoe ahead like a busy steamboat.

In mid-afternoon we came to the tidal pool. We pulled our canoes up on the bank and climbed into the open. 'This is the place to come if you want to find Frenchies,' Duggie said. He went looking but came back empty-handed. The pool, which was simply the Pool, lay brown and salty in the sun. Green water from the creek ran into it down a rock slide overgrown with slime. All around were willow trees and gums. We lay in the grass at the top of the bank and brooded on the water, seeing tribes of sprats and eels in there. Cries came up from Moa Park. Canoes nosed round the corner but could not mount the rapids to the Pool.

When a jeep drove up from the gate we slithered further back. Two marines and their girlfriends carried rugs and beer down to the flat place by the diving board. The girls were permed and had painted nails, which my mother had told me was a sure sign a girl was no lady. Duggie and I slipped into our spying role but Beak half rose and swayed like a praying mantis.

'D-do you think they're going to do it?'

'Get down,' Duggie snarled.

The men opened bottles of beer and passed them to the girls, who drank manlike, ladylike. A lump grew in my chest, hard as a cricket ball.

'Yanks always fuck their sheilas,' Duggie said.

These ones went to the bathing shed and changed into swimming togs. They came back with their clothes neatly folded. One of them put his cap on his girl. She rubbed his thigh. That was more like it. But again reality let us down. The man walked on to the diving board.

'Hey – hey –' Beak Wyatt squeaked.

'He knows,' Duggie said.

'Sure,' I said.

The Yank bounced high in the air and seemed to hang there, arms outspread. The old board rattled and chattered. On the bank the girls clapped.

'Bloody skite,' Duggie said.

I did not think so. He seemed to touch the sky. Then, bending his knees, he made the board go still. He strutted to the rug and slapped the girls' behinds. They ran away to change while the men lay on their elbows, drinking beer.

'They're not going to do it,' Beak Wyatt said. He was relieved.

The girls ran back. Seeing them made the day go brighter. One was in red, the other in yellow. They looked as if they had stepped out of magazines.

'Wow,' yelled one of the Yanks. He made curvy shapes in the air with his hands.

'Dirty bugger,' Duggie said.

But, like Beak, I was relieved they weren't going to do it. The pressure was gone from my chest. I wished the Yank would go on the board and bounce. And soon he made that strutting walk out there. The board rattled, the big long-legged Yank hung in the air. 'Zowie,' he yelled.

The other one stood up and took a final swig from his bottle. He was smaller and whiter and had bones standing out in his elbows. 'Move over, Joe.' The big Yank came back and stood aside. He smoothed his hair and winked at the girls.

'I'll show you how we do it back home, baby,' the small one said. He flexed his shoulders in a clowning way. He was skinny but he was strong. His back was shaped like a cobra's hood. Joe grinned and whacked his bum. 'Go man,' he said.

The small man ran. I see him still. He was Munro Gussey from Bay City, Michigan. I can feel the day break apart. Something broke in me, like snapping rubber. I was half-way to my feet, suspended there. My head was in my shoulders, my mouth hung stupidly, squeaking a word that was never finished.

The board shot Munro Gussey high in the air. I see him grinning as he began to fall. His arms came round and chopped the water. Yellow splashes flew, sharp as glass. His body went down cleanly.

The girls yelled their zowies, but after a little time became uncertain. 'He's swimming under water,' Joe explained. 'You watch the other bank.' Munro Gussey floated up. His buttocks surfaced like a jelly fish. Then his white back showed, and his pale head, spilling a fan of blood on the water.

Beak Wyatt had run. I saw him sprinting high-kneed to the gate. Duggie and I started down to the board. We made jerky progress;

we believed, and could not believe, and did not know what to do.

Joe ploughed out to his friend. 'There's no water here.' It came as high as our waists as we went in to help him. He turned his face at the sky. 'There's no water.'

'The tide's out,' Duggie said. 'We thought you knew.'

We wrestled Munro Gussey up the bank and laid him on the rug. The girls hovered. 'Gus,' they whispered.

'Jesus, Jesus,' Joe cried. He was in a rage and he was weeping. The girl in the yellow togs knelt beside Gus and stroked his face. She got a handkerchief from her purse and dabbed the top of his head.

'Don't touch him,' Joe yelled. He went down on his knees and looked at the wound. A cut like the split in a melon showed in the crown of Gus's head. Blood oozed in his pale hair. Joe felt the back of his neck. 'There's a lump there big as my fist. Jesus,' he yelled at the sky, 'there was supposed to be water.' He walked away and knelt in the grass. Then he jumped up. 'We've got to get a saw-bones.' He started to run to his jeep.

'I'm coming too, Joe,' cried the girl in the red bathing suit. Her bottom wobbled as she ran. Her friend looked round wildly and half rose to her feet. 'They're going.'

'They're getting a doctor. I think I'd better –'

Duggie beat me to it. There seemed to be space behind his eyes. He took a dozen backward steps from Gus. 'I'm not staying here.' Grass tangled his feet and made him lurch, but he scrambled four-legged. 'I'll show you where.'

When the jeep had gone the girl sank on to her knees. She looked at Gus and she looked at me. 'I was with Joe.' She began to cry, rocking back and forth as though doing exercises. She cried with closed eyes, through a mouth shut tightly, making a steady hum, an insect buzz. Joe's cap was sitting on her hair. I saw she was not pretty – her prettiness was gone. Red spots stood out around her mouth. I wanted to tell her to use her handkerchief but she kept it in her fist, down on her thigh, where it smeared her skin with blood. Once she leaned at Gus and slipped her fingers under his neck. Then she set up her rocking again, and her buzzing grief.

I started to ease away. I did not like being tangled up in this, I thought it unfair; and I was wild with Duggie for leaving me. I felt hollowed out every time I looked at the man on the rug, so I let my eyes go quickly over him, and collected a series of images: his eyes staring up with a faraway look; the wound in his head, oozing like a boil; and the lump on his neck, white and shiny as an egg. I remember his name tag lying in the damp hair on his chest. His fingers were broken and their nails bleeding. But the little finger on one of his hands was bent back at an angle and the nail there was a lady's, white as milk and beautifully clean.

I soft-footed away. 'Don't go,' said the girl. Every time I moved she spoke again. 'I didn't want to come. My friend made me.' So I shuffled up and down. I edged around her, careful not to step on the rug. She was young, I saw with fright, not an adult. She could not have been more than seventeen. But she held me. It was as if every time I moved she reached out and gripped me in my chest. I felt if I ran away she would make me die.

I straightened the edge of the rug. I picked bottle tops up in my toes and lobbed them into the water. The yells of children came from Moa Park. I thought that was wrong. I walked on the diving board and looked at the canoes nosing in the rapids.

When we heard the jeep coming the girl jumped up and collected the beer bottles. She hid them behind the changing sheds. Joe and Doctor Walker ran down to the rug. Duggie was not there. Another car arrived. He was not in that one either. I watched for a while, circling away, and heard Doctor Walker say Gus was dead. The girls walked to the jeep, holding each other. Joe stood with his hands on his hips, staring at The Pool and talking to himself. Gus was covered up. No one took any notice of me.

At the top of the bank I turned and ran. I ran through the main street of Loomis and along Millbrook Road. I came charging into the kitchen. 'Where's Duggie?' I yelled at my mother.

'What's the matter, Raymie? You look flushed.'

'Where is he?'

'Heavens, I don't know. Go and wash your face.'

When I saw him next he looked at me with his eyes distended. 'I didn't want to be in the way. There were plenty of people there.' He did not know whether he was lying or telling the truth. I saw his face change like that of a person who has picked up something ordinary from the ground, and rubs it, and sees it shine.

4

We told our story to the Loomis constable. He wrote it down on sheets of yellow paper.

'Now, you saw him go on the board?'

'I didn't know he was going to dive. I thought he was going to bounce.'

We agreed on that; even Beak Wyatt, with Adam's apple jumping. The constable went tsk, tsk and looked at us sadly. There was nothing he could do so he sent us home.

My mother hovered over me for a while. She thought that seeing a man die might scar me mentally. She worked me into a state of tears about this young American dying so far from home. I felt better after it. I'd done something to please her, passed a test.

Tears marked the stations of our day. She cried in the morning and at night, and at intervals between. My mother was coming to terms. What she felt was less than a cosmic grief but more than private. My father had gone off to the war before his papers came – that was one thing. And mankind had gone mad and killing was everywhere. She had taken my grandfather's faith in man's becoming Man, but in her it was sentimental, it had no under-pinning, it was simply an image of Man and Woman, naked and sexless, walking into the Dawn. She cancelled it and could discover nothing to fill herself with. I find myself wanting to use her language. It was full of cuts and wounds and fractures and dark night.

Before long she had what used to be known as a nervous breakdown. For six months we had to tiptoe round her. She lay in her bed, she drifted about the house. She sat on the floor and tears dripped in her lap. Bobby and Becky and I did our best. We knew she might go mad and that placed a terrible weight on every word we spoke. Grandpa tried hard too. He was impatient of 'female matters' but saw that this was more. For the first time in his life he made his own cup of tea. Becky did the cooking. She was twelve. Aunt Esther came as often as she could and Aunt Mirth now and then, or sent one of her older girls to help. And my mother, by some means unknown to me, began to get well.

Bluey Considine lent her his gramophone. In the evenings she sat on the back veranda looking down at the creek and played *Lindy Lou* over and over. Each time it came to an end she felt a little less, a little better.

> Lindy, did you hear dat mockin' bird sing las' night?
> Honey, he was singin' so sweet in de moo-oonlight . . .

Paul Robeson: one of the gods in her pantheon. The flatness in his voice increased its feeling. When the record ended she lit a cigarette – a Camel from Esther – and smoked a while. She rested her hand on mine where I sat in the other seagrass chair. Then she leaned to the little table and wound the gramophone.

'What a wonderful voice, Ray.'

Scratch went the needle.

> Lindy, did you hear dat mockin' bird . . .

She had believed in this and was looking as one looks at old photographs.

> . . . I'd lay right down and die
> If I could sing like dat bird sings to you-oo,
> My little Lindy Lou-oo.

Tears trickled on her cheeks. She squashed them matter-of-factly. 'Well Ray, I think we've had enough of that. What would you like?'

I chose *Phil the Fluter's Ball* and we had a laugh.

'But remember Ray, there's another side. Life is beautiful.' My lesson for the night. 'Go to bed now.' As I changed into my pyjamas I heard *Lindy Lou* again.

Aunt Esther took my mother to parties. She went as though to the dentist. And when Esther brought Yanks to Peacehaven on Sunday afternoons and they sat on the lawn drinking Dally wine Mum would come up to the house and sit in the kitchen with her put-upon look. 'I wish she'd take them home.' But when she went back she laughed and smoked and drank and enjoyed herself. Once a Yank who looked like Errol Flynn tried to kiss her. 'Please Bob, I don't want that.' She tried to get her hand free but he held on hard. I looked at him murderously. If my father were home he would knock him into the middle of next week.

I knew what went on. In spite of her talk about the love of husbands and wives being beautiful and pure and not having a great deal to do with bodies I knew that with her body she had done it with my father. I was proof of that. And with the novels and poetry on her bedroom shelf was *Married Love* done up in brown paper like a recipe book. I had sneaked along by her bed and read it, cover to cover. Marie Stopes had the trick of sliding away from things; but I made out in spite of her exactly what adults did. I was sickened and excited.

So I watched the Yank Duggie and I called Errol. He was not going to get my mother. I thought of writing to Dad but felt if I worried him he might be careless and a German sniper would shoot him. I prowled from my bed in the night, making sure that Errol was out of the house. I crept along to my mother's window and peered at her white bed floating on the night. She was alone. Her hair made a smudge on the pillow. Once I heard her weeping. Once I heard her snore.

And one night she said to me, 'Go back to bed, Raymie. Everything's all right now.'

After that things were almost all right. She managed to get through her day without those tears that began so deep in her they seemed to come out black. She did some spur-of-the-moment crying of course: for a broken plate, for a kitchen range that would not draw properly. Errol went back to the war. My mother kept on smoking, and drank a glass of wine now and then. I took that hard and dared to mention it. She spoke of moderation and the power of the mind over appetites. But she had made a puritan of me and could not undo it.

When I visited Grandma Sole, which I did once a week – Mum insisted – she asked me how 'poor Meg' was getting on. She hammered questions into me like tacks. 'Does she have many visitors?' 'Do any of them ever stay all night?' I don't know what she wrote to Dad, but if he had been killed I would have blamed her. She never left off working when I called, and made me follow with a bucket as she washed the ceilings – tiny, spindly, at the top of her ladder – and made me turn the wringer while she fed in clothes. If I sat down she was at me with a duster, wiping the arm of my chair, and while I ate a biscuit was kneeling at my feet brushing up crumbs. As a treat she would let me have five minutes in the front room.

It was a box, ten by ten; but for us, Aladdin's cave. It was her treat as much as mine. She softened in there, she blossomed. She never turned the light on and never drew back the curtains. Clack went the door behind us. I heard her breathe. Her eyes shone in the dark, her face opened like a flower. And the room took on a magic for me. The firescreen, the tongs, poker, andiron, gleamed like gold. The knick-knacks on the china cabinet were rich as the crown jewels; and the crockery inside – plates like shells, cups like butterflies – seemed to me the finest in the world. I could not imagine the king and queen having better.

'See, Ray. Here's your great-grandma and pa. And this is Ted and me on our wedding day.' Whiskery great-grandpa, great-grandma black and lacy, as stuck-up as Queen Victoria. I thought I was special having them. The wedding photo – well, it was interesting: Grandpa Sole like a forward missing the match and Grandma thin as pea-sticks, neat as a doll. She was the kitchen Grandma Sole, not the front room one.

I touched the 'sweet', sat primly, fingers folded, in a chair. She sat in the one next to it – 'just for a jiffy' – smiled and wrapped her arms around herself. Then she was up and lifting the lid of her box. I took the other end. We leaned it on the wall and gazed on the treasures – rolls of linen, heavy as folded lead and cold as stone; towels of pink and blue and royal purple; embroidered pillow cases; embroidered table cloths with birds and roses. Lace like spider webs. It seemed right to me they were in the box and never came out.

'I've never showed your mum these.'

We went out quietly and closed the door. Ha! – we let our breath out and blinked in the light. Then her face began to close. A sharpness came on her. She saw something that needed doing, and rushed at it, and snapped at me, 'Don't get under my feet, boy. Go and see your grandpa in the garden. He wants some weeding done.'

I went, with a last glance at the door. I'm glad I never saw that room with the light on.

Grandpa Sole did not want weeding done. Today when people say 'your grandfather', it's Grandpa Plumb they mean, but Ted Sole who comes into my mind. He may not stay there long but he comes first. I see his grimy head and porous cheeks and granite chin. His hairy ears. His body clothed in railway black. He was a great block of a man and he stands at one side of my childhood like a wall I could lean against. He had little clear blue eyes. I wonder if I loved him so much because I did not have to share him with Duggie. He was a railway blacksmith. Soot was in his scalp and forehead, in his nose and cheeks. It was deep in his hands like a million black prickles. I longed to take a needle and dig them out.

Grandpa Sole showed me what order might achieve. At the back of his railway house was a patch of garden made with a fierce geometry. Everything was there, space and angle; and last year, next year, in his head. He had less than a quarter acre but no farmer knew the seasons better than Ted Sole. Order, knowledge, patience. He would not have cared for my language. All he did was what his old man did. Deep digging, natural manures, plenty of air round the roots. And squash them snails. And move your plants around son. Cabbages here one year, over there the next. I went out with him, riding in his barrow, and climbed the hilly paddocks around Loomis. I prised up crusted cow-pats from the grass while he scooped up the wet ones in his shovel. We made liquid manure in an oil drum. And squashed butterfly eggs. And staked tomatoes, trained the runner beans. I folded back the sacks where he bred worms and counted them out in dozens and planted them like seeds in the earth.

One day we boiled water in Grandma's copper and washed three dozen bottles till they sparkled in the sun. In the garden shed we bottled his home brew. I used the capper he had made at work: set a silver crown on each brown bottle, gave a press with all my body in it, felt a firm resistance and a beautiful give, and was fulfilled. I could have stayed there working with him forever.

But Grandma Sole came out and sent me home. 'What are you doing Ted, letting the boy see that beer?'

'Now mother, it's all right.'

'It is not all right. He'll tell those wowsers round there. That Reverend and that Meg.'

'Mum drinks wine.'

'She does? How much? Who with? Does some man bring it for her?'

'Now mother, don't ask the boy questions. Get off home, Ray. Come and help me next weekend. I know where we can get some horse manure.'

I went home to that Meg and that Reverend. Bobby and Becky. Duggie Plumb. They were in a different world from Ted Sole's world, where hidden things, tears and violence, suddenly leaped on you. It was more real in the end. It was where I had to live.

For a spell of several months Duggie stayed with us at Peacehaven. There was, I heard, trouble at the orchard – something Uncle Willis was up to. 'More of his shenanigans,' Mum said. That did not sound too bad and I could not see why Duggie had to come. But although Mum never cared for him she thought I spent too much time alone. She had become suspicious of solitude. 'Things' happened when you were by yourself and company was a kind of medicine.

So Duggie came and shared my room and was like a piece of grit in my eye. He chipped round the edges of our family. When he watched and turned away I knew he was grinning. And some piece of our behaviour that I had never given any thought to was in question. I came to doubt my mother. Was she right? Was she, even, good? While Duggie was with us I began to see she was not pretty. I saw her crooked teeth and skinny throat. I blushed at the little belches she hid behind her hand. And when she said, 'That's not a table topic,' I had to join Duggie in a smirk.

He did not know he was damaging me. He did not know that in another way he made me free. He had no plan, no programme. Anarchy was as natural to him as affection was to Grandpa Sole.

I asked him what the trouble was at home. 'Dad's rooting some sheila in town. Mum beats him up when he comes home.'

At school I would have been at him for details. But in our living-room I shied away. It was as if I'd caught him doing his job on the hearthmat. Next day when I was ready he chewed his nails and looked at me dark-eyed and turned away.

He was built like his father: short legs, big behind. (Cartoonists came to label it GNP and stuck a little head and limbs on it.) At school he was Plumbum, a name you pressed like a button: he went berserk and fought with a monkey gabble and spit frothing on his mouth. I ran for his brother Cliff, who saved him and washed his face with water. Then Duggie went away and hid himself. I hunted in the dunnies and slit trenches but he pelted me with clay, he climbed on the seat and punched me when I looked over the wall.

Bluey Considine heard of our fights and tried to teach us how to box. He showed us the English style, straight left, right cross, and the Yankee crouch. Five minutes of it had him purple-faced. He sat in his chair and talked about the fighters he had known. 'Say we're in a pub. Now, who was the first New Zealander to win a world boxing title?'

'Bob Fitzsimmons.'

'The Freckled Wonder.'

'You're a pair of ignoramuses. He was second. The first one was Torpedo Billy Murphy, the Little Tailor. He knocked out Spider Weir in San Francisco, 1890. I knew Ike Weir. He was a Belfast man. And too good for Billy. He made a fool of him. Turned a somersault, danced a jig, and kicked him in the bum. Then he'd give him the left and give him the right. Poor Billy didn't know what town he was in. But he kept on swinging and in the thirteenth Ike walked into one. He never saw it coming. Billy put him down five times and in the fourteenth knocked him out stone cold. I can still see Ike's head banging on the canvas. So the Little Tailor was featherweight champion of the world. He was the first. Now if we were in a pub you'd owe me a beer.'

Duggie loved those tales, those fighters Bluey had seen in the States in the 1890s, and loved their names; and I liked them. The kids at school never knew what we were talking about as we sparred around the playground shouting, 'Here's Young Griffo. Here's Little Chocolate. Here's the Nonpareel. Here's George La Blanche, the pivot puncher.' Duggie practised the solar plexus punch, Bob Fitzsimmons' favourite. 'When Fitz knocked out Jim Corbett he got him with the solar plexus punch,' Bluey said, 'and Corbett lay there paralysed while the referee counted him out. He heard it all. One, two, three . . .'

'They've just got to lie there watching,' Duggie said.

Sutton also drew him to the cottage. Sutton was hump-backed and club-footed. Bluey had picked him up somewhere and taken him under his care and Sutton had a pure love for Bluey and an impure passion. We never knew of that but sensed something black in him, some cause beyond his hump and foot for his hatreds and his bitterness. Sutton had a head too large for him. His legs were jockey's legs and his hands wide as dinner plates. His mouth and gums were red as rubber. One of his eyes was tea-coloured and the other baby-blue. Here was a bogeyman handy to my door but I was never scared of him. Though once or twice he chased me in my dreams in the daytime he was only a joke. But Duggie found more than that in him. And something in Duggie gave Sutton pauses in his bitterness.

'Round the back with Roger,' Bluey said. 'They're doing the snails.' He looked at me sadly. 'I wouldn't go round there.'

I crept to the corner. There were Sutton and Duggie, squatting one each side of the chopping block. Duggie had a biscuit tin in his hand. I had seen Sutton with it in the garden hunting snails but never thought about what happened to them. Duggie took them out one by one and put them on the block, where Sutton hit them with a hammer. 'Forty-three,' Duggie said. He scraped the remains off with a garden trowel. 'This one's a baby.' 'Doesn't matter what they are, the buggers,' Sutton said. Duggie's face and Sutton's shirt were splashed with bits of snail. Their mouths were set in grins. 'You said I could do the last one,' Duggie said. Sutton gave him the hammer. 'That's a grandddaddy. That's the boss. You kept him on purpose.'

I backed away and sat with Bluey. 'He's a strange one, Roger. I think I'll have a chat with the Reverend.' We went up together. 'Don't tell Meg about the snails.'

Uncle Willis 'came to his senses' and Duggie went home. It was too soon. Mirth and Willis had been happy, and would be happy again. She had not worried about his women when she knew he liked her best; and when they were old they became infatuated with each other. But Willis was in his mid-forties and jumping out of his skin. Mirth was close to sixty. He explained to her that she should be thinking of other things. He told her how young women affected him; and, kindly, that she had done that to him not long ago. He advised her to enjoy her memories.

I waited for Duggie on Millbrook Road the morning after he left. I knelt among the pine-roots ready to ambush him. He came along barefooted, carrying his books and lunch in a cutdown sugarbag. I shrank into the roots, for Duggie was crying. Tears made slug tracks on his face. He stood in the dust ten feet away and threw stones at the insulators on a power pole. He threw with a quiet ferocity, broken only by sobs and gluey sniffs. Grey heads of snot slid from his nose and he sniffed them back. He was throwing there five minutes. Then one of his stones hit a cup and chips of porcelain rained down. Duggie wiped his nose on his forearm. He picked his sugarbag up and walked on. I did not come out of the roots until he was over the bridge into Loomis. I knew he would kill me.

He told me nothing about his life at home. But one day Mum sent me up to the orchard with a message and I saw. It was four miles up the road, a walk through yellow cuttings and gorse fields. The road crossed a railway line and passed a Dally vineyard, where the old Dally was out shooting blackbirds with his shotgun. After that it climbed into the hills. Willis's orchard lay on a north-facing slope. It *looked* like the Garden of Eden. I went along a drive through trees so green and glossy they seemed to be modelled in wax. The house increased my sense of unreality. It was a railway carriage, blue and red, with lean-tos stuck on it. Mirth was in the yard with babies.

My mother made a myth of Mirth and Willis. That pair always made her soft and blind. They had the same effect on Grandpa Plumb. He elevated the orchard into a temple and found there natural wisdom, lessons in acceptance and fruitfulness. Mirth was priestess/Mother. He thought those naked children in the trees – 'dryads, fauns' – were Mirth's, but they were grandchildren of her first marriage, and later on of her second.

As for natural wisdom . . .

I gave Mum's note to Mirth and went looking for Duggie. I found him in a shed in the grapefruit trees, sweeping the floor with a witch's broom. For a moment he looked as if he would take to me, but I told him about my message and he calmed down.

'Who sleeps here?'

'Dad.' When he had finished the floor he made the bed. 'Mum's kicked him out of the house.' He began to fold clothes heaped on a chair. I saw in his eyes the black fall into emptiness I had seen when Munro Gussey died. 'I tidy it up so Mum'll think he's done it.'

'Ah,' I said.

'There's a tap up at the tank-stand. Give that cup a rinse. Don't let her see you.'

I did as I was told. When the shed was tidy we went into the trees and lay in the grass. 'He's got another sheila. She's only thirty-five.'

'That's old.'

He gave me a look of contempt. He was years ahead of me in many things. 'He told Mum he can't keep his hands off her. He's in his prime.'

That gave me a picture of Willis hanging naked on a hook like a side of beef. I was still contemplating it when Mirth's shouting started.

'Jesus,' Duggie said, 'he's home.' He ran through the trees. When I came to the yard he was hopping round them, making cries. Willis was on his knees – not easy for him with his peg-leg. His hands were praying. Mirth knocked his hat off with a swipe. His head shone bald in the sun and she cracked her knuckles on it.

'Look at him. What woman would want him?' She was flopping in her clothes, her breasts and buttocks jumping.

Two of her girls came out of the house. 'Come on, Mum. Don't bother with him,' but they looked amused.

'It's in my nature. I can't help myself,' Willis whined.

Mirth slapped his face.

'Yes, I deserve it. Hit me again.'

'He's got her on his pants,' Mirth screamed. 'He hasn't even done his filthy fly up.'

'Mirth dear, Mirth . . .'

'Mum, Dad,' Duggie squeaked. His eyes were popping from his head.

'I'm going to cut it off. She's not having it.' She rushed into the house, scattering babies.

The two girls, Irene, Melva, took Willis's arms and heaved him up. 'She means it, Dad. You'd better start running.'

'Dad, Dad, lock yourself in the shed,' Duggie wept.

Mirth burst out of the house. She tumbled down the steps and fell on her knees. The carving knife in her hand glinted in the sun.

'Dad,' Duggie screamed.

Irene gave Willis a push. 'Go,' she laughed. Willis started running, hopping, away. He went behind the tank-stand and came round the other side, but found Mirth crouching there. Her knife flashed as she swung it like a sickle. He backed away and tumbled down a slope into the trees, rolling like a boy. Irene was shrieking with laughter, and Melva, laughing too, tried half-heartedly to take Mirth's arm. Mirth pushed her away and started down the slope.

Duggie got in front of her. Tiny sounds came out of his mouth. Mirth hit him back-handed. She ran into the trees, where Willis was flitting like a satyr. His peg-leg tangled in the grass and down he went and banged his head on a tree-trunk. Mirth stood over him. 'Ha!' she cried, ripping at his stained fly with her hand. He wriggled round the trunk like a swollen snake, and was up and off again, making cries and plunging in the leaves. He had forgotten the shed but it came at him and knocked him flat. Mirth tumbled over him. The knife stabbed the wall. She tugged it out two-handed and turned her great balloon face at her husband. But he was gone. He had crawled round the corner and in at the door of the shed and as Mirth came rushing he slammed it in her face and bolted it.

Mirth went berserk. She stabbed the door. She kicked it. She hit it with her side and with her bottom. 'Mirth love, Mirth,' Willis cried. The shed was rocking. She left her knife embedded in the door and found a length of four by two and smashed the window in. She hurled the wood at Willis, pale on the other side. 'Mirth my love, have a snooze and you'll soon feel better.'

She ran up to the house. Irene and Melva, Duggie and I, waited by the door. We heard her heaving things around.

'She's going to chop the door down,' Melva said.

But Mirth came back with an armful of firewood and some crumpled paper. She stacked it against the door.

'Gee whizz,' Irene said.

Duggie fell on his knees. He wept into his hands.

Mirth struck a match and lit the paper and flames climbed up the door.

'What's happening?' Willis cried, putting his head out the window. He sniffed the smoke. 'Mirth, you're burning me.'

She said nothing. A collapse was starting in her. Air rushed out her mouth with a whistling sound. Irene and Melva took her arms. Melva winked at me. They put their hands on Mirth and seemed to hold her in a piece. Carefully they walked her to the house, where a sound of wailing babies came. 'You'd better do some wees on that,' Irene said over her shoulder.

But it was Cliff, coming from somewhere, who threw a bucket of water on the fire. He pulled the knife out of the door, going tsk tsk tsk like a policeman.

Duggie went round to the window. His face was streaked with

tears. I did not like the look of him. There was Willis, framed. He had a wild look in his eye, but he managed to smile.

'Dad,' Duggie croaked.

Still I was the only one to see him.

'My word Duggie, how that woman loves me. She's a princess,' Willis said.

5

That was one Duggie story I never told my fellow reporters in the Parliamentary Press Gallery. They often asked me for a Duggie story. I kept them short and I kept them clean. I mean, no sex; though they were keen for sex. I told them how Duggie dared anything. We had a friend at school, I said, who had a nasty habit. One day I dared Duggie to tell the teacher. He looked at me a moment, then put up his hand. 'Please Miss Hoyle, Beak Wyatt's stuck a steelie up his bum.'

They liked that one. A game grew out of it. 'Please Mr Speaker, Keith Holyoake's dropped an aitch.' 'Please Mr Speaker, Norman Kirk's eating a pie.'

And I told them one I called Duggie Plumb Practises Politics. It happened at Loomis school in standard six. Duggie and Beak and I and a couple of others were eating lunch in a corner of the playground when Duggie pulled a matchbox out of his pocket. He opened it and showed us a little heap of yellow flakes and bits of grit in one corner.

'That's just a week's worth,' Duggie said.

'What is it?'

'Sleepers from my eyes.'

I felt sick. I threw away the sandwich I was eating.

'Ha,' Duggie laughed. 'Arsehole doesn't feel good.'

The others tried to prove they were no sissies. One of them bet he could get more. So Duggie got a competition going. We had a week. And no cheating, no dandruff.

I went in it too. I wasn't being left out. I even asked Becky for her sleepers and she told me what a filthy pig I was.

After a week the four of us got together and went to Duggie. Beak Wyatt had the biggest pile but none of us had done badly.

'What's this?' Duggie said.

'Our sleepers. Let's see yours.'

'Sleepers?' Duggie said. 'You mean sleepers from your eyes? You filthy buggers.' He walked away.

We dropped our matchboxes in the rubbish tin. No one ever mentioned them again.

The gallery boys liked that one too. Some of them loved it. 'My God, he'll make Prime Minister one day.'

After Loomis school I saw less of Duggie. We went on to Rosebank College, half an hour's ride on the train, and there Duggie took a commercial course, book-keeping in place of my French and Latin. I wasn't as 'smart' as Duggie but Mum told me I had a better mind. Rosebank College was in its first year. The Americans had built it as a hospital and the Education Department took it over in 1946. Our classrooms had been wards. The gym was made for indoor basketball. There was more light and air about than we had been used to, but no more than the usual amount in the teaching.

By late April the sports grounds were ready and we had a ceremony to open them. Only the day before, Ormiston, our headmaster, had sent the girls out of assembly and spent an hour lashing at us boys for moral filth. Someone had drawn dirty pictures on the lavatory walls. Sex, he glittered at us, leads to madness. These suicides you read about in the newspapers, they're all people who've been obsessed with sex. That's the way you boys will end up. We came out and pretended to swallow poison and jump off bridges. I played along, although it was no joke to me.

On the cold autumn day when the grounds were opened Ormiston showed he was out to get us. He made us parade barefooted, wearing shorts and singlets. The wind was blowing over the new grass and asphalt courts as he introduced the speaker, the Hon. H. G. R. Mason, Minister of Education. I felt a little better that he was Labour but as he went on – our privilege, our splendid grounds, the fine traditions we must build – I started to hate him. I thought I was going to fall over. The wind got up my shorts and made my balls shrink. Two rows down I saw Duggie gritting his teeth. The boy beside me was crying quietly. Ormiston's glasses caught the pale sun. Blue sky looked at us, expressionless. The Hon. H. G. R. talked for forty minutes. Then he smiled kindly and said he thought we were getting cold and he'd better let us go. But these splendid grounds, how privileged we were . . .

'Jesus,' Duggie said, 'I'm going to be a politician.'

He hated Ormiston. He hated most of his teachers. I liked mine. I even said Ormiston wasn't too bad – if he'd only smile. He never smiled in the five years I was there. But he came to look on Duggie with approval. Duggie managed it. We fell under his notice on the same day. The school went into town to see *The Way Ahead* at the Roxy Theatre in Queen Street. The war was being kept alive for us and we approved of that if it meant going to the pictures. Stanley Holloway and his platoon walked into the desert smoke with bayonets fixed and faces ready. Comradeship. Heroism. My dad had done that. 'They'll get their heads shot off,' Duggie said. We came out into the sun and lined up for our trams and he talked me into sneaking down an alleyway and spending the afternoon at the Tepid Baths. We hired togs and splashed about in the warm salt water and when we looked up there was Freddie Shanks our Phys. Ed. teacher smiling down at us with gleaming teeth. Ormiston had sent him out to round up Rosebank strays.

The suburbs rolled by in reverse. Freddie enjoyed himself. 'Any last messages for your folks?' He thrust us in by our necks to face the moral glitter of Ormiston.

'Well, I'm disgusted. I'm appalled.'

Then Duggie set about saving himself. He opened up his face. His cheeks grew round and seemed to shine and his eyes grew larger. He stood up straight.

'It was my idea, sir.'

'I don't believe that, Plumb.'

Ormiston looked at me and I looked at the floor. In those years I was eaten with sexual guilt. Guilt was the big thing in my life. I knew I was filthy and doomed to madness. Meeting anyone's eyes was more than I could manage. Glimpses showed me how Ormiston loathed me.

'We shouldn't have done it, sir. Not after that picture,' Duggie said.

'I'm glad you understand, Plumb. But I think you were led astray. I don't know what to say to you, Sole. I wish I didn't have you in my school. I hope this punishment will be a lesson. Though I doubt it. Hold out your hand.'

He hit me six times with his whippy cane. On the last blow I shrieked.

'Don't blubber, boy. Be a man.'

Duggie got one hit.

'I advise you to seek out other company, Plumb. Cousins or not. Now clear out, both of you.' He opened his windows.

Duggie and I walked side by side to the lavatories. 'My fingers are broken,' I wept.

He looked at them. 'They'll be all right.'

'Why did he give me six?'

'Search me.'

We ran our hands under water. 'You only got one.'

'I told him it was my idea. It's not my fault if he didn't believe me. And you'd better stop crying. Teachers don't like it when you cry.'

Nobody seemed to like it when you cried so I learned not to. Even Mum wasn't keen on it any more. Dad thought like Ormiston, men didn't do it. He would not let Mum write to him about my swollen hand. I'd taken a chance and been caught and that was that.

It was good having Dad home. I found that I'd remembered him pretty well and I got used to him being not so big and more bad tempered. I could not talk to him about the thing that worried me – tortured me – but I took his company as a holiday. I went with him to his parents' house and sat on the lawn with him and Grandpa Sole while they drank home brew. Dad let me have half a glass and I seemed to glimpse as I took it that what was happening on the lawn was true and the world outside was full of lies and that I might come out of my pain and find that I was not sick after all. I leaned on my elbow like a man, sipped my beer – finding it sour but not saying so – and listened to Dad and Grandpa talk about plumbing. Dad was trying to start up in business and he wanted to ask his brother-in-law Fred Meggett for a loan. Grandpa was against it. He advised Dad to save his money and do things on his own. In his opinion Meggett was a crook. It was the middle of the war surplus scandal. Surplus made Fred rich – jeeps and GM trucks, and piles of 'scrap' that turned out to be worth thousands of pounds. Fred bought cheap and sold dear and soon he was swimming in money. It was spectacular, and very fishy, and a Royal Commission had been set up to look into it. 'Keep away from him, son. You'll get tarred with the same brush,' Grandpa said. Dad frowned and fidgeted. He stood up and practised cricket strokes. His wrists and arms and legs and pale blue eyes and jet-black hair made me think him tough and dangerous. I could not see Fred Meggett ever getting the better of him.

We rode our bicycles home past the shunting yards and the jam factory and freewheeled down to Millbrook Road with our hands dangling at our sides. All along Millbrook Road we competed making skid marks. Becky and Bobby were on the lawn with tennis rackets, practising lobs over the summerhouse. Dad rode off the drive at Becky, trying to grab the ball. She gave a shriek and tumbled him into the rhododendrons. We went into a tangle, struggling for the ball. Our yells brought Mum out to the veranda, holding her breast. 'Oh Becky, come out of that. You look like . . .' Becky, flushed and shrieking, gave Dad a shove that sent him tumbling almost to the creek. She darted off with the ball and Bobby brought her down with an ankle tap. I wrestled him over the top of her and the three of us rolled into the wall of the summer-house, where Grandpa Plumb was sleeping with his handkerchief over his face.

'You'll wake Dad,' Mum cried.

'A buzz-bomb wouldn't wake him,' Dad said, stealing the ball. He ran over the bridge into the orchard with us at his heels. We ended rolling in the swamp and had to hose each other in the garden, where Mum caught us.

'Fergus, you! I'll never understand you. And Becky, look at you. You're supposed to be a lady.'

'Who told you that?'

'Ray, I thought you had more sense.'

Dad gave her a squirt with the hose and she fled into the house. He had an instinctive wisdom with her. That wetting made her part of us and though she ran away she was humming a tune when we came into the kitchen.

She sent me down to bring Grandpa in. He had not wakened though his handkerchief lay on his chest like a bib. The lace of one of his sandshoes was undone and I tied it up. His eyes shot open, fierce and lonely. He touched my head. 'You're a good boy, Raymond.' He seemed to have grown very old lately and his statements of approval and disapproval were mundane. They kept the weight of moral dogma though. I saw even at fourteen that his was a simple view of things.

Lunch. I made the shape with my mouth.

'Mealtimes are a great robber of time. Sleep,' he said, seeing my objection, 'there's a better nourishment than food. Sleep that knits up the ravell'd sleave of care. *Macbeth*. You know that play? Well, you'll come to it.' He took my arm and we went along by the rose garden, where he stopped to sniff a bloom. 'Roses are the most beautiful flowers.' More dogma. If I had disagreed he would have been outraged.

Mum sat him at the head of the table. Sunday lunch she termed 'a family time' and she made him join us. He took all other meals in his study, which never seemed to strike him as unusual. His hatred of tyrannies did not extend into the home. Mum did not have the energy, or even the desire, to make more than small dents in his comfort. But she would not let Becky even rinse a cup for him.

Dad carved the roast. 'George?' He put the browned first cut on Grandpa's plate. It happened every Sunday, and still we resented it. Grandpa never ate more than a bite and the rest sat on his plate oozing juice till the end of the meal. Then the cat got it. Mum saw to that. Eating scraps from other people's plates might be all right for Bluey Considine but we were supposed to be civilized beings.

We ate, remembering our manners. Gentility had infected us through Mum and though she struggled to be free, Sunday lunch brought a flush like fever on her cheeks at the 'niceness' of her family. We passed the salt and passed the gravy boat. We remembered not to rub our hands and say how good the food looked.

Grandpa was outside this. He ate as much as he wanted, then he stopped. He dabbed his lips with his serviette and drank from his glass of water. He did not bring his ear trumpet to table but now and then dropped some remark into our talk. Sometimes they were to the point. Seeing Mum angrily wiping a gravy spot from the cloth – 'A man – or woman, Meg – is as big as the things that annoy him.' And to Becky, holding out her bowl: 'The hunger of a fresh young heart.' It had affection but it had an edge. He said to me, 'The sick dog refuses all food.' My heart began to thump. I wondered what he knew. 'I'm not sick.' But he was looking into the distance at some landscape none of us could see. He had this way of coming and going. 'World, world, I cannot get thee close enough.'

'Jesus,' Bobby muttered, turning up his eyes.

'Prithee, let no bird call,' Grandpa said. 'Meg dear, may I be excused? That was a lovely meal.' And off he went to his study to scribble something down, leaving us sniggering; confused; or in a state of wonder.

In the afternoon Esther and Fred Meggett called to see us. We went out to the lawn and sat in the sun. I lay a little way off, brooding on Grandpa's remark. Mum had set Becky to watch the Meggett child, Adrian, but he seemed to like me better and he came and sat on my chest. Esther leaned over and gave him a sip of wine.

'Esther,' Mum protested.

'No harm in it. Get off your cousin you little horror.'

'He's all right,' I said.

'You'd sooner have a girl cuddling up. Tell me about your girls, Raymond.'

'I haven't got any.'

'You're leaving it a bit late. What do you do, just think about them in bed?'

I looked at her with horror. How had she known?

'Thinking's OK. But doing's a lot more fun.' She breathed wine on me and I found I was getting an erection. I rolled over and lay on my stomach. Adrian went sprawling. Esther stood him up and grinned at me. 'Get a girl. I'll bet you're big enough.'

'Leave him alone,' Mum said. 'He's got plenty of time.'

'Now's the time,' Esther said, but she left off tormenting me and listened to Fred telling Dad about the Royal Commission. It was in recess for a day or two.

'They've got nothing on me. I just knew good business when I saw it. It's the civil servants getting it in the neck.'

'What are you going to do with all your loot?' Mum said.

'Wouldn't you like to know.'

'Tell her, Fred.'

'I'm going to build Loomis.'

Mum looked puzzled but Dad sat up straighter.

'Shops,' Fred said. 'The city's got no place to go except out here. So I've taken an option on the land between the bridges. Two years time you won't know Loomis.'

'Who's going to do the building?' Dad asked.

'Me. I'm starting my own construction company.'

'You don't know anything about building.'

'I'll buy people who do know. Might be some plumbing in it, Fergie.'

'Fergus is happy where he is,' Mum said.

'Don't miss your chance, boy. You mightn't ever get another one.'

'I'd have to . . .' Dad said.

'I know what you'd have to do. So come and talk to me. What's a family for?'

'Listen to him!' Esther said. 'But if you can show him some way to make money you're in Fergie.'

Bluey Considine walked by on his way to visit Grandpa. He raised his hat. 'Meg. Esther. Becky. Gentlemen.'

'That old bugger owes me fifty quid,' Fred said.

'Slow horses,' Esther laughed. 'You'll never see it.'

'He's under Meg's protection.'

'Remember that. I won't have betting.'

'I've written it off, Meg. I'm in the big time now. Going places.'

'I'm going too,' Esther cried. She swallowed wine and winked at me. 'Here's a cobber of yours. Tell me what the pair of you talk about.'

It was Duggie, coming uncertainly over the lawn. Esther had her usual effect on him. While everybody looked at him I scuttled to the creek, hiding my condition. Duggie came after me when they let him go. I was all right by then.

'What's the matter? What did you clear out for?'

'I can't stand that Esther.'

'Me neither. Fat bitch. Is anyone in the house?'

'Grandpa and Bluey.'

We went into the living-room. Duggie loved getting in there, especially when no one was about. He poked at things and weighed them in his hands. His eyes gleamed with desire but he kept a sneer on his mouth and threatened to smash vases and tear books. We had nothing grand; no treasures, real or supposed. Unlike Grandma Sole's front room ours was for living in. But something in it drove Duggie wild. He called it stuck-up and called it pansy. He kicked the chairs and joggled ornaments on the mantelpiece.

'Lay off, Duggie.'

'I suppose you'll get all this one day.'

'Why should I? Bobby'll get it.'

'You'll get this house. You'll be rich.' He jerked the edge of a picture, setting it askew. I ran to straighten it.

'Lay off.'

He went into the hall and listened outside the study. 'There's no one in there. You stand guard.'

'No . . .' But he was gone, bent at the waist, tip-toeing. My world began to tremble, then was still. I put my head in at the door and saw Duggie moving round Grandpa's desk trying the drawers.

'Duggie . . .' I wanted him to go on. I wanted him to defile the study. He flicked things in a drawer and gave a grunt.

'Where does he keep his sovereigns?'

'I don't know.'

'Maybe they're in here.' He picked up Grandpa's trumpet from the desk and looked in it. 'Empty. Hey, I reckon you could piss through this.' He stuck it on the front of his trousers. I gave a burst of laughter. Duggie grinned. He put the trumpet to his eye and tried to look at the shelves. 'You reckon he's got any hot books here?'

'I don't think so.' I was deep in betrayal. 'Mum and Dad have got one in their bedroom.'

But Duggie was skimming along the titles. 'It's all dry stuff.' He went to Grandpa's Buddha and looked at it. 'This joker eats too much. He's not made of gold is he?'

'Brass.'

'Who are these sheilas?' He had come to a row of plaster figurines.

'Goddesses. Minerva. Venus. Diana's the one with the bow.'

'Venus has got nice tits.' He fingered them.

I had a touch of my trouble and turned away. Duggie looked at the books climbing to the ceiling. He mounted half-way up Grandpa's steps and stood looking round. 'All this must be worth thousands of quids.'

'I suppose so.'

'Yeah,' he said bitterly. 'Jesus, I'd like to smash this place up.'

I saw that he might come down and begin. I might help him. But as I waited he climbed to the top of the steps and sat down. 'I'm going to have a place like this one day.'

'Let's get out, Duggie.'

'I like it here.' He put the trumpet to his mouth and blew a fart.

'He'll come back.'

It was too late. Grandpa's voice sounded in the hall. I nearly fainted. But Duggie only gave a blink. He climbed down the steps and set the trumpet on the desk. 'Get one, quick,' he said, snatching a book. I grabbed one, not knowing why. 'Read, you stupid bugger.'

Grandpa came through the door. It was not Bluey with him but Wendy Philson. 'Hallo,' Grandpa said, 'a visitation.' He came in, frowning, then started looking pleased. 'You see Wendy, books are a magnet to the young.'

Duggie raised his head and blinked his eyes. 'Grandpa.'

'What are you reading? Ah, Wordsworth. The Child is father of the Man, eh Wendy? And what about Raymond?' He turned to me and took my book. 'Ovid? I didn't know your Latin was that good.'

'He was reading it upside down too,' Wendy said. Grandpa went to his desk and picked up his trumpet.

'You kids get out while the going's good,' Wendy said.

We started for the door. 'Boys. Whenever you want a book come and see me. But I don't recommend Ovid, Raymond.'

'No, Grandpa.'

'Thank you, Grandpa.' Duggie made oriental bows.

'Scram,' Wendy said softly.

'Boys. Ask when you want to come in. Many of these books are valuable.'

'Yes. Sorry. Thank you. Goodbye.'

We got out and ran up the orchard. Duggie rolled in the grass and laughed his head off. 'Jesus, he's a stupid old bugger. Jesus, we fooled him.'

I lay in the grass and said nothing. I did not know what I thought, or what I felt, or even who I was. I loved and hated Grandpa. I loved and hated Duggie. I was terrified of myself and fascinated with myself. I wished that I was dead, but soon ate an apple and was happy. I joked with Duggie.

When we came down Aunt Esther asked if we'd taken measurements.

6

Dad and I bicycled round to the Soles with a paper bag of kumaras. Grandpa handled them like pieces of sculpture. 'Yes,' he said, 'beauties. I'll dig some potatoes for you, Fergus.' They played a game of exchanging produce so that they might praise and boast.

We sat on the lawn drinking beer. Grandpa gave me a full glass now and I had learned to like the taste. Dad was happy. He had his own business at last. Fred Meggett had started him and Dad had done the plumbing in the Loomis shops. Then he had paid the loan back and was free. Mum stopped worrying and so did Grandpa Sole. He was proud of Dad. When it was time to go he dug a root of potatoes.

'Beauties,' Dad said.

'You pick 'em up, Ray. I've been feeling a bit off colour.'

I was putting the last ones in the bag when Grandpa fell down beside me. His face was bulging and his lips flapped like rubber. Dad got down on his knees and tried to hook Grandpa's false teeth out. 'It's a heart attack. Get the doctor.' Grandpa's heels went drumming in the earth. Then he was dead. It all happened in less than a minute. 'Too late, son. Too late,' Dad said to me. He crouched there looking at Grandpa's face.

'Help me get him on the lawn.'

'Are you sure he's . . .'

'I'm sure. You take his legs.'

We carried Grandpa to the lawn and laid him down. Dad took out the false teeth and put them in his pocket. He wet his handkerchief at the garden tap and washed Grandpa's face.

'You wait here, Ray. I'm going to tell Mum.'

I knelt beside Grandpa, and could make nothing of it. He looked like an old man sleeping. Grains of dirt were in his hair.

Dad came back with Grandma. She stood a little way off and

looked at the body. Her face had gone thin but her eyes were dry.

'Bring him into the house.'

Dad and I carried him again. He was heavy and loose and I made hard work of it. Grandma held the bedroom door open. She followed us in and turned the coverlet down.

'He's got dirt on him.'

'Never mind.'

She took off his boots, then sat on a chair by the bed and took his hand. Dad and I watched as she laid her cheek on it.

'Mum . . .'

'Thank you, son. I'll be all right now.'

'I'm going for the doctor. Ray will stay.'

'It's too late for doctors.'

'I'll get Meg.'

'I don't want Meg.'

'Mrs Cooper then.'

'Or Mrs Cooper.'

'He'll need washing.'

'I'll wash him.'

'Mum –'

'No one is touching Ted but me.'

Dad drew me out of the room. He looked as if he had been struck in the throat and could not breathe. 'You go home, Ray. There's nothing you can do.'

So I cycled home to Peacehaven. I tried to feel something as I went but it took me two or three days to understand. Then I was faced with a great hole in that part of my life I'd been certain of. I circled round it trying to see in, and then backed off and looked for things to keep my mind off it. I felt shrunken and dry and felt there was a stranger in my skull laughing at me. What I had loved was taken away. Ha, ha! He seemed to have my brain squeezed in his fist.

Mum had not known I cared so much for Grandpa Sole. I think she found it unreasonable; and possibly perverse, with Grandpa Plumb handy to admire. She was kind to me and we discussed death and the possibility of a life beyond, but reached no conclusions. Both of us were concerned with now. Usually she finished by jumping up and saying, 'Well, I must do the dishes. Life goes on.'

That was more wisdom than I could accept. But something or other, life and death, went on. Bobby was some help. He still gave me the Chinese burn. Now and then we caught a bus and went to a Saturday afternoon movie in town.

One day as we came out a voice murmured at our shoulders, 'Enjoy the picture, boys?'

We turned and saw a man with a chest and throat both soft and strong, and a mouth that was my mother's, and the Spitfire-pilot eyes of Grandpa Plumb.

'You remember me, Bobby?'

'Sure,' Bobby said, 'you're Uncle Alf. I met you at Esther's.'

'And this is Ray? Raymong. Has your mother told you about me, Ray?'

She had, and she had not. What I did not know made me blush, and Uncle Alf laughed. 'You're charming when you blush. How would you boys like to have a milk shake?'

'Sure,' Bobby said. He winked at me. We trooped off to a milk-bar and Bobby and I sat down while Uncle Alf bought our drinks.

'Is he . . . ?'

'He's the pansy. The one Grandpa kicked out.'

'We shouldn't –'

'Free milk shakes. Just make sure he keeps his hands on the table.'

Uncle Alf did not stay with us long. He saw someone beckoning from the window. 'I've got to go now, boys. But I'm often at the pictures on Saturday. We'll meet again. My love to your mum.'

We met several times, then Bobby started Training College and was off after girls. Duggie and I got into the habit of Saturday movies. We played morning sport for Rosebank College, then took a bus or tram and headed for Queen Street. Duggie was after girls too and sometimes picked up a pair of them and dragged me off to milk bars, where I sat silent and miserable, listening to them giggle as he tried out double meanings.

Twice we met Uncle Alf. 'So this is Duggie? What a tribe of nephews I've got. But what's that in your bags? Not muddy gear? You boys are really so masculine. I can see I'll have to take you in hand.'

He was not usually like that. Just the sight of Duggie was enough to make him perform. It was, I think, a kind of self-defence. All the time he was with us he acted like a girl; and hurried away when he saw people watching from other tables.

'So that's a homo,' Duggie said. 'What a laugh.'

'I don't think he actually – I don't think –'

'How dumb can you get? They suck each other. They go up each other's bums. Grandpa found him doing it in the orchard.'

'No,' I said. There was no Marie Stopes to make me believe that.

Next time we met, Duggie asked Alf for a loan.

'Money?'

'Sure. A couple of quid would do. I'm taking a girl out.'

'A couple of quid! Well! A couple of shillings.'

Duggie smiled at him. His ginger eyelashes made him look sleepy. 'I haven't told anyone we've been meeting.'

'Meeting?'

'On Saturday afternoons. You know? In milk bars.'

'I see.' Alf took out his wallet, trembling slightly. 'Two "quid", you say? I hope you have a nice time.'

'I will.' Duggie rolled the notes and slipped them like a pencil into his pocket. 'So long Uncle Alf. Watch yourself, Ray.' He whistled a tune as he went into the street.

'He'll go far,' Alf said. 'He'll be a great man one day.'

I began to say I was sorry, but Alf stopped me. 'It's not your fault. But that boy makes me shiver. I want to keep well away from him. You take my advice and do the same.'

But Duggie, like Bobby, had had enough of my sort of Saturday. There was a natural falling into groups as we grew older and his was made up of boys with knowledge beyond their years. They knew all about sex, and the way the world worked, and knew exactly what they were after. I was in a place for discards; giving my superior grin but turning with bewilderment inside.

I still met Alf. Two or three times I went to his house – keeping it secret from Mum and Dad. We met in town and he drove me to Herne Bay. His friend, his lover, John Willis had died several years before and left his money to Alf – 'I can spare two quid.' Alf had bought an old villa and spent 'far too much' doing it up. I sat in the living-room and talked to him, sipping a glass of wine that made all my secrets tumble out. I felt that Alf was an outcast like me. In the beginning my confessions were loaded down with contempt for us.

He saw it and was angry, but kept quiet. And I got on the other side of contempt. I saw he understood me, I could say *everything* and not be judged, and relief made me break down and cry. He patted my back and left me alone for a while.

Then, with his glass topped up (and a shake of his head for me): 'This manic organ of yours? Where does it happen?'

'Anywhere. In buses. At school. In my School Cert. maths exam.'

'Did you pass?'

'Yes. It happens in the pictures all the time. When people kiss. And when I'm reading books. And when I'm eating. Sometimes I can't leave the table.'

Alf laughed. 'And Meg doesn't see? No, she wouldn't. What goes on in your head?'

'All sorts of things.'

'Like what?'

I told him.

'Pretty hot stuff. Ha, saying it's given you a stiffy. Put a cushion over it, that's right. Some of it's not possible, Ray. Not for human beings. Well, we've got to get it out of your head.'

'How?'

'This partner of yours – these partners? You're sure they're always girls? Never boys?'

'No. I'm sorry, Uncle Alf.'

'Don't call me uncle. And don't be sorry, you're not my type. Do you go to dances?'

'I can't.'

'Why not? Oh, you'd have to hold them at arm's length. Has it crossed your mind they might like the feel of it? I'm not joking.'

'Am I sick? Has it got a name?'

'Everything's got a name. But some things aren't as bad as the names they've got. Priapism. That's,' he raised his forearm, 'all the time. A mild case. And sex in the head.'

'It sounds terrible.' But I laughed.

'Pretty usual with boys. Do you come?'

'What?'

'Do you go off pop?'

'Sometimes.'

'Embarrassing, eh? It used to happen to me. I used to get erections on parade in the school cadets.'

'What did you do?'

He shrugged. 'Do you diddle yourself?'

That was hard for me to admit. He waited until I said yes.

'Well, keep it up. Have fun. But try to be less extravagant here.' He tapped his head. 'The real cure is real girls. Sit in the back row at the pictures, Ray. Put it in their hands. Girls like it. They really do.'

'I know that. I know. But I can't *believe* it.'

All the same, because of that talk and several others I came to believe. It put me back in the human race. And though it did not get me close to girls I was a little readier in my mind. It put the girls up there in the human race too. I kept on meeting Alf from time to time. I think he found me fairly heavy going; but kept his patience, kept his smile, enquired how I was getting on.

In most things I was getting on well. I was in the first fifteen at school. I edited the school magazine – and laid a clutch of sonnets there demanding that Nature satisfy me. My English teacher called them sensitive. As for Duggie, he left Rosebank College at the end of his sixth-form year. Grandpa Plumb had helped Willis with money to keep him there and he was not pleased when Duggie went into an accountant's office and started doing Accountancy I at the university. He wasn't pleased either when I became a prefect in 6A. I didn't like it myself but I didn't know how to say no. Ormiston pinned my badge on me but did not smile. For a year I wandered around giving detentions. I never wore my prefect's badge at home. If Grandpa saw it he spoke about 'the aristocratic embrace'.

Since Grandpa Sole's death I had turned to him. In my confused state it was a natural gravitation. I overlooked his confusions and saw him as a kind of monolith, an Easter Island god frowning at the horizon. He took me out there with him and for a time I was safe. We talked in large terms and never questioned their meaning. Generalities lapped me round and buoyed me up. When we got down to cases they were in another age. I spent much anger on dead villains and was heartened by story-book victories of George Plumb. Grandpa mythologized himself. Later in my life I was cynical; but these days I would not be without him.

He told me how he had battled his church. I saw his resignation as a victory for Man. His voice was modulated beautifully. It rang and boomed and whispered over the lawns. It made my spine prickle and made me catch my breath. I thought of Paul Robeson singing

Lindy Lou. But this was better. This was heroic. Even when he'd known they were after him he would not stop his lectures against the war. Policemen came and wrote down what he said, and he lectured at *them*. 'No ground is too stony, Raymond.' In Paparua prison he made converts. These were victories. I believed in them. I even managed to carry them back to the place where I suffered my defeats. So I had something. I came to believe I was descended from a special line. It helped explain my loneliness and helped me fix my superior smile.

A year or so before he died Grandpa met Uncle Alf round at Esther's. I had not known how much Alf hated him. Grandpa came home and sat in the summer-house. There he was, a little withered man in a grey suit and tennis shoes. Peering from the edge of the lawn I saw he was stunned and patient. He was waiting to die.

Mum beckoned me to the veranda. 'Alfred smashed his trumpet.' I did not let on I knew Alfred. 'It was so horrible. He was, he seemed, all wet and red. Dad was like a child.'

'Shall I play draughts with him?'

I went to the summer-house and set the board up on the table. I put out my fists and Grandpa tapped one. He did not make his usual remark about the symbolism of black and white. I had beaten him several times lately but that day I made sure he won. He seemed to me childlike. He forgot Alfred, and his trumpet, and set his eyes darting round the board. 'Crown me,' he said when I was slow.

Soon Mum came and led him in for tea. He had it in his study and that night I saw no more of him. Aunt Felicity, who was up on a visit, sat and smouldered during our meal. She had gone with Mum and Grandpa to see Alf and she was full of rage at 'that stupid old man'. Now and then she broke out but Mum shushed her angrily.

Felicity had the effect on me that Esther had on Duggie. She set me off balance. She took on a complacent air in talk about religion or 'the mind'. I felt second-rate. Nothing I managed to say ever surprised her. She looked at me and said, 'Well, you'll grow up.' It pleased me that Mum wasn't scared of her. Mum got very blunt, almost crude. That day she said, 'Don't get all Catholic and sniffy.'

'Catholic? –'

'How can you listen to those blue-chinned priests?'

'Now just hold on –'

'If you ask me what they need is a bit of loving from a pretty girl.'

We looked at her with astonishment. Felicity laughed. 'I do like your way with a *non sequitur*.' We relaxed – which might have been the end Mum was looking for. None of us knew what a *non sequitur* was but we were pleased Mum was good at them.

My talks with Grandpa changed. He stopped booming at me about his battles and seemed to recall, with a kind of wonder, that other things had happened in his life. I learned more about my grandmother than I had known before. But he stopped frequently and seemed to listen, and he turned as though someone was creeping up on him. Now that his trumpet was broken he was more eager to hear than he had been before.

'Can you hear the creek, Raymond? I haven't heard a creek for fifty years. What does it sound like?'

'Music,' I cried. 'Wind. A breeze,' mouthing like cheese.

'Like an Aeolean harp. Is the thrush singing?'

'No. There's a skylark over the orchard.'

'What?'

'SKY-LARK.'

'Ah.' He looked up in the wrong direction. 'Hail to thee, blithe Spirit! Your uncle Alfred looked like Percy Bysshe Shelley when he was young. Is it still there?'

'Yes.'

'Your grandmother loved skylarks. She said their song was snow flakes turned into music.'

He was burning a candle to her. She was his personal saint. He did not seem to regret the pain he had caused her, but put it down to the springs of wickedness in him. There was some complacency in his recognition that he was like other men.

He told me of an experience called vastation and found me William James's account of his experience of it. Vastation had come on Grandpa several times. Only recently he had been felled by it – yes, he had actually staggered as though a fist had struck him between the eyes. He had fallen to his knees. It was at the sight of Sutton's face looking at him from the cottage window. Sutton seemed to peer out of a cave; and yet the pane of glass was a mirror. Primitive man, man the brute, squatted in the dark, with nothing learned through the millennia. He picked fleas from his armpits and crushed them in his teeth. With vacant eyes he was the world, and now and then gibbered with fear and hatred. Grandpa was knocked to his knees. He saw himself and the human race.

I thought he had dressed it up. It was too poetical. 'What about the other side of things?'

He watched my lips. 'Ah, mystical experience. Illumination. I've had that too. And it was real. I won't deny it. Unforgettable, Raymond. And yet I forget. There's too much there, too much light, we can't hold it, and what we can hold becomes the enemy of life and the human emotions. There's the rub. No, reason is more use to man. That's his weapon, because the irrational is in us – the dark side is here' – he struck his breast – 'in the best of us. And so we've got to hold on to reason and good sense.'

'Ah,' I said, 'I see,' although I did not. He seemed tired of it too. He sighed and shook his head; and began talking about his wife again.

When he was dying I lost interest in him. Something was going on but it was too far from me. He was a little yellow man in a bed, too weak to lift his hands or talk to me or even look at me. I sat a while, then I went away, worrying about my lack of feeling. I could no longer believe in him as a man, he was something else, some product of his end. What he had been he had put away.

He died. I did not feel the loss I had felt at Ted Sole's death. Today: I think of Ted Sole first, and think of George Plumb longer.

7

I was writing a Political Science essay in the university library when Duggie came up to me and said, 'Put that stuff back on the shelves. We're going to Wellington.'

'What?'

'Do you want to come? We're leaving in half an hour.'

'I can't come to Wellington.'

'Or Mummy might be cross.'

'Lay off, Duggie.'

He looked at my books, flicked their covers closed. 'All these jokers are dead. I'm offering the real thing, boy.'

People were frowning at us so I gathered my notes and we went into the foyer. 'What is this, Duggie?'

'There's five of us going down in Tim Gibbons' van. We need one more.'

'What for? How long are you going?'

'The weekend. Back on Sunday night.'

'I haven't got clothes. Or a toothbrush.'

'You'll be worrying about your pyjamas next.'

'Who's going?'

'Me and Tim. A couple of sheilas he knows. And Miss Gobbloffski.'

'Who?'

'Myra Payne. Myra pain in the arse. Wait till you see her mouth, boy. She's like a vacuum cleaner. You'll find out.' As simply as that he reeled me in. 'How much money you got, Ray?'

'Just my bus fare home.'

'Pity.'

'I've got my Post Office book. I can be back here in half an hour.'

'You'd better run. Tim's arriving in a minute.'

'How much shall I bring?'

'Twenty quid should do it.'

Even that did not stop me. I ran all right. I ran all the way to the Post Office and all the way back, stopping only at Milne and Choyce's to send a message home with Becky that I was off to Wellington. Then we waited two hours for Tim Gibbons. It did not bother me that Duggie had lied. With girls on my mind I did not care. He broke one of my fivers on draught beer and after two drinks I felt the world was a fine place. I trusted Duggie. Words like friends, cousins, went running in my mind.

'What about these sheilas? Is one of them for me?'

Duggie shrugged. 'Try your luck. You'd better lay off that beer, Ray. You're not used to it.'

'One more, eh?'

At six o'clock we walked through Albert Park to the university. Tim Gibbons was waiting in his van, and two girls sitting high with him, straight and pink and white and porcelain. I peered at them and smiled but they kept the inhuman look girls saved for me and my smile sank into my jaws.

'You're late,' Tim Gibbons said.

'We're here now. Give us a tenner, Ray.'

I handed over two fivers carelessly and Duggie gave them to Tim. 'One for him, one for me.'

'What about? –' Tim gestured at the back of the van.

'She pays for herself.'

'She hasn't yet.'

'She will.'

'OK. Hop in.'

Duggie opened the rear doors and there was Myra Payne as advertised. She was sitting on a blanket, on a mattress. She smiled at Duggie; and she frowned at me. I had expected a slut, with that gluey lipstick that sluts wore. This girl was elegant and pretty. She wore pale lipstick and no paint on her nails. She had what my mother called a generous mouth. I knew there was no way she would look at me and I made little nervous bobs of my head.

'This is Ray,' Duggie said. 'Myra.'

'You didn't say anyone else was coming.'

'Plenty of room. Hop in, Ray. Shift your arse over, Payne.'

I put my satchel in the van and clambered up. Tim Gibbons locked the doors and we started out of Auckland.

'Hey Tim,' Duggie yelled, 'push one of those sheilas back for Ray.'

But the cab was a substantive world and had no connection with ours. Down the Great South Road, over the Bombay hill, my sense of unreality grew until I was in a panic. Where was I going? How had I got into this? I was on the point of yelling for the van to stop. I leaned on the doors, thinking it would be a release if they sprang open and threw me on the road, shattered me.

Myra sulked. Duggie winked at me. He felt in her bag and conjured out a bottle with a horse on it. 'Presto! Gee up, Payne.' She gave a defeated smile and drank from it and gasped and rolled her eyes. It placed her for me as surely as if she had spoken dirty words. The glugging sound marked her equally. But I made no return from my limbo. Drink, women, conversation – everything was beyond me. When she offered me the bottle I shook my head. I watched while she and Duggie started kissing. When it was dark they did other things. I saw them in flashes from the street lights. I saw locking forearm and bald knee and heard soft cries. They sat up smoking cigarettes. Myra offered her packet. 'No thank you.'

'He's got a mummy,' Duggie said. Myra whispered something in his ear. 'She reckons you must be sublimating, Ray.'

In Te Kuiti we bought pies and coffee. Tim Gibbons and his girls ate high in the cab. 'You should be doing law. They'd be all over you,' Duggie said. We went across to the station lavatory. 'Did you see her gobbling me off. Then she wanted to kiss me. Dirty bitch.'

Back in the van. Down through the hills to Taumurunui. Down past the mountains. More things were going on. I tried to sleep and managed it in snatches. Somewhere south of Taihape Myra and Duggie hissed a quarrel. She gave a screech of pain. 'All right, all right.' I saw her crawling at me like a hedgehog. In flashing lights I saw her face was wet. Her hand was at my fly. I got those buttons open with a rip, and had her hand on me as I said kindly, 'You don't have to.'

'Shut up,' she moaned.

'Compliments of the management,' Duggie said.

It didn't take long. I censored anger from her hand and shame from me. She crawled away and huddled in a corner.

'Nice?' Duggie asked. His face had an elevated look. He was

benevolent and careless. Later Myra shifted back to him and did some more of what he liked. 'You like that?' 'Sure I like.' 'I'm the only one who'll do that for you.'

We came into Wellington at dawn. Tired, half-sick, tormented by shame, I saw the hills and harbour and felt their shape and stillness cleansing me. I told myself I would live in this town. Duggie and Myra were sleeping. She looked smeared and swollen. Her prettiness, her elegance, were gone. She made little farts and twitched her hands. Duggie looked seedy too, but dangerous in his sleep.

The van climbed into a suburb of tall houses and narrow streets. Tim Gibbons came round and opened the doors.

'Out.'

Duggie did not wake up.

'You've had your ride.'

'I'm staying here.'

'Listen –'

'I paid a tenner. So you piss off.'

Tim Gibbons blinked. He shrank. The two girls stared at me.

'Well if that's how you feel,' Gibbons said. They went into a house.

'Good on you, Ray. You told him,' Duggie said.

We slept in the van for most of the morning. Then Duggie wobbled Myra awake. He had a bag with him and he took out a clean shirt and underpants and a toilet bag. I was not surprised. He had his toothbrush.

'Let's go in and twist old Timothy's arm. Stay here Ray till I get the lay of the land.'

He came back in half an hour, clean and shaved. 'Get in and wash, you scruffy bugger.'

'I'm staying here.' I was determined to be dirty. I was going to sit this weekend out, get myself through it by sitting still, and back in Auckland I was going to write Duggie out of my life.

'Suit yourself,' Duggie said. He went away.

At midday I walked down into the town. I ate another pie and sat on the wharves watching the black mountains over the harbour. A wind was raising white caps and blowing gulls in curving falls out towards an island with yellow cliffs. That, I guessed, was Somes Island, where they had kept enemy aliens in the war. It looked like a haven more than a prison. In the wind and sunlight I began to feel better. I followed the wharves and the waterfront road and came to Oriental Bay. There I sat in the bandstand, watching yachts, watching hills, until I began to be cold. Wellington, I thought, I'll live here one day. I told myself I would start again.

The rest of the afternoon I sat in the movies. Then I followed my nose back up the hills and found the van still parked by tall thin houses. I opened the doors and there was Myra again, wrapped in her blanket. Her hair was down and she looked like a squaw.

'Where's Duggie?'

'How would I know?'

'When's he coming back?'

'How would I know?' Tears rolled on her cheeks. I offered my handkerchief. She shook her head. 'Please go away.'

'Have you had tea?'

'I can't eat.'

'I'll get some fish and chips.'

I walked down town again and found a fish shop and came striding back with my warm packet. It took an hour but Myra was still there. We ate fish and chips.

'He just went away and left me.'

'It's the sort of thing he does.'

'He's a bastard.'

'You don't have to tell me. I grew up with him.'

'You're cousins?'

'Yes.'

'I love Duggie. I know he's only eighteen. I'm twenty seven.'

'Age,' I said, 'doesn't make any difference. If you're in love.'

'That's what I think. I'd do anything for him. Why does he treat me so badly?'

She cried quietly. I knew I should put my arm round her but I could not do it. I sat there being helpless, sentimental. She was pretty again, and pitiable. Not elegant. Grease and tears were round her mouth.

I did not expect to see Duggie again but he came as dark was falling, in a car with a young man and two girls.

'Oh-uh, oh-uh,' Myra wept. 'Please don't let him see me.'

Duggie jumped out of the back seat, leaving a girl who seemed at a distance beautiful, cool, composed. She had blond hair falling on her cheeks.

'Ray.' He drew me up the road past the van. 'Is Myra there? Look, take care of her eh? I've got this little piece. I don't want Miss Gobbloffski on my back.'

'What am I supposed to do?'

'Just look after her. I need a fiver. You still got some money?'

'No.'

'Come on, Ray. A fiver and you can have Miss Gobbloffski.'

'Listen –'

'Joke, joke. This Glenda's real class, Ray. I've got to have some money.'

'She looks about fifteen.'

'She's old enough. Come on, I'll pay you back.'

I gave him my last note.

'Thanks.' He dug me with his elbow and jerked his thumb at the van. 'Get in there boy.' He ran to the car, the blonde girl drew him in, and they were gone.

I climbed into the van. Myra was a bruised shape in the dark.

'Where's he gone?'

'I don't know.'

'Who was the girl with him?'

'I don't know. He took my money.'

'She was young.'

'He sold you to me for a fiver.'

She lay in her corner and sobbed evenly, making a sound like tearing paper.

'Myra.'

'Leave me alone.'

I sat on the edge of the mattress and listened to her. After a while she said, 'Have you got that hankie?'

I gave it to her.

'I wish I could kill him.'

'Myra, I'm sorry.' I had begun to smell her. She was wet and pungent. I moved close and touched her cheek. A throbbing started in me. I was tumid with lust and pity. 'Myra, I'll help you. I really like you.' I took her hand and put it on my trousers. The bulge there was the size of a cucumber and I felt her hand take notice of its shape. Then she gave a yelping laugh. She pulled open my fly and got her hand inside my underpants. I was dizzy with excitement and exultation. This was me. This was happening to me. Then I screamed. I had never felt worse pain. She had my balls and was twisting them and digging her fingernails in.

'You creepy little bastard,' she yelled; and gave another twist.

I screamed like someone murdered and she let go.

'Get out of here. Get out, you creepy sod.'

I got out. Somehow I fell out. I was on my knees at the back of the van, holding myself, whimpering with pain. She put her foot on me and sent me sprawling. I got up and stumbled down the road, running bent and throwing up my hands like a capuchin monkey. I wept as I ran. I was destroyed.

After a while I went out of houses into trees and blundered in the dark, sobbing my name. I smelled pine trees, and lay on needles, curled up in a ball. The pain had a beat in it like drums. Sideways, I saw the moon on water, and I thought of going down to the wharves and tumbling off like a shot man, sinking into the clean cold, not coming up. I saw my body in the harbour mud, crusting with mussels; and played that several ways, increasing its attractions, until I was able to get clear of it and snigger with self-contempt. This was not the night I was going to die. If I killed myself it would be without self-indulgence.

When I was able to walk I went higher up the roads. On the hills over the city I found myself on a country track. Cold air. Pine trees heaving in a wind. Lights burned in Oriental Bay and pricked in suburbs at the back of the island, on the lower rim of huge black hills. The sky was clear, the moon was lemon-shaped. Stars trembled on the edge of going out. The harbour seemed to turn itself on and off. It was two things – flat white plate, porcelain and lovely – then a hole that opened into nothing. I watched it flick back and forth. Pain, humiliation, had me in a mildly visionary state, and this was my vision: people showing glow-worm lights on the edge of nothing. I thought it was a good one – it would do me. I promised I would live in Wellington.

I came down a different way, past houses on wide lawns, down a zig-zag angling twenty times. I looked at names of streets but they meant nothing. When I came to the place where the van should have been I gave a laugh. Of course it was gone. Finding it there would have broken the pattern. I stood under a street lamp and looked at my watch. I counted the silver in my pocket. Eight and sixpence.

Then I walked down to the city. It was eleven o'clock. I had been playing at desolation. Even when I ran down the street holding my balls I knew I had relatives in this town. One of the names I had seen high on the hill came back to me: Wadestown Road. I had seen Mum write it on a letter to her brother Oliver. But I grinned with fright at the thought of that icy man. At the station I looked in the telephone book and found the address of M. J. and F. E. Waring. It was in Khandallah. I liked that name. Sitting in the taxi, heading into family, I said it to myself. I tried to keep the night alive. What had happened to me was at least *something*.

I paid and had a shilling left. Then I stood among gnome houses and could not make connections. Where was I? What had brought me here? The moon sailed in the sky as strangely as if it sailed over continents of ice. There was nothing I wanted but to sink into warmth. I ran to a letterbox and found my number. If they were not at home I would curl up on their door mat like a dog. I ran up a path through hump-backed shrubs. Steps sent me sprawling on hands and knees. I saw a light somewhere at the back, in a second-storey room. It shone like the sun on me, enfolded me, it brought me home. I stood up easy, smoothed my hair and hoped I did not smell, and I checked my fly that had come undone so easily; and when I was all right, grubby but sufficiently a Plumb, I knocked on the door.

Max Waring came. I had met him at Grandpa's funeral. He peered at me over reading glasses. He was wearing a dressing gown and pom-pommed slippers.

'Hello, Uncle Max.'

He put his tiny woman-hands at me. 'Raymond. Raymond Sole. Well I never.'

'I was just in Wellington so I . . .'

'Come in Ray, come in.' He had black darting eyes that took me in head to foot. 'Is something wrong?'

I stepped into the hall. Aunt Felicity leaned over the rail. She wore a hairnet and her face glistened with cream. 'Who is it, Max? Good grief, Raymond. How did you get here?'

'I was in Wellington and I ran out of money, so . . . I'm sorry it's so late.'

She came down the stairs and kissed me. Brisk. No nonsense. 'Something fishy, Max.'

'I think so, dear. But let him have a bath. And a sleep. We can talk in the morning.'

'Yes. A bath.' Max scuttled away. 'Come under the light, boy.' She turned on the hall lamp and dragged me to it. 'Is this one of those escapades? Girls at the back of it, I shouldn't wonder. Does your mother know you're here?'

'Not exactly.'

'Good grief, you smell. How long since you changed that shirt?'

'Only two days.'

'I'll bet your underclothes are a mess. Is anyone with you?'

'Duggie. I don't know where he's gone.'

'Attila the Hun. That explains it.'

I was back in my place, nobody; with no desire to argue. I let myself be turned around and prodded to the bathroom. If she had undressed me I wouldn't have minded.

Max said, 'There, nice and hot. Have a good long soak.'

I lowered myself in: sour feet, smelly armpits, tender balls. I washed out fish smell, sex smell, cigarette. I washed my hair. Then I wrapped myself in a towel and pulled the plug. Max must have been waiting at the door.

'You out, Ray? You decent?'

Felicity came galloping up. 'Don't worry about that, man. Here, give me those.' She burst in with pyjamas. 'Put these on. They were Peter's, they should fit. And then to bed.' She turned my dirty clothes with her toe. 'Leave those. I'll wash them in the morning. Have you got that toothbrush, Max? Listen young fellow, I'll be wanting your story. Lock stock and barrel. And no lies.'

'Yes, Felicity.' I cleaned my teeth and went to bed. Max had put a hot water bottle in. I lay and sighed and smiled into the dark. My balls throbbed pleasantly. I thought with admiration of Myra Payne. I approved of what she had done and wished that she would do the same to Duggie. There wasn't any malice in the thought. I wondered how he was getting on with the blonde girl, Glenda.

The morning wasn't such a happy time. Mornings seldom are. A weasel had my testicles and would not let them go. The bite turned into aching as I woke. Swellings, yellow bruising, had given me a strange unhealthy fruit between my legs. I examined it with fatalism. If she'd ruined me for life that was that.

I covered myself and lay back. There was another thing, less easy to accept. No matter how I cleared my mind it turned there on the blue; a great black bird. *Creepy*. She'd called me *creepy*.

Max came in with porridge and tea. 'Sleep well?'

'Yes. Thank you.'

'Felicity's gone to mass. What's the matter? You don't look well.'

'It's a headache. Maybe if you've got a couple of Aspros . . .'

He ran off and got them. I saw he enjoyed doctoring and wondered if, after all, I should show him my balls. I could see him compassionate, putting on ice packs; and I had a moment's hope that he would cure creepy.

'Eat your porridge while it's hot. Is the tea how you like it?'

'Just right. Thanks very much.'

'I'll lend you a razor when you've finished. It would be an idea to be out of bed when Felix gets back.'

'Oh. Sure. OK.'

I ate, and kept my troubles to myself. Max found me some old clothes that had been my cousin Peter's. Shaved and dressed, I went downstairs. My movements all that day were measured, stately. I gave white smiles and enjoyed my pain; and talking humorously, being wise, I managed to believe I was not creepy.

Felicity sat in her chair and let Max fuss around her. She pointed to where she'd like me and I sat there. 'Stop fussing, Max. Sit down. Right young man, spill the beans.'

I told them most of what had happened, leaving out the sex. I made them laugh. Once when I began to complain I saw they liked me less so I dropped that. I praised Duggie for at least knowing who he was and what he wanted.

Felicity snorted. 'He's a little crook. This girl of his – he went off with someone else. What happened to her?'

'She cried. Not much else she could do.'

'Why didn't you bring her here?'

'She didn't want me. I tried.'

'Tried what? Girls get a bad time, Ray. Remember that.'

'We all get a bad time,' Max said. 'The only thing is to keep bouncing back.'

'How's that for a philosophy of life?' Felicity said.

'Now Felix, don't get on at me. I'm a humanist, Ray. She doesn't like it.'

So we got past my adventures on to the meaning of life and Max and Felicity scored fondly off each other – Max more fond than Felix and more gentle. Neither was touched by any witticism; by logic or by doctrine; they simply put on their show and I was confused. So much that both of them said seemed right, even when they contradicted each other.

Max cooked lunch. Afterwards we went for a walk in Khandallah. They went along more quickly than I liked but I grinned and kept up and gave them all the family news from Auckland. Felicity made sharp remarks – she had everyone's number; though, as Max told me, she loved them dearly. Coming back, licking an ice cream, she asked me about myself: what was I doing with my life? what was I looking for apart from a good time? I told her about university, how sadly I was lost there. I had not told my parents. It's easier to confess to someone interested than those who love you. I described my feelings on climbing the stone steps, entering the stone hall under the wedding-cake tower. I felt I was stepping out of my life into some icy marriage. The riches I'd been promised, those feasts and satisfactions of the mind, were not there. I felt like the ghost at the wedding. People seemed to shy away from me. I had been at varsity two months, I said, and spoken to no one.

Felicity laughed. 'You're dressing up your shyness in some pretty fancy clothes.'

I was offended and tried to explain it was more than shyness. I had to believe there was something in me too fine for the place I'd found myself in. But Felicity raised her eyes and gave a laugh, and I saw how ridiculous I was; and was filled with envy of those easy boys who sat in the cafeteria, who walked in the cloisters and the park, holding girls by the hand. I had an image of myself wrapped in a sticky membrane.

'I'm going to leave. I want to get a job.'

'What as?'

'I'm going to be a journalist.'

'Ah,' Max said, 'that's good. I wanted to be a journalist. You'll meet people that way. You'll have to talk to them.'

'It'll bring you down to earth,' Felicity said. 'But your mother won't be pleased. She wants to see you in a cap and gown.'

'I've got to do what I want.'

'Yes, you have.'

Back at the house Max brought my clothes in from the line. He finished drying them in front of a fire. At half past six I was fed and dressed and ready for the Limited. Felicity patted me and gave me a kiss.

'You've got a lot of growing up to do.'

'Yes. Goodbye. And thank you.' She was a tough old thing and I was lucky to have her.

'Keep clear of Duggie. You don't need him.'

'I will.'

'And get away from that blessed Peacehaven. It's a big wide world out there.'

'Stop bossing him, Felicity. He'll find his own way.'

She came out to the steps and watched Max get the car out. No 'drive carefullys', no watching us out of sight. She went inside and closed the door. Max drove me to the station. He bought a ticket and a pillow and gave me a pound note – 'In case of emergencies.'

'Thank you, Max.'

'There's something I've got to say.' This little man who did not come to my shoulder; bright-eyed, bright-faced, sharp as a pixie. 'I've noticed the way you're walking. If you've got anything wrong down there, see a doctor. The minute you get home. Don't delay.'

I blushed. 'It's not that. I got a kick. From a girl. Well – she twisted them.'

'Ha! Ha!' He blushed too. 'I'll keep it to myself. Ray, this business with girls, if you'll excuse me, you can't go into it with most parts missing. A doo-dah on its own won't get you far.'

'No, I see that.'

'One day you'll want a woman like Felicity – with a mind.'

'Yes, I suppose so.'

'Just thought I'd pass it on. Well, all aboard. I'm glad it's not the other thing.'

The train rolled along the harbour front and dived into a tunnel. Towards Paekakariki I saw Tim Gibbons' van running parallel with us and caught a glimpse of Duggie next to him. I wondered what had happened to the girls. They were not the sort to be sold off like Myra. The van drew ahead and flicked away under a bridge. My satchel was in the back with my library books and Pol. Sci. essay inside. I was pleased at the idea of them heading off, and the essay finishing in mid-argument. I did not mind if I never saw them again. I did not mind if I never saw Duggie either.

Then I felt a grief like the passing of innocence. It was as if I had believed in magic and now saw tricks for what they were. I was in a world where things were worked by wires – where people had a single shape and ended at their fingertips.

That was no visionary moment but a flash of conviction. It burned an epidermis off my mind and left me free of its sudden grief, and fresh, and ready.

Through the night I watched the towns go by. There was, as Felicity had said, a big wide world out there. I was going to prove I was not creepy.

8

So I missed seeing Duggie's metamorphosis. I had no clear view of mine. I woke one morning in a rusty bed in a boarding house called Primrose Hall set behind Phoenix palms off the main street of Gerriston on the edge of the Hauraki plains. A man called Don snored and farted in a bed over the room. His teeth grinned in a glass of yellow water. He had shown me his hernia. Twice in the night he had got up and pissed out the window. I hugged myself and grinned at the ceiling. Maps of South America up there. And fleas in the mat. There were fleas all over town. A circus had come through and now we had a plague of them. Don had sat with his bare feet on the mat and caught them with a wet piece of soap as they jumped aboard. That was a trick worth knowing. I felt I was away from home at last.

My job was with the *Gerriston Independent*. I was proof-reader and cub reporter. The *Independent* came out on Mondays, Wednesdays and Fridays. Its old press clanked and slapped in a shed with an iron roof at the back of a stationer's shop. The editor's office was ten by ten. The reporters' room was ten by ten. Fleas were in the mat there too. They had our girl reporter Iris in tears. We tried to help her make a joke of them but she was from a good home and fleas meant dirt and she wasn't laughing at that. Trevor Barley, the editor, wrote his Wednesday leader on the need for better public health measures to combat invasions of this sort. The chief reporter, Morrie Horne, wrote the news report. And I did a humorous piece called *The Democracy of Fleas* – how they bit the highest with the low. Trevor Barley cut out several adjectives and ran it – my first article. I posted a clipping home to Mum.

Trevor Barley was pleased with me. I was willing to do just about anything. I would have made the tea and swept the floor. Although my sense of having begun kept my voice firm and my shoulders straight, I was also very humble and had rushes of gratitude that made me want to open doors for people and wash their cups. 'Stop being such a goddam girl,' Morrie Horne snarled. That cured me. I was sensitive to how people saw me. Humbleness troubled me no more, and gratitude became too generalized for me to hold. It caught me now and then and made me grin; but soon I was more pleased with myself than with other people.

The pay was forty-five shillings a week. When people asked me why I didn't leave Primrose Hall for private board I replied that I couldn't afford to. But nothing would have made me leave the Hall. I shifted from the double room into a single one. That was as far as I meant to go. I pinned a few prints on the wall and screwed a bookcase up for my Penguins, and bought a strip of Feltex for the floor; and left it at that. I did not want to change Primrose Hall. I was there two years and was nervous all the time that fire or flood or Health Department would take it away from me.

The landlady was Mrs Fitz – Fitzwater, – simmons, – hugh, I never found out. She boiled the flavour out of everything. We ate grey cabbage, grey stew, grey tripe, even grey carrots. On Friday nights she came home from the pub with a giant packet of fish and chips and opened it on the kitchen table, where we helped ourselves. Most of her boarders were back from the pub and did not mind. Mrs Fitz had rolling buttocks and a cupid's-bow mouth. Painted nails were the first thing I saw. They made my heart jump. She was a divorcee, disowned by her sons. She cried about it on Friday nights; and then said, 'What the hell, I've still got me,' and brought out her gin bottle and drank past midnight with whoever was around. I drank with her now and then and we competed in self-pity and unconcern. She took me up to the front room where she had a bed deep as a basin. It was said you could buy Mrs Fitz for a pound. She never asked any payment from me. She showed me what to do and said I needed lots and lots of practice.

In the mornings I came into a dining-room so genteel I felt I had been jerked out of my time. It was as though nature had gone wrong. Mrs Fitz came in with a tray of porridge bowls and set them out. The porridge steamed in the chilly air. She said, 'Good morning, Mr Sole.' The room made her formal, it restored her, and though she had found it ready-made when she bought Primrose Hall it was fixed and beautiful among the floating pieces of her life. You paid your respects there to Mrs Fitz. You did not raise your voice. You watched your manners.

'A chilly morning, Mrs Fitz.'

'You'll have to buy some gloves, Mr Sole.'

I felt a little dizzy from my about-face jerk into the day. I'd spent the dark hours cosy in her bed. Done it – what? – seven times? I'd had her breasts, white and warm and spongy, smothering me, and hands that put porridge down and mouth that said Mr Sole busily making me hard for more and more. It helped me when I smelled the porridge burned, and saw the red on her nails flaking off.

'Or you could find a girl to knit you some.' That was better.

'I'll have to do that, Mrs Fitz.'

She went back to the kitchen.

'They say you can have her for a pound,' wheezed an itinerant plasterer.

'Don't you believe it. Good woman, Mrs Fitz. Very moral. Look around if you don't believe me.'

The wallpaper might bubble, even breathe, but it was rich gold and rich maroon. Ornate mouldings curved into the ceiling, where a coloured-glass chandelier turned like the minute hand of a clock. Illuminated verses – *We are nearer God's heart in a garden . . . I think that I shall never see . . .* hung above oak chairs and rosewood cabinets and a black piano with yellow teeth. Over the fireplace was a huge red painting – *Soldiers of the Queen* : Victorian arrogance, moustachioed and paunchy, and the little queen like a chip of ice in it. There was a Maxfield Parrish too, glaring back in blue at the red: naked maidens, gelded youths, in Greek columns, by a lake. It made me think of my mother.

'Ah,' wheezed the plasterer, 'I seen some joker coming out of her room the other night.'

'You sure?'

'Wednesday. After the pictures.'

It was not me. I did not care.

At Primrose Hall we had 'some dodgy types', said Mrs Fitz. She did not seem to like them less for that. Maintenance dodgers, tax evaders, passed through. Some were not sure what name they were using. We had a con man in a Tyrolean hat and a porno king with his suitcase full of cyclostyled yarns. The local police sergeant looked in often. He shook his head at finding me still there. One night detectives from Auckland came barging in and arrested the quiet chap in the room next to mine. It turned out he was a tank man. He had his gear and loot in a laundry bag under his bed.

Iris's mother offered me board. She felt it was her duty. I thanked her and said I liked the freedom at Primrose Hall.

After a while I stopped sending clippings home. I tried to stop using the word, believing that it did not suit my style. I went up to Auckland for Becky's wedding and her sugar-cake dress and pink bridesmaids seemed to come out of a fairy-tale book. I had grown out of her, and Mum, and Bobby, and my love for them had become a burden. I took it back to Gerriston, feeling it under my ribs like indigestion. I saw myself like a dog on a running-wire, getting just so far then finding nowhere to go but back to the kennel. For a while I was violent in my mind, inventing fires and drowning at Peacehaven. But that soon passed, and I was scribbling notes about the weather, and saying I couldn't come for Easter – because of this, because of that. Mum wrote that she understood.

Morrie Horne became a drinking mate. Later we worked together on the *Evening Post*. Trevor Barley taught me how to write. He was a patient man. But it was the owner of the paper, Charlie Kittredge, who became my only real friend in Gerriston. Charlie, a returned soldier, started the *Independent* in 1919. He kept it alive as a broadsheet in the depression, and used sausage paper in World War 2. He edited it for twenty-five years, but when he hired Trevor Barley agreed to limit himself to an article a week. We called it Charlie's porridge. He wrote on political economy and the social contract. *The Wealth of Nations* was his holy book and his weekly article was a hymn of praise to free enterprise. When I told him I was a Socialist he said I had some growing up to do. Socialism was a young man's disease, a part of wild oats and Dad-bashing. He warned me that past a certain age it grew malignant and held up 'poor sick Britain' as an example. It did not trouble him to see the Empire breaking up. Empire was a malignancy too. But he insisted on a hierarchy within the state. His ideas shocked me. I had not done Pol. Sci. long enough to discover their pedigree and thought at first he was Sid Holland's man. But Charlie loathed Sid Holland and 'that crew'. They muddied his ideal. He saw them as selfseekers. 'There's not an ounce of greed in Adam Smith.'

Charlie found no heroes in the waterfront dispute of '51. He saw corruption and betrayal. His view was almost theological. Evil had lurched out into the open. The bright god was dying. In other words, passion conquered order. Trevor Barley was unhappy too. After the February Emergency Regulations he decided the *Independent* would run no letters on the strike. 'If we can't have both sides we'll have none.' His editorials were among the few in the country that kept a tone of reason.

As for me, I went out in the night painting slogans. My favourite was $id ⇕olland. I painted it on the brewery gates and the town water tower. Up there I felt like a hero of the revolution. I hung over an eighty-foot drop with my paint tin on my thumb and made a fat dollar sign and a swastika like a running man. The tin slipped off and crashed into the paddock. No matter – I had done it. In the morning Gerriston would read my message. I took my torch out of my windbreaker pocket and played it on the words. I was swollen with accomplishment. Grandpa Plumb would be proud of me.

I dropped my brush down to join the tin and climbed on to the roof of the tower. It was past midnight and most of the town lights were out. I sat and grinned at Gerriston, feeling it was mine; but soon became disturbed by its smallness on the plain. I felt that I was on the edge of nothing, hanging on with fingernails and teeth. I was afraid of my tininess. The town was made of cardboard. It was accidental. Raymond Sole, sitting on this tower, was accidental.

Then the picture broke and reassembled. No shortage of significance now. That was a police car turning in at the gate. Its lights came stiffly round and settled on the tower base. Flattened on the roof, I heard tyres rasp on gravel, heard doors thump. Torch beams angled up from the rim of the plate where I lay spread out like frog awaiting dissection.

'Sid Holland. It's that bastard.' Sergeant Whittle.

'Shall I go up, Sarge?' Constable Toomey. I sometimes had a drink with him. He thought I was a smart-arse. I looked around but there was nowhere to go. I had the urge to climb into the sky.

'Here's his paint tin, Sarge. The bugger's done a bunk.'

Whittle gave it a boot. 'I'll do the sod over when I catch him. Get out there Frank and have a look in the bushes.'

Toomey went off with his torch and I saw its yellow puddle working along the trees by the cricket field. Whittle prowled round the foot of the tower. I heard him muttering. His boots rang as he climbed a dozen steps up the ladder. He shone his torch up. Toomey came back from the trees. 'Nothing, Sarge.'

'It's the same bloke. He's got his bloody swastika the wrong way round.'

After a while they drove away. I lay on the iron lid watching their car slide into the corners of Gerriston. Sometimes it floated like a fish; then its lights would leap at distant things and I felt the menace of it and its power to break my life. It seemed the car was after me, not men.

At three o'clock I lost it. Suddenly it was gone, and then I saw it parked and empty in the police station yard. I climbed down gripping with numb hands, treading on dead feet, and swam home through the streets, working my mouth. I lay in bed with my hands like ice, my frozen buttocks missing from my body. No more slogans, I said. I dreamed I was dying.

In the morning council workmen scrubbed the tower. I wrote a report on 'our phantom slogan-writer' but Trevor Barley would not allow me that or Sid Holland, even when I made the swastika right. 'An anti-Government slogan' was as far as he would go.

The following day I took my lunch into the park. The water tower stood up over the trees like a martian machine. The ghost of my message was on its side and I drank my bottle of fizz to it, wishing it a long life. Iris and her girlfriend from the Loan and Mercantile office sunned themselves on a bench along from me. When I had finished my lunch I sat with them. The girl from Loan and Merc. was dumb, pretty, remote, and I had grown sure enough of myself to make a game of getting nowhere with her. I had just seen her glaze over and her goldfish mouth contract when a man on the bandstand steps stood up and shouted, 'Brothers! Comrades!'

'My God,' I said, 'a wharfie.'

'Brothers, I want to tell you the true story about what's happening in our country . . .'

'Iris, get your camera. Run.'

'What for?'

'This is a story. We can get pictures.'

'It's no good getting pictures you can't print.'

'We'll print them. Go on. You're supposed to be a reporter.' I was making little runs at the bandstand and running back at Iris. She did not move.

'Someone should get the police,' the Loan and Merc. girl said. She stood up suddenly, her face gone red. 'Communist,' she screamed at the wharfie. 'Why don't you go to Russia?'

'Go on, Iris.'

'Too late. Here's the cops. Plain clothes, eh?'

They came from a car by the fence, slow as Jersey bulls ambling in a show-ring. One of them was eating a pie and he flicked the crust to seagulls on the cricket pitch.

'They're not local. They must have followed him.' I ran across the grass and fell in step. '*Gerriston Independent*. Can you tell me who you are?'

'Buzz off, sonny.'

The wharfie began a gabbling shout. He was a fat man in a tartan shirt and a red tie. 'Here they come. Here they come. The minions of Sid Holland's fascist state. Watch them, brothers. Watch them put the boot in.' He remembered his message. 'This is not a strike, this is a lock-out. The ship owners have bought Sid Holland and his crew. They've bought the newspapers. Don't believe the papers. They're printing lies. We have been locked out. We are not on strike —'

'Come on, Joe.' They mounted into the bandstand without hurry. One took him by the back of his neck, the other bent his arm in a hammerlock. The wharfie's hat fell off. I saw his ridged scalp coming down the steps at me, waist high.

'Ow! Ow! You don't have to . . . No need . . .'

'Shut up, Joe. Move.' They kneed his buttocks.

'*Gerriston Independent*,' I gabbled.

'Out of the way, sonny.'

They took the wharfie to their car and pushed him into the back seat. One got in with him and the other behind the wheel. 'What's your name, son?'

'Ray Sole. *Independent*.'

'You hear that, Mick? His name's R. Sole.'

'Don't go printing any stories, R. Sole.'

They drove away. I saw Mick sitting sideways and saw his fist come up and fall like a club.

'Did you see? They're beating him up.'

The three or four watchers took a dead look.

'Come on, Ray,' Iris said. 'You'll get yourself in trouble.'

'You saw it.'

'Serves him right,' the Loan and Merc. girl said. 'They should shoot them all.'

'It's nice to find you've got a voice, Doreen.'

'They should shoot you, too.' She ran over the grass to the wharfie's hat and gave it a kick that sent it looping in the air. As it came down she caught it and tried to tear the band off. I thought she would attack it with her teeth. Her face was thick with rage. But she worked her fingers in and the stitches popped like corks.

'Come on,' Iris said. 'Into the office.' She pushed me along.

'They can't do that. Not here. Not in New Zealand.'

'They can. They did. They'll do it to you if you make any trouble.'

'I'll make trouble. Stop pushing me.' I ran ahead and had paper in my typewriter before she came in.

When Trevor Barley arrived my story was on his desk. Trevor had been at the pub for his lunchtime stout. It usually made him grumpy but today he just looked tired. He came to our room and closed the door.

'Anyone else see this?'

'I did,' Iris said.

He gave her the story to read. 'That how it happened?'

'More or less.'

'OK. Do me one column inch. Police arrested a man under the Emergency Regulations. That sort of thing.'

'Just a minute,' I said.

'Shut up, Ray.' He threw the story on my desk. 'Keep that for your memoirs. Have you done the stock sale report?'

'No, but listen –'

'You listen. I'm not running a kindergarten for revolutionaries here. You want to write that sort of stuff join the *People's Voice*.'

'Trevor, it happened that way.'

'You say. They'll say different. Get on with your sale report.'

He went out but I passed him in the corridor and ran through the shop to Charlie Kittredge's office. 'Mr Kittredge,' I said, bursting in, throwing down my story on his blotter. Charlie blinked at me. He had been drinking stout with Trevor Barley.

'I wrote this and Mr Barley won't print it. This is an important story.'

Trevor came in. He sat down in a chair and took his glasses off and wiped his eyes. 'Better read it, Charlie.'

'All right.' Charlie read. He hunched his shoulders a little and sighed as he went on. Like Trevor Barley he seemed to grow tired.

'You really think the wharfies are the good guys? There aren't any good guys in this thing.'

'That's not the point –'

'The point is Ray, under the Emergency Regulations we can't print it.'

'I wouldn't print it anyway,' Trevor said, 'until you took all the sob stuff out. You're supposed to be a reporter not a novelist.'

'But,' I said. I got myself together. 'A man was giving a speech. In a free country. Policemen came and arrested him.'

'Not a free country now.'

'That's my point. And they beat him up. And how do we know they were even policemen? They might be some sort of secret police.'

'Come on, Ray.'

'I'd like to follow this up. I'd like to do a proper investigation.'

'And get the paper closed?' Trevor said.

'I'm sorry,' Charlie said. They were both sorry. They had a shrunken look and would not meet my eyes. Trevor went back to his office. Charlie sat and talked at me aimlessly – telling me he didn't agree with Trevor, my story was well done. He was dithering in himself, there was a question in him and he could not say yes or no. I was too upset to be sorry for him. I feel sorry now. He knew what he should do and could not do it. He had been proud of the *Independent*.

How did it end? I walked out of the paper. But I went back, and wrote my sale report. I was pleased with myself for walking out; and felt a cold satisfaction in going back. I did not feel diminished. This was how life had to be played. I would play along. But I wouldn't pretend to like it. I would keep my eyes open.

Soon afterwards Iris became my girlfriend. We went to pictures and we went to dances and when those preliminaries were done went to Primrose Hall instead and spent the time from ten to one in bed.

Iris learned not to mind dirt too much. She liked sex, but liked it slow and tender.

With Mrs Fitz and Iris I began to have some perception of normal feeling between a man and a woman.

9

I cannot be so definite about Duggie's progress. He kept on at the university and in the accountant's office but in the two years I was in Gerriston worked changes in himself that made him barely recognizable. Who was this fellow in the yellow waistcoat, talking like the lord of the manor in some drama club farce? I asked my mother when it had happened, how? But she had seen very little of him. 'He's always been like that. Hasn't he?' Now that she thought about it she wasn't sure. Nobody was sure. Duggie had such belief in himself and engaged you so fully that memories of him would not come clear. I had the advantage of our shared childhood. And I had been away, so the gradations in his change were less fine to me. From this time I was the only one to know him.

'Where did you get the voice, Duggie?'

'How do you mean?'

'That's not Rosebank, that's Kinks College. It's damn near Eton.'

'I've always talked like this.'

'Have you been taking elocution lessons? The rain in Spain . . .'

We were in a private bar drinking bottled beer. I watched Duggie fill his glass. He would never be elegant, but there was a measure in him; he had stopped charging.

'It's a good act, Duggie. Who's it for?'

He looked at me over his glass. 'Cheers.'

'Come on. I'm not one of your girls.'

He gave a little nod. I had shown my limitations. 'You know what I've found out, Ray? You don't have to sit and take it. You can make things happen.'

'I thought you'd always known that. And where does the voice fit in?'

'The way you talk is important,' he said vaguely.

'Are you looking for a wife? Some Remuera dame?'

'Ah, Ray.' His mildness was deceptive. He was assessing me; and because he was fond of me could not believe I had any substance. My mistaking of his ambitions was further proof of it. Almost by accident I became indispensable to him. He licensed me to point out his mistakes.

'People will think you're a poof. And listen Duggie, get rid of that Karitane waistcoat. It makes you look like a con man.'

'Maybe you're right. I didn't like it when I put it on.' He picked at it with his fingers and told me about his girls. They had names like Antoinette and Miranda and they seemed to own little cars and call their fathers Daddy. Some learned ballet or the violin. Nevertheless they 'turned it up'. As usual this sort of talk made me discontented. I told him about Iris and Mrs Fitz. He was not impressed; and I was not. So I boasted of my slogan-writing and my decorating of the water tower.

'Keep quiet about it,' he said.

I drew a dollar sign and a swastika in beer.

'Grow up.' He smeared them with his hand. 'They could still get you. Listen, I'll tell you some news. Beak Wyatt's married.'

'Who to?' I had seen almost nothing of Beak since he left Rosebank College. All I knew was that he had gone through a motor mechanic's apprenticeship in a Loomis garage.

Duggie grinned. 'I reckon you could sit here all day and you'd never guess.' He swallowed some beer. 'Miss Gobbloffski.'

'You're kidding. Myra Payne?'

'Poor old Beak, he'll be quiet now.'

'She's ten years older than him.' I could not marry them in my mind.

'So he's got a mummy. Maybe she'll stick marbles up his bum.'

Duggie had bumped into Myra in John Courts – 'there was nowhere to run' – then Beak came along. He pushed them at each other and got out of there – 'left them sniffing each other's bums'. Now there was this photo in the *Loomis Gazette* – Beak wearing a carnation and Myra dressed in white. 'In white!'

'I still can't see it.'

'She must have been getting desperate. What do you reckon we tell old Beak the sort of girl his wife is?'

They did not matter to him, he was relaxing. I felt more alarmed than privileged at seeing a part of him hidden from others. Then I had a sense that this Duggie, the old one, Millbrook Road boy, was not real. He put the face on like his yellow waistcoat; and I felt myself thinning out, I became as ghostly as Beak and Myra. He picked me up; put me down; forgot me.

'Well, Ray . . .' He looked away from me at the door.

I guessed he was waiting for a girl, and I made a rush at substance: I would see her, I would get her, I would show him I was real.

'You've got a bus to catch,' he said.

'There's a later one.'

'I'm waiting for some friends, actually.'

'Eckchewlay.'

'Don't push it, Ray.'

I watched him fidget as I drank my beer. Then he gave a small grin over my shoulder and said to me softly 'Buzz off, eh?' I turned and saw two young men coming along the room. They were almost as interesting as a girl. The ferrety one in the suit and Calvinist glasses was Mark Brierly. The pink and white hearty in marmalade tweeds, Tony Smith. I saw where Duggie had copied his waistcoat from.

'Ho ho,' Tony Smith said as we shook hands.

'My cousin's a journalist,' Duggie said. He spoke as if explaining my awkwardness.

'What paper?' Brierly asked.

'The *Gerriston Independent*.'

'Ho. A two-minute silence,' Tony Smith said.

Duggie gave him a cold look. 'He's just got a job on the *Dominion*.'

'I'm going down next week.'

'First-rate paper,' Brierly said. 'They did a good job for us in the strike.'

'Us?'

'We're the Junior National Party. Ball Committee,' Tony Smith said.

'Duggie too?' He must have found a way of making money out of them.

Brierly smiled. 'Douglas is co-opted. He's very useful. Does the accounts. It's nice to have someone who can add up.'

Duggie took this insult without blinking. He simply looked at

Brierly, and then at Tony Smith, who suddenly seemed nervous and gave his plummy laugh. I wanted to get Duggie aside and ask him what his game was.

'Let's get on with it,' he said. 'Raymond, keep in touch. Now, what have we got?'

I caught my bus; and walking by Loomis creek, hearing the pines sigh, I had a sense of Duggie as the boy who had lived on the citrus orchard, and I found that it connected with him now – I knew by a premonition what he was after. The voice fitted in, the clothes fitted in. It was far bigger than I'd thought; and I grew afraid. He had a long way to go, but he would get there. I restored myself by laughing in advance at his mistakes, then thought of Smith and Brierly and was on Duggie's side.

'When did Sebastian join the National Party?' I asked my mother.

'He's not? Not Duggie?' It could not happen to a Plumb.

'He's on the ball committee.'

'They'd better watch out, he'll pinch the takings,' Dad said.

'I don't believe it,' Mum said. 'Not a Tory.'

'Duggie was never a Plumb. A wolf suckled him.'

Dad coughed. He did not like the 'fancy talk' Mum and I indulged in. 'I'll tell you one thing about young Duggie. Fred Meggett's got his eye on him. And Fred picks winners.' He blushed. 'Not that I mean me.' Dad was part of Meggett Enterprises. He ran a subsidiary called Sole Construction – a sore point with Mum.

I said, 'Duggie'll end up owning Fred. But politics is where he's really going.'

'He'll want some money first.'

Dad took me into the paddocks where the orchard had been. We walked among partly built Sole/Meggett houses. Dad seemed happy and he seemed unhappy. 'Forty houses, Ray. I feel like a bloody magician.'

'They all look the same.'

'They're pre-cut. We're first in that. Most of it's done in the factory.' We walked on the hill at the back and looked over new roofs, blinding in the sun. Up this end one or two families had moved in. 'It wouldn't have suited my old man. Did you ever see him work a piece of iron? Still, there we are. Houses for people.' It was the Sole Construction Company slogan but Dad could not make it sound convincing. 'Your mother says it's like toytown.'

'Mum's a bit of a snob.'

'I'd have put them up one by one. But I'm not blaming Fred. They're good houses, Ray. They'll last.'

'Sure. You drained the swamp, eh?' I looked at the front yards running down to footpaths. 'Where's all the topsoil gone?'

'Well, you see, you've got to get a contour.'

'Fred sells it, I suppose.'

'That's about the strength of it,' Dad said.

We met Mum on the brick bridge. That was as far as she cared to come now.

'What do you think, Ray?'

'Houses for people.'

'I wonder if I clap my hands will they all fall down.'

'Grow up, Meg,' Dad said.

He started mowing the lawns, using the old hand machine Uncle Robert had owned. It made a pleasant chatter as he closed on Mum and me in the summer-house. To make up for Duggie's defection I told her how I had painted my slogan on the tower. She was pleased, though the danger of my falling worried her. I gave her a version of my life at Primrose Hall.

'I don't think I'd like Mrs Fitz. You'd better be sure you always wash your hands there.'

'I do.'

'What about girls? You must have a girl by now.'

I had not known my backwardness troubled her. 'I'm not like Uncle Alf if that's what you mean.'

'I don't mean that. Bobby started so early. Becky too.' She talked fast for a moment, getting us by the dangerous place.

I said, 'I've got a girl called Iris.'

'That's a nice name. Is she . . . ? Is it . . . ?'

'Serious?' I had thought it might be. I had even thought I might marry Iris. There was no chance of that now. I had boasted about her to Duggie. 'It helps pass the time.'

In the afternoon I went down to see Bluey. He had turned eighty-three the week before. I took him a packet of pipe tobacco and he lit up straight away, puffing out aromatic smoke that overcame the meat smell of his kitchen. He had a priest with him, Father Pearce. Bluey had got free of his Church and stayed free fifty years but now he was back inside, rolling comfortably like a basking shark. I shook hands with the priest, uncertain how to address him. I had that trouble even with Protestant clergymen. But with Catholics I had the fear they sniffed my secrets out. I liked to believe they were jolly Irishmen or starved fanatics; but all were celibate and had an extra sense.

Father Pearce did not look starved. He didn't look jolly either. I saw where my mother had got her jibe about blue-chinned priests. He and Bluey had the *Herald* open on the table and were picking horses. Pearce went at it fiercely: fanaticism there.

Sutton put the kettle on. I told him Duggie had joined the National Party.

'What's that?' Bluey boomed.

'Duggie's joined the Junior Nats. He's organizing their ball.'

'Ah, he'll be after the girls. He'll plough a furrow there.'

'I don't know the young man,' Father Pearce said. He was not put out by the talk of sex. I had the impression he wanted more.

'Duggie,' Bluey said, 'is a walking cock and balls. If you'll pardon me, Father.'

'There's something in it for him,' Sutton said.

Bluey and Father Pearce went back to their horses. I took a book from Bluey's shelf and browsed in it: *The Growing Point of Truth*, one of my grandfather's. I looked at the chapter on Walt Whitman – Whitman as 'new man', as exemplar of Man – and wondered if Grandpa Plumb had known that Whitman was as ready to go to bed with men as women. Perhaps at that point he had put judgement aside; just as he had deafened himself to daily noises. I turned a page and came on Edward Carpenter, new man too. Now Carpenter, I had read, was Whitman's 'friend'. Would Grandpa have banished them like Alf if someone had forced him to know?

'You'll have tea, Ray? Put another cup out, Roger boyo,' Bluey said.

Sutton snarled and did it. I watched him secretly, remembering he had brought on Grandpa's experience of vastation. He was ugly all right – but primitive man in his cave? I could not see it. I found his played-out hatreds rather sad. He put leaves in the teapot and hissed with satisfaction as he poured boiling water in. I watched from behind my book, admiring the way he hopped about and the unlikely deftness of his hands. He threw a sidelong look at us, lifted a cup, and dropped a gob of spit in. I heard the little smack as it hit the bottom.

I guessed at once the cup was for the priest. He was the one who had stolen Bluey. But I watched it carefully, watched every move Sutton made. He had never had any liking for me and could spit in two cups as easily as one. It was only my wish to see the priest drinking that kept me there.

'Milk?' Sutton asked. Then he balanced the tray on his fingers and came to us posing as a waiter and doing a little jig that banged his surgical boot on the floor. He was quick as a boy.

'Ah, tea,' Father Pearce said. He put his pencil down and reached for a cup; and Sutton was suddenly Irish, giving a leprechaun grin and brogueing extravagantly. 'Now don't be getting off with Bluey's cup, Father. I'll be thanking you to see the shamrock on it.'

'Stealing my tea, are you?' Bluey said.

Then I looked at Sutton with fear. I saw the richness of his life. This was his way of having Bluey and of forcing Bluey to have him. Each tea-drinking was a communion. I stood my cup on one side and watched Bluey sucking greedily, 'Ah,' in his swagman way. 'Now that's a brew. You make a lovely cup, Roger boyo. Drink up, Ray.'

I got my tea down and said goodbye. Sutton gave me his reddest grin. I wondered if he knew that I had seen. I went out the door sideways. Grandpa had been right: Sutton was in the cave. He was terrifying. But Grandpa was wrong. Sutton was at the other end too. He was a man of subtleties. Along one of the branches he was Man.

The next day I went back to Gerriston. I had three days left on the *Independent*. Love, I thought, took some twisted shapes. The betrayal I was guilty of was not worth noticing alongside Sutton's love.

Iris said, 'You're not going to write to me, are you?'

'Well,' I said.

'Just tell me, Ray.'

'I suppose I'm not.'

'I could tell.'

'Was it different?'

Rain boomed on the roof of Primrose Hall. We were in the hollow of my bed. Now and then it took my breath away. Look, I wanted to cry out, I'm in bed with a girl, we've got no clothes on.

'I knew this was going to happen,' Iris said. I did not know she was crying until I touched her cheeks. 'I don't mind. Really,' she said.

'I'm sorry, Iris.'

'No you're not.' Tears rolled like glycerine. I swung between remorse and delight. Look at me, I'm hurting a girl. Look, she loves me. This paid Myra Payne for twisting my balls.

Iris dried her eyes on the sheet. I began stroking her and nuzzling her. 'Iris,' I said; and whispered things I would like us to do.

She got out of bed. 'It's no use starting that when it's all over.' She pulled on her clothes.

'It's early, Iris. It's only eleven o'clock.'

'Too bad. Don't get out.'

I ran down the hall in my underpants and watched her walk away in a tropical storm. The Phoenix palms thrashed over her. Power lines hissed and swung. She did not look back. It was like being in a movie.

Later I saw how it really was. I betrayed myself as well as Iris. I had stepped a long way back. That was my last time with her and, as Max Waring would have said, I had gone into it with only my doo-dah.

Justice, a true balance, would have had Gerriston end for me there. But the rain kept on all night and blocked the roads. Primrose Hall stood in a puddle six inches deep. I borrowed gumboots and waded out to look at the river. It was bucking like a cable. It swelled greasily and ate the stopbanks. Posts and gates and cabbage trees floated by and tangled in the understructure of the railway bridge. The mayor and the town clerk and the borough engineer were watching it. Morrie Horne was squatting, trying to keep his pad dry as he scribbled. Iris was there with her camera, snapping away.

Soon trucks arrived from the Council depot. Men started sandbagging round the ends of the road bridge. I wished I was still with the *Independent*. I wanted to be with Iris and Morrie Horne. If the stopbanks broke this would be the biggest story in Gerriston since the gold rush. I wondered if I should be writing it for the *Dominion*. Instead I went back to Primrose Hall and changed into my oldest clothes. I borrowed an oilskin and went back to the bridge and helped with the sandbagging. I hoped Iris would photograph me.

But soon she was gone with Morrie in his car. The old bridge south of town was washed away.

I stayed with the sandbagging team all that day and half the night. We filled bags at the depot and later at half a dozen yards and drove out to strengthen weak places in the bank. The rain rattled on our oilskins and the river brimmed at our feet. Trees rose in it lazily and crashed down in slow motion. Drowned cows floated by like lost footballs. At midnight farmers with shotguns stopped the engineer from dynamiting the banks on the side away from town.

I slept three hours and went out in the dawn. The rain was heavier. It struck my coat like bird-shot and dented it like copper on my skin. Stormwater was up to the porch of Primrose Hall. I met Mrs Fitz wading back from town.

'We've got to evacuate. They've run out of sandbags.'

I helped her get the boarders out and we trudged up to the higher part of town and stood on verandas watching the river, still inside its banks, lurching past level with the shop roofs. It seemed mindlessly happy, like a monster broken through from an unknown world.

At nine o'clock it pushed the bridge aside and sucked it down. At half past ten it broke the bank, punched through like a fist on a corner west of town. It came down curving like the Huka Falls. We saw a man run out of a house. It swallowed him. Then easily, like water, it ran through all the streets and took charge of the buildings up to their window sills. I saw it pouring into my room at Primrose Hall. It was neat and fairly lazy by that time.

They found the drowned man floating by a door with his fingers tapping. Cats and dogs and guinea pigs and budgerigars were drowned. Out on the farms sheep and cattle died in hundreds. Cars died and carpets and furniture.

I stood in her dining-room with Mrs Fitz. Silt lay inches deep on the floor. The naked girls and boys and swollen soldiers hid in corners. The water in Primrose Hall had lapped the door heads. All the happy verses lay in mud.

'I'll never get this back the way it was,' said Mrs Fitz. I held her hand but she did not cry.

'I knew I couldn't keep it. Come on, Ray. Let's see what's happened to my gin.'

10

'You see,' I told the girl over the table, 'the way I look at it is that we've got a longing in us for happiness but the world is silent, or else it gives us back this idiot chatter. We've got a deep desire, a deep nostalgia really, for unity and the world disappoints us. Now in the face of this, all we can do is struggle. The only weapons we have are strength and pride. The only truth we have is in defiance. Meaning is defiance. If there's any meaning. Ha! Another cup of coffee? Well anyway, that's how I see it.'

'It's how Albert Camus sees it too.' This was Glenda. She punctured me like a bladder. My borrowed air came out in a rush. 'Everyone I know is reading *The Myth of Sisyphus*. I wish they'd find another book.'

'It's a matter of making what you read your own.' I tried to sound Olympian and sounded pompous. Glenda smiled at me. 'Perhaps. I won't have another cup. I'll have to go.'

'Camus has taught me a lot. He's made things clear. And Kierkegaard.'

'I'm pleased. They're too hard for me.'

'They're really quite simple –'

'I mean the way is too hard. I want some fun in my life.'

'Well . . .'

She gave a tiny smile at my comic eyebrows. 'Groucho Marx. I really think you should acknowledge your sources.'

'Can I ring you? Can I see you?'

'I'm rather busy.'

'I've met you before. Nearly met. Four years ago. You were in a car with Douglas Plumb.'

'I don't know any Douglas Plumb.'

'Early nineteen-fifty. Up in Wadestown.'

'You've got a better memory than me. Thanks for the coffee.' She walked out of my life – so she thought. I might have let her go if she hadn't forgotten Duggie.

Kierkegaard did not deny happiness was possible. My melancholy was a result of breathing air thick with disappointments and defeats. Naturally I came to generalize. No girls – at least none of the sort I wanted – and not much money. Had it gone on I would have turned to ideology. Thought was too difficult. Action was difficult, but within my means. I went after Glenda and I got her. I caught her like a disease. I had been after happiness, but I became filled with uncomfortable sensations. I planned my getting of her anxiously and spent the nights dreaming of triumphs I could never make quite honourable.

'How did you get here?' she said at the party.

'I told them you invited me.'

'The cheek!'

'Are you going to kick me out?'

'A gate-crasher, Di. Shall we kick him out?'

'He looks quite nice.'

'You look after him then.'

Plump Diana looked after me. She pointed out Glenda's boyfriend, a poet in a beret and red cravat. 'He's had poems in *Image*.'

'Good poems?'

'They're all about thighs and breasts. That's how he sees the hills.' She leaned close to me. 'Derivative. *Landfall* turned him down. Over there by the door –' she pointed at a fat little man rolling a cigarette '– that's Alan Webster. He's a real poet. He's after Glenda too. You'll have to stand in line.'

'Not me.'

'I don't think you can compete with Ron O'Connor.' That was the bereted poet. 'He's got, well, flair. Besides, he's a renegade Catholic. That thickens up the brew.'

I began to like Diana. But over the room Glenda pushed her hair back with a gesture almost monkey-like. She took a neat two fingerfuls of dress and gave her pants a hitch. Her laugh chimed out and I watched her in a way that made Diana give her own laugh.

'I really should go and live in another flat.'

'I'm sorry.'

'Don't be. I wish you luck. I warn you though, she's Mariana in the moated grange.'

'Meaning?'

'There's no quick way. You'll find out. If it's any consolation Ron O'Connor's finding out.'

She told me she and Glenda were finishing their BAs. Then they were going to Training College.

'Secondary?'

'Of course.'

'That means Auckland.'

She smiled with malice. 'It means you've got six months.' But she was a jolly girl – jolliness was a style she'd adopted – and she sat and joked with me about flat life and dieting and randy poets while I watched Glenda. Ron O'Connor lit two cigarettes and gave her one. I was astonished by his cheapness and by the flush of pleasure that came on Glenda's cheeks.

Diana said, 'He's been seeing too many movies.'

'So bloody obvious. Do girls really fall for that stuff?'

'We've been known to.'

'He pinched it from Humphrey Bogart.'

'So? She's smoking a ciggie he held in his own two lips.'

'No she's not.' Glenda stubbed it out in an ashtray. She beckoned Diana and went to the kitchen.

'Saved by the gong,' Diana said. She followed Glenda out. The other girls sharing the flat cleared dirty glasses off the table. Glenda and Diana carried in plates of sausage rolls and cheese and pickled onions.

I found myself by the door next to Alan Webster and a young man with sunken shoulders and limp hair. Except for his air of premature bitterness he reminded me of Beak Wyatt.

'Bourgeois bitches,' he said.

'What?'

'They know what we want and they bring in supper. Little bits of pineapple and cheese stuck on toothpicks. Bourgeois bitches.'

'Stay with it, John,' Alan Webster said.

'Bloody culture snobs. I write stories. That's the only reason I get invited. But I can't compete with Webster, the great poet. He's had the lot of them.'

'You're thinking of Ron O'Connor,' Webster said.

'The young solicitors get the Karori girls and you and O'Connor get the culture snobs. We should send the pair of you out on grummet-chasing expeditions. You could send the ones you don't want back to base. I wouldn't mind leftovers.'

'John suffers,' Webster said.

'I suffer from these bitches. They don't want cock they want promises. I can't afford promises. We're running against the hounds boy and we can't take on extra weight.'

'Put it in a story,' I said.

'Nobody'll print the things. Will you look at those bums. I'm aching. O'Connor will get the lot. The mould of their creativity is the womb so before all the squawling and shitting starts they're determined to experience the prick of the great poet.'

'Easy, John.'

I had supposed they were doing a comic-and-straight-man act but I saw a look of such misery on John's face I thought something in him must have broken.

'I've got to get out of here. I can't stand it.'

He rushed out. Webster gave me his drink. 'Hold this.'

Diana came over with a tray of sausage rolls. 'Jolly John fallen to pieces, has he?'

'It looks like it.'

'Alan will put him together. He's good at that. It's what he does instead of having girls.'

'John says he has them.'

'I've heard that. Him and Ron. All of us together and one by one. Do you believe it?'

'I don't think so.'

'Just as well.' She sent a furtive glance at Glenda. 'John tries to kill himself. They had to pump him out last week. He puts it all in stories but nobody publishes them.' She wasn't a jolly fat girl. 'I know what you're thinking.'

'No –'

'I could be "nice" to him. Oh, brother! Take one of these damn sausage rolls. I spent all afternoon making them.'

Glenda came over to us. She had a way of pointing her chin and looking at things sidelong that reminded me of my mother.

'What went wrong with John?'

'The usual thing.'

Glenda blushed on her cheeks but her forehead stayed white. 'Did you say something to him?' she asked me.

'No.'

'John Jolly is disturbed.'

'So Diana said.'

'We try to help him.'

'Not the way he wants.'

The blush mounted to her forehead. 'I can see the sort of mind you've got.'

'What sort?'

'Rather grubby.' She went to sit with O'Connor on the sofa. I watched his over-ripe face and soft red mouth and wondered how we'd get on in a fight. He was large round the shoulders but his hands made lifts and gestures that set me wondering about his sex. I said to Diana, 'Are you sure it's girls he likes?'

'You're clutching at straws.'

'I don't know.'

'That hand stuff is part of his style. French or something. Read his poetry if you don't believe me. All his hills have got nipples on top.'

I put down Alan Webster's glass and wandered away with my sausage roll. People were dancing in a room over the hall. The air was grey with cigarette smoke and the crush of bodies left me no way through. I went down the hall and found a lavatory with fish painted on the walls. Opposite were bedrooms; piles of raincoats, varsity scarves. I tried guessing at Glenda's bed and chose the one with a dark blue counterpane and a mobile of blue fishes over it. She must lie in bed and sleep as though under water. On the bedside stand was a photograph of a middle-aged man with the same over-ripe look Ron O'Connor had. I wondered where I had seen him.

'Who's this?' I asked Diana, who came in the door.

'Glenda's father.'

'He's got a boozer's face. So this is her bed? Nice mobile.'

'Glenda made it. She's got a thing about water. The moving waters at their priestlike task etcetera. Would you like to hold her nightie?'

'I like you, Diana.'

'Don't let my mind fool you. The important thing about me is my excess of adipose tissue.'

'Don't say that.' I stroked her arm.

'Get your hands off me. And get out of my bedroom, I've decided to have a cry. Close the door behind you.'

I did as I was told and the man in the photo seemed to wink at me as I had a last look at Glenda's bed.

'Excuse me,' I said to one of the flatmates, 'is Glenda's father famous for anything?'

'Why don't you go home?'

'Yeah, piss off,' her boyfriend said.

'Friendly place.' I went into the sitting-room. And there the name I heard was Uncle Alf's. It hit me like a punch. I was trying not to think of Alf. He was beaten to death in Moa Park in Loomis. A bunch of boys hunting queers had got him. The trial was just over and the boys had been acquitted. I had used a lot of anger on that, evading my guilt at dropping Alf. He had helped me when there was no one else. 'If you can't get in to see me, drop a line. Let me know how you're getting on.' I had not done it. His death troubled me in several ways.

'You're wrong,' I said to O'Connor. 'Alfred Hamer never chased little boys. You'd be his style.'

'Who the hell are you?'

'Alfred Hamer was my uncle.'

'Oo la,' O'Connor said, 'so it runs in the family.'

'He was a good man.' I wondered how soon I would hit O'Connor.

'Boo hoo,' he said. He was not going to stand up though. Glenda watched me with a look of calm I took for superiority.

'He's the one who's been on trial, not those thugs who killed him. I'm buggered if I'm going to stand here and listen to him being run down by half-baked poets and their arty girlfriends.'

'Go home then,' someone said.

'Yeah, go home.'

'You can't deny,' O'Connor said, 'that he was out there chasing little boys.'

My mother had an explanation for that and in her grief had written it to me. I said, 'My uncle was committing suicide.'

I heard a hiss of outrage. A girl behind the sofa hooked her hands on Glenda's collar bones. Another put her face down and rubbed her cheek on Glenda's. 'Glenda, love.'

'I'm all right.'

'Bastard,' someone squeaked.

'Boot him out.'

I did not know what I had said but it filled me with delight. Somehow I had broken their rules; and now their boyfriends scrummed me out of their house. O'Connor dug his fingers in my neck and gave the knee that sprawled me on the path. The door slammed but I wasn't having that. I found a stone and threw it at the wall.

'We're calling the police,' O'Connor yelled.

I gave their letter-box a kick and ran up the road. I could not understand why I was laughing.

Alan Webster found me leaning on a concrete wall in the Terrace. I was licking blood from my wounded palms. 'They kicked me out.'

'It happens now and then. The boys don't like too much competition.'

'Is O'Connor really a poet?'

'He tries. He'd do better if he didn't have to pretend.'

'Yeah, I thought so.'

'Glenda feels safe with him. Glenda needs to feel safe. You want my advice?'

'Maybe.'

'Diana's the best of them. Go after her.'

I wrapped my handkerchief round one of my palms. 'What did I say wrong?' I told him about Alf and he laughed.

'You shouldn't have said suicide. You know who Glenda is?'

The face in the picture had a name. 'God,' I said. 'Goodlad.'

'Graham Goodlad was her father.'

'Someone should have told me.'

'Suicide is the dirty word in that flat. But I'm glad you've said it. I'll make a prediction.'

'What?'

'You'll have her on your doorstep in the morning. Ray – that's your name, isn't it?'

'Yes.'

'Go easy on her, Ray.'

11

Graham Goodlad was a racing journalist. He wrote a column called *Goodlad's Hot Tips* and was one of the first tipsters to go on radio. Dad used to listen to him on Saturday mornings. That must have been in 1947. In '48 Goodlad left his paper and started *Horse Talk*, a weekly form guide padded out with stable gossip. *Hot Tips* was part of it and Goodlad's whisky face grinned at New Zealand. That was where I had seen him. Goodlad was in half the houses in the country.

Then a brewer called Mottram brought a divorce action against his wife and named Graham Goodlad as co-respondent. It was in the days when adultery in the courts became a floor show. The Mottram/Goodlad case sent a delicious shiver up our spines. Famous people. High society. It gave us a licence to talk about sex. Graham Goodlad was our hero/victim. His name passed into the language. I still hear people use it. From the *New Zealand Dictionary*: goodlad *noun* (*informal*), a penis: 'I gave her a bit of *goodlad*'. It appeared in limericks on lavatory walls. And everywhere were pictures: Goodlad in the saddle, Goodlad's hot tip.

For me the case had an extra dimension: Uncle Oliver was the judge. He was famous for his moral homilies and he did not spare Goodlad. His remarks about 'the cancer eating home and family' were as talked-of for a time as the Mazengarb Report.

The trial lasted for two weeks and the papers printed every scrap of it. In the end Mottram got his divorce. Mrs Mottram sailed away to England. Graham Goodlad went out to his woodshed, put his shotgun in his mouth, and blew the top of his head off. That's the story. I knew it well. I could not find a place in it for Glenda.

On Sunday morning I lay in bed waiting for her knock. I thought it better not to be polished up and I ran my hand over my stubbly chin, shivering with lust and pity as I thought of the mark I would leave on her. Every sound in the street had me ready. Her knock.

Her timid knock . . . It did not come. Webster and I had forgotten she did not know where I lived.

At midday I got up and shaved and tidied my rooms. I hoped they'd have a big effect on Glenda. Today the building is gone. The motorway tunnel comes out where it stood in Ghuznee Street and four lanes of traffic pass over the garden where I grew my radishes. In through a high wooden wall, in through a red door in the iron cladding: there was the kitchen – tiny stove, rag mat from my mother, built-in table with a bamboo screen. Up a ladder through a hole in the ceiling: bedroom, painted red. Bookshelves, desk, hand-basin, built-in bed running the width of the room, six feet. A shower in the corner – cold. No lavatory. That was outside through the yard. At Ghuznee Street I learned to pee in preserving jars.

By two o'clock I had to admit Glenda was not coming. I went out to a phone box and rang the flat.

'Is Glenda in?' I asked one of the flatmates.

'She's gone to visit her aunt.'

'Oh.'

'Any message?'

'No message. Is she all right?'

The girl gave a hiss. 'I thought it was you.' She hung up.

That made me happy. I saw how it might push Glenda at me. I walked down Willis Street and Lambton Quay and struck up into the hills. I went through the street where Myra Payne had wrecked me and climbed clear of houses into the pines. The white harbour, the hills like black steam trains: I had not grown used to them. Wellington lifted me and blew me about. It still does that. I came down through a wind that tore my hair and tore my coat, making me flap like a bird. In Wadestown Road I buttoned up. I found a still spot and combed my hair.

'Hallo,' I said to the woman – nurse it seemed – who opened the door, 'is Mr Plumb at home? I'm his nephew.' I had been here only once before, with Felicity and Max. Oliver had asked me to call again but a sniffy elevation in his voice had warned me off. I followed the woman in with the feeling that I was back at Ormiston's door.

'Hallo Uncle Oliver. It's Raymond Sole.'

'Raymond. Yes, I see. What brings you here?'

'I was passing. I thought I'd drop in.'

Oliver frowned at such casualness. His eye took in my tie-less throat as I shed my raincoat. He had not risen from his chair at the fire.

'Can I sit down?'

'Very well. I can't offer you tea.'

'That's all right. How's Aunt Beatrice?'

'Unwell. She's most unwell.'

'I'm sorry –'

'My own health is good. In spite of the trials my family bring on me.'

I understood he was referring to Alf. 'That was bad. An incredible verdict.'

'The verdict was quite proper. Your newspapers need not have reported the case so fully. At least we can be thankful he changed his name.'

Uncle Oliver took my breath away. I was helpless with him, I could find no place of attack. He was in his professional prime. Judgement was his habit; and moral disgust, a disgust I believe encompassing everything not himself, had thrown him into a mental stance so bent that I came to see him as a kind of brother to Roger Sutton. He was riddled with self and hatred. He was the most freakish man I have known.

I said, 'I liked Uncle Alf.'

He said, 'You're not speaking of anyone I know.'

'He was –'

'You will kindly not mention him.'

'He was your brother.'

'Is this what you came to see me for? What then? I'm a busy man.'

'Do you remember a case – the Goodlad case?'

'I do.'

'What was Goodlad like?'

'I never knew him. I took no notice of him. I took notice of the facts before me.'

'You talked about the moral squalor of it.'

'Goodlad was an adulterer. He was a man who drank, a man who gambled. I said as much. Beyond that I said nothing.'

'Did you know he shot himself?'

'I heard of it.'

'Did you know he had a daughter?'

He looked at me with a coldness, a needle sharpness, that made me prickle.

'I can see that this is the point of your visit. No doubt you have met this daughter. I see you have. I can only advise you, as my sister's son, to have nothing to do with her. I remind you of what her father was. Now Raymond, I'm busy. If you decide to visit me again please give me warning. I'd like it too if you dress suitably.' He had me at the door. 'Mrs Barrett will see you out. Remember me to your parents. I understand your father's doing well.' He closed the door, and there I was in the hall, reeling with disbelief. He had got me out of there like a schoolboy.

Mrs Barrett drew me down the hall. I stuttered at her that I was all right, I was going; but she gave a cheery smile, gave a wink. 'Dodge along through the garden. I'll open the French doors. Your aunt wants to see you. Don't worry about old Sourpuss, he won't know.' She opened the door and pushed me out. I did as I was told; squelched along the lawn through winter shrubs; let her draw me into another room. She smiled and said, 'Easy-peasy. Now take off your shoes. Tippy-toes.'

We went into a room looking over the harbour and there was my Aunt Beatrice, monkey woman in a wooden bed. Her face was like crinkled paper. I thought there was some hideous mistake. I had met my aunt but not this woman before.

'There we are Plumduff,' Mrs Barrett said, 'your nephew's come to visit you. Give him a smoochy-smoo.' She pushed me over the bed and the woman kissed me, light and sharp as bird claws.

'Raymond? Raymond Sole? You're Meg's son?' *She* did not know *me*. 'The newspaperman?'

'Yes. I'm sorry you're not well.'

'I've had the jaundice. I can't seem to get better.'

'She's only five stoney-oh,' Mrs Barrett said. 'She used to be thirteen. That's why I call her Plumduff.'

'I'm so very tired,' Aunt Beatrice said.

'I'm sorry . . .'

'Raymond, listen. I want you to do something for me. You work on a newspaper, so you can find things out.'

'Well . . .'

'I want you to find my daughter. I want you to send her to me.'

'Aunt Beatrice –'

'Call me Trixie. People called me that when I was young. Even Oliver. I called him Ollie.'

'Aunt. Aunt Trixie. I don't know whether I can trace people.'

'I've written it all down. Barry will give it to you. Barry dear . . .'

Mrs Barrett gave me a paper covered with wispy writing. *Helen Plumb. Born in Palmerston North 1921. Adopted 1921 by Oliver and Beatrice Plumb* . . .

'Her mother was an educated girl. Oliver made sure of that.'

'Aunt Beatrice, I wouldn't know where to start.'

'He pays her money to stay away. I've written it down. You'll know her by her eye. Help me, dear.'

I did not know whether she spoke to me or Mrs Barrett. Mrs Barrett knew. 'Righty-ho. Outski. Back in a wee mo, Plumduff.' She nudged me at the door. 'Tippy-toes.'

'Aunt –'

'I saw her last in 1942. I want to say I love her. We must tell people we love them.'

'Yes, I see.'

'Now let's play little mice,' Mrs Barrett whispered, easing me out. Aunt Beatrice, Aunt Trixie, smiled tiredly. Even her teeth were yellow. There were yellow stains on the paper in my hand. Later I sniffed them and found they were orange juice.

'Put that in your pocket, just in case. He'd go right through the roof,' Mrs Barrett whispered. She waited while I put on my shoes. 'Help her. She's had a dreadful life married to that cactus.'

'This daughter . . . ?'

'It's worth a try. To help a poor old lady. She won't last long.'

'How long?'

'Oh, she's dying. Of thirst if you ask me.'

I went down Wadestown Road with her whispered 'Cheerybye' in my ears. I wondered how I was going to get out of this. All the time I was getting to know Glenda it troubled me like a boil. I was scratching it, worrying it, when Glenda tapped on my door the following night. I opened, said hallo, let her in. My smile was cool but my heart was banging and it came to me that her visit marked out the rest of my life.

Glenda had got my address from the office. She said she had come around to apologize. 'For Ron talking like that about your uncle.'

'He wasn't to know.'

'All the same, he shouldn't have said those things. And I want you to know I'm not arty.'

'I didn't think you were. I was trying to hurt you.'

'What for?'

'For liking Ron O'Connor more than me.'

'I don't. He's company.'

'I'm sorry I threw a stone at your house.'

We went on for a while in that way. It was a verbal current over still deep waters where we met. (Her words, later on.) I showed her round my bach. She thought it 'marvellous', the upstairs room like a magic cave. She said it was too bare though and needed treasures in it and said that she would bring me some polished stones from West Coast rivers. She walked about the room, turning on her heel. 'Rude,' she said of my Modigliani print. When she looked at my books she found Camus and laughed.

I took her downstairs and made a cup of tea and while we were drinking it she asked about Alf. I told her he had been my wailing wall when I was 'mixed up'. 'No,' I said, 'not that way. I like girls.'

'I never doubted it. Your uncle was crucified in court.'

'Yes.'

'I'm sorry.' She did not go on to talk about her father and I was offended not to be given that. Instead she asked about my job. And as I talked the gloss I had put on her fell away and I began to see her. With Mrs Fitz and Iris I had learned a good deal, but I'd forgotten. When Glenda came I started to remember, I grew up. I had taken backward steps, but I took them forward again, then took another. I *saw* Glenda. I forgot about sex.

We walked up Ghuznee Street and up the Terrace.

'Am I going to see you again?'

'I'll only throw my rotten apple at you.'

For a moment I was afraid. 'I don't mind.'

We went into the flat. 'You've jumped the queue,' Diana said.

Glenda was round at my bach almost every night. She brought me polished stones. She made a lantern from paper and bamboo and fitted it on the naked bulb in my bedroom. It turned the room purple. I did not tell her the light was now too dim for me to read. Sometimes she brought Diana or Alan Webster. I treated them with condescension, believing them unqualified for happiness of the sort we had.

Webster was there the night Ron O'Connor called. O'Connor banged on my door, howling for Glenda. She was Holy Spirit, Holy Mother. Only she could save him from the Pit. O'Connor's voice rose melodiously. It reminded me of Duggie Plumb's new voice. We pulled him in and let him weep at my table, where his beret fell like a tent on the sugar bowl. Alan Webster washed his face with water. Glenda tried to make him drink some tea. Then Ron O'Connor vomited on my floor. Webster washed him again and took him away, while Glenda got some rags and wiped up the vomit. 'No,' she said, 'don't touch it.' When she was finished she went upstairs and used my shower. It was a winter night but she stood in there five minutes and then sat wrapped in towels in front of my heater. I made tea. I rubbed her hands and she put her head on my shoulder.

'I collect lame ducks.'

'I'm not one.'

'That's why I like you. Alan's a lame duck. He's a lame duck who collects lame ducks. He's trying to get rid of me. I'm graduating.'

She took off her towels and I gave her clothes to her piece by piece. Later I was astonished. There had been no sex in it.

Walking home, she said, 'That cousin of yours? Duggie Plumb? He had a big behind.'

'That's Duggie.'

'He tried to maul me in the car. I had to get out and catch a taxi home.'

'That's Duggie too. Why did you say you didn't remember?'

'He had the same name as the judge at my father's divorce case.'

'Oliver Plumb. He's my uncle.'

'Yes, I worked that out.'

The next night she brought me a mobile of blue and yellow fishes and hung it on a cup hook over my bed. It turned there dreamily.

'Lovely,' I said.

She took off her clothes and slipped into bed. She looked like a fish herself in the purple light. 'Come in with me.'

So that part of it started. I can't really sort it out from the rest. Later things came apart but in the beginning there were no divisions. Our times in bed were nothing out of the ordinary. There was no 'sex-book fucking', in Duggie's phrase. Nor did our talk go anywhere unusual. No Camus or Kierkegaard. We talked about my job and her exams; and laughed about Duggie now and then. She showed me how he had mauled her – savage stuff. I gave her his new voice, and hopped out of bed to fetch a clipping from the *Weekly News*. It was hard to see in the dim light, but there was Duggie, no mistake: bum out, belly in, dancing at this year's National Party Ball with Miss Jennifer Gibbs, who looked rather like Kim Novak and a little bit like Glenda.

'Do you ever see your uncle?' Glenda asked.

'Never again.' I told her about Aunt Beatrice and my search for Helen Plumb. 'Not much of a search.' I had gone through the records at the Registrar's Office and through the Wellington electoral rolls. Apart from that I had written to Mum, who told me the story. Aunt Beatrice had given the girl her name – slipped it past Oliver's guard somehow. The child was pretty, clever. She had her education at Marsden School. But at sixteen she started running away (looking for love, Mum said) and at seventeen ran away with a *Maori*! At that point Oliver stopped fetching her home. She came of her own accord on her twenty-first birthday – 'for my present'. She was wearing a black eye-patch. One of her eyes was gone after a fight. Oliver gave her a cheque, and probably at that time made his arrangement to keep her away. He saw her only once again, drunk in Lambton Quay, arm in arm with a *black*! American sailor. He put his newspaper over his face. 'But do try and find her,' Mum wrote. 'Felicity says Beatrice is wasting away.'

'I feel sorry for your uncle,' Glenda said.

'He wouldn't like that.'

We put on our coats and I took her down through the yard to pee. I waited barefoot on the gravel, then she waited for me. Upstairs we made love hours on end, with tiny tiny movements, and no movements, simply joined. Then Glenda told me about her father . . .

Graham Goodlad loved three things in his life – horses, women, Glenda. Four if you counted whisky. He did not love his wife, an Englishwoman he'd met on a trip Home in 1922. He was bowled over by her arrogance. It was as if, he said, he was watching it on a stage. He thought she was from 'the upper class'. Actually her father was a clerk, but she was a climber. She'd learned some tricks and she played them well. That didn't stop her from making the great mistake. She was pregnant and the cad would not marry her. But along came this young New Zealander, rough but presentable; with, it seemed, a little bit of money. He was too nervous to put his hands on her. But all told he would do, though poles away from what she had expected. By this time she too felt she was on a stage. Things had begun that could not be reversed. Dulcie Titheridge spoke the lines left to her. She quickly got the young man over his fright.

Glenda told it like that. Young Graham Goodlad amused and enchanted her. I held her in my arm and stroked her breast and watched her face staring up at the lazy fishes. I did not think she could keep it up. But she put detachment in place of humour, choosing words.

In Wellington the Goodlads settled down. Graham went into his father's importing business. He bought a house in Karori not far from the old Beauchamp place. The baby was named Gordon. He grew up looking English, speaking county. Dulcie Goodlad worked very hard at him. She made as much of her own life as she could, near the top among the second best. Then the depression came. New Zealanders over a certain age all say that: the depression came. *Goodlads* went down early. Grandpa, who had not spread his money out, worked for the Council painting white lines on the roads. He was almost cheerful about it. Graham did this and that. He wheeled and dealed. He got by. Somehow he became connected with horses. But the car went, the house in Karori went. Glenda had her infancy in a little house in Tinakori Road – quite near the other Beauchamp place.

Dulcie Goodlad never forgave her husband for the late baby. Glenda remembered her mother in little words: cold, sharp, neat, grey, thin. Her father – he was Daddy. He filled all the cold and empty places. Still, there were quarrels; there were shrunken silences and icy dislike; there was reek of whisky and smashing of chairs. 'Why go into it?'

Graham Goodlad became a racing writer. In the war he sank out of sight in a department of government. The Goodlads shifted to Brooklyn. Glenda saw the harbour and the mountains. People called her old-fashioned but she was quiet and still. Quiet and still, she floated over the harbour. Albatross, she was tossed by storms. She sat and watched her mother. News came that Gordon was dead in a battle in Italy. She touched her mother's cheeks and felt hands as cold as ice and sharp as claws push her back and down and out of sight. Her father cried round tears. 'Poor little bugger, poor little bugger.' 'You weren't his father,' Dulcie Goodlad said.

Then the war was over. Graham Goodlad went back to his newspaper. That was not all. He had, he said, a finger in several pies. There was money to send Glenda to Queen Margaret College. Soon there was enough to shift to Kelburn. Mrs Goodlad sat there, upper-class. It did not matter that she was the only one to see it.

As for Graham Goodlad: race-courses and stables; whisky; women. And there was his lovely daughter Glenda. She was 'Princess'.

'He took me on a holiday,' Glenda said. 'We rented a house in the Marlborough Sounds.' Mr and Mrs Mottram had the house round the bay. They came over every day in their launch. 'Daddy seemed to know them pretty well.'

At nights she heard her father creeping out. At last she followed him. She sat in rocks at the end of the bay and watched him swimming with Mrs Mottram. They ran up from the sea. They were beautiful. She saw Mrs Mottram's long breasts swinging. There was a gleaming in their thighs.

They went by Glenda, blind and close. She heard their feet padding and breath hissing. She saw her father's penis long and white. On a beach robe on the dry sand they knelt down. They were horrible and beautiful, making love in the moonlight. They seemed to fight each other and become each other.

Glenda watched. When it was over they saw her in her nightie. She was sitting with her hands folded in her lap. They pulled on their clothes and her father ran to her.

'Darling, Princess, I wouldn't have had you see that for the world.'

She wanted him to touch her. She wanted to tell him that she did not mind.

'Princess. Princess. Try to understand. We love each other.'

She understood perfectly. She was perfectly happy. But she could not smile. She could not do it, even though, with still face, she looked like Dulcie Goodlad.

Mrs Mottram put her palm on Glenda's cheek. It was soft and cool and smelled of salt. 'I want to tell you this. I love your father.' She walked off along the sand in her beach robe, with her towel about her hair. She looked like an Arab in the desert.

'Princess,' Goodlad said. He sat by Glenda and put his arm around her.

'Then,' Glenda said, 'Daddy loved me.'

I gave a jerk. Whatever I might have expected, this was not it.

'No, no, no,' Glenda cried.

'I'm sorry –'

'It's my fault. I said it the wrong way. He showed me that he loved me. He's the only person who could ever do that. Just by being with me.'

I began to dislike this clever man. Glenda felt it.

'Please, Ray. Understand.' She heard the echo of her father's word and gave a laugh, not doubting then that I would see. I pulled her close. She was clear – clear to me as water. Goodlad? No. I tried to hide that I could not see him. He was always lost in a cloud of laughter; deep in cleverness and quick emotions. I came to see his death as quick and cheap.

What came next? The Mottrams sailed away in their flash launch. Glenda and her father stayed three more days. They walked and fished and swam. He told his daughter how happy Josie Mottram had made him and said that she had made him twenty again. 'But if I was twenty, Princess, I wouldn't look past you.' They swam off the end of the Mottrams' jetty. Under water, in the slanting sun, they bubbled and made faces at each other. Her father's diamond eyes flashed at her. Silver fishes darted in the piles.

And next? The divorce. Still Glenda chose her words with care. It was as if exactness cancelled pain. Dulcie Goodlad did not wait but put things in her lawyer's hands and left for Home, which turned out to be Exeter, on the first ship she could catch. She went through the forms by 'insisting' her daughter go with her but gave a smile, at once relieved and bitter, when Glenda said no. 'You were never mine. Stay in this wretched country if you must. With that man.' Glenda went to her father's sister in Scorching Bay. They sat there being jolly, being brave, while Graham Goodlad and Mrs Mottram became figures in a comic strip. Glenda watched the sea. She watched ships steaming in and out and read their names and home ports with her father's racing binoculars. Graham Goodlad came for dinner every evening. He had sold his interest in *Horse Talk*. *Hot Tips* had a new name, but *hot tip* was everywhere: scratched on walls, painted on railway bridges. *Goodlad* too. Glenda found it written in the sand at Scorching Bay under a penis squirting pipi shells at a vagina.

'Princess, I'm sorry,' Goodlad groaned. He was sorry, he was groggy, he was hurting. Mrs Mottram sat in court with a smile on her lips. She was cool, inviolate, wrapped in furs, and he knew she was gone. Everything was gone. He had loved being famous and popular; but now, Glenda said, his life was like a photographic negative reversed. What had been dark was light, what had been light was dark. At times his eyes sank deep into his head, at others they strained out, blue and bursting. She pictured hands in there squeezing his brain.

On the day Judge Plumb granted the divorce Glenda sat waiting for her father. Aunt Rose had cooked him a fillet steak – a small one, grilled medium. Blood, he said, made him feel sick. Aunt Rose was a teacher at the Girls' College. She had not been to school all week. It was no fun being Miss Goodlad at a time like this. She thought her brother a fool, but tried to take a larger view and talked a good deal about *hubris* and *nemesis*. She advised Glenda to keep her chin up.

Graham Goodlad did not come. Aunt Rose tapped her foot and began to look dangerous. 'He's somewhere with his cronies getting drunk.'

What Glenda told me next had a quality of neatness that kept me still for fear that I should break it and break her. It was as if she were taking two-footed jumps, landing her feet in squares marked on the floor. The game was to get to the wall without being eaten by crocodiles – or rolled soundlessly screaming into space.

'When he was five minutes late I knew he was dead.'

She took his binoculars and watched a freighter coming in from the broken sea by Barretts Reef. Up in Kelburn Graham Goodlad walked through the yard with his brand new shotgun. Mottram had promised to take him duck shooting. He sat on a pile of coalsacks in a corner of the woodshed and put the barrel of the gun in his mouth. He pressed the trigger with a piece of kindling wood.

The phone rang. 'That'll be him,' Aunt Rose said. 'I'll give him a piece of my mind.' Glenda smiled. The freighter went by from Liverpool. Before Aunt Rose came back she locked herself in her room.

'I've never blamed him, Ray. I thought it was the proper thing to do.'

12

Another proper thing, considering our love, was to take no precautions. She did not want anything between us. And those things, rubber, were so horrible. And fizzy pills to stick up there – she would sooner use a bottle of coke like those girls at Naenae. I agreed. No precautions. Considering our love.

She sat her exams with morning sickness and was capped *in absentia*. I put a payment on a house in Wadestown, an old villa with rust holes in the roof and weatherboards dry-rotted light as balsa and wallpaper flopping off its scrim. I took her there in January from the registry office and Glenda grew round as I tore tobacco-coloured roses from our walls and nailed up sheets of gib board. We were up towards the pines on the Tinakori Hills. Our bedroom looked over the snooty part of Wadestown – Oliver's house – and over the harbour at the Orongorongos. We lay in bed and watched them browse like herds of elephants.

'I love it up here. I never want to leave.' She made new mobiles and hung them round the house: octopuses in the lavatory, a school of silver sprats over our bed. When Sharon was born she hung clouds of butterflies over her cot. I lay in bed with my wife and practised happiness. Our balsa walls kept out the southerlies and our web of affections kept out the world. Love turned back time and fate. These are phrases from the poems she wrote.

Glenda had some money from her father. We spent it on the house: re-roofed, re-piled. I put in a retaining wall where the back of our section was slipping into the neighbour's. There on a new little lawn Glenda and Sharon basked in the sun, watching ladybirds and lizards, watching mountains and the sea. On summer evenings we sat on our veranda drinking home brew made from Ted Sole's recipe, while lights swelled from silver to golden across at Eastbourne and Days Bay. Our visitors were polite about the beer; but our house, our view, our marriage seemed to delight them.

Glenda's Aunt Rose had been less upset by our 'mistake' than by Glenda's 'tossing away' of her career. The girl should at least have qualified, then if anything went wrong . . . Rose was a believer in things going wrong. Experience had taught her. But she came to acknowledge that ours was out of the common run of marriages, and she 'saw Glenda's point' that happiness itself was a career. When she came to visit us she brought gifts of food and books and pottery, calling them 'a little contribution'. It seemed to us that she helped herself to pieces of our contentment in return, but we had plenty so we did not mind. She was a crusading rationalist and watched us for signs of belief that more was in our union than met the eye. Glenda, she observed, had 'a tendency'.

Rose became dry and exact when she found Felicity calling on us. They were full-rigged ladies and should have fired broadsides at each other. But Rose advanced only her common sense and Felicity brushed it off in a friendly way. It seemed that she too shared in our contentment.

'How's Aunt Beatrice?' I asked. I did not really want to know but she troubled me.

'Oh,' Felicity said, 'so so.'

'Is that Barrett woman still there?'

'She is. I suppose we should be grateful Trixie has someone. But she's like one of those Yankee ra-ra girls. Twirling sticks.'

'No news of her daughter?'

'None. That's a hopeless business.'

'I tried. I don't know where to go next.'

'It worries Ray,' Glenda said.

'Don't worry. Life's too short.'

That was also Rose's philosophy but she wasn't going to agree with Felicity. 'Rather brutish without conscience, wouldn't you say?'

'Is conscience part of the doctrine?'

'She was at Marsden,' Glenda said. 'You might have taught her, Rose.'

'Who?'

'Helen Plumb. She had one eye.'

'Not when she was at school,' Felicity said.

'I remember Helen Plumb,' Rose said. 'She was the daughter . . . yes,' looking at Glenda. 'A pretty girl. Always in trouble. I hadn't realized . . .'

'She's Ray's cousin.'

'Yes, I see.' She studied us, wondering if this might be a crack in our happiness. In spite of the pleasure she took in us the moment satisfied her.

'And you remember her?' Glenda asked.

'She's coming back. She had a kind of – eager quality. Yet even then she was somehow beaten. It was all blunted somehow. Helen was a very troubled girl.'

'What happened to her?'

'Oh I don't know. She left. They have a way of leaving. That's the end. They don't come back. And I left Marsden myself. I never enjoyed being in a church school. Visits from the bishop and all that. I wouldn't have minded if there'd been more to it than a kind of fancy dress show. Some intellectual distinction. Instead of all that watery piety. And moral precepts dangling kitchen objects round their necks. Egg beaters and fish slices. We had one chappie visit there who was always going on about sponge cakes that failed to rise. Because, you see, something was left out. Love of God, apparently, is a kind of baking powder.'

Felicity laughed. 'Suitable for girls. Plain-ness without plain thinking. Hard thinking, I mean. Why, I heard a fellow on the air . . .' and she mimicked him: 'Have you ever noticed we have two eyes but only one mouth? I'm sure God made us that way on purpose.'

It was Rose's turn to laugh. The two ladies beamed at each other. Glenda made tea and offered biscuits.

'Buy your biscuits Glenda, don't waste time making them.'

'Read books instead.'

They cleared the plate. And disapproved when Glenda gave Sharon her bottle to stop her crying. It was time, they agreed, that the child faced up to things. Parents must not play the role of *deus ex machina* endlessly. In the last analysis a short sharp smack . . .

Glenda said, 'What rot!' She picked Sharon up and cuddled her.

'You'll spoil the child.'

'Like a sponge cake,' Glenda said.

'This is a serious matter.'

'It is. It is. Come on, love. It's your mummy you want not that old bottle.' She opened her blouse and Sharon latched on. That was a time when breast-feeding was frowned on. Rose and Felicity were enlightened women, so they frowned. The child should be broken of *that* habit.

'You pair of silly old noodles,' Glenda said.

I asked Rose more about Helen Plumb but she had told me all she could remember. Well, let's see. The child liked Wordsworth: an unusual taste. Usually it was Keats and Shelley. When it was anything. And – music? She played the piano rather well. I rang the secretary of the Marsden Old Girls Association but Helen Plumb was not a member. There I stopped again. There was nothing else I could do. I left a message with Mrs Barrett that I had reached a dead end. She let me know she was 'a wee bit disappointed'. Beatrice, it seemed, spoke of little else now but her daughter. It worried me, but I wanted to find Helen less than go down to Oliver's house and give the old bugger a talking to. When I thought of him in his study, by his fire, and all human feeling locked outside, and misery and love and desperation tapping like the drowned man at his door, I was filled with rage, and I wanted to do more than tell him he, not the world, was leprous – I wanted to smash him.

Glenda reasoned with me and calmed me down. I saw her as Oliver's victim too; but she cured me, for I believed I had saved her. She saved me. I had a sense of *us* that filled my days. When we sat at the breakfast table, or worked side by side in our garden, or when I pulled her by the hand up the steep hill home, it seemed to me we were making love just as surely as when we coupled in our bed. Everything was easy, there was no intensity – even in our quarrels, which were noise. She went to bed early and sometimes was asleep by nine o'clock. When she brushed her teeth she put paste on my brush – a message for me. I found it there even after our quarrels. Often she was on my side of the bed. That was a message too: I was to wake her and make love. Still no precautions, though while she breast-fed Sharon we hoped she would not conceive.

One night we heard a knocking at our door and there were Diana and Alan Webster, come to tell us they were getting married. We had not seen much of Diana since her year in Auckland. She was teaching out at Naenae and finding it fun. In spite of what *Truth* and Mazengarb might say, the kids were not monsters of depravity.

'They're just plain bored, poor little buggers. I try to keep them laughing.'

She called our house 'The Nest', which offended us. 'Alan and I will call ours Cosy Nook.'

'Waiwurri,' Alan said. 'And talking of *Truth*, have you heard about John Jolly? He's got a job there. We'll get some seedy stories from him now.'

'And Ron O'Connor's gone into radio. Producing plays.'

'Don't talk about them. They make me depressed,' Glenda said.

'Ron's writing religious verse,' Diana said. 'All about Christ with BO and the Virgin Mary missing her period.'

'Please.'

'Sorry, sorry. Where's the baby. I want to get some practice holding her.'

'She's clucky,' Alan said. Later he showed us *Numbers* with some poems he had written for her. I told him they were beautiful – controlled, shapely, passionate, eager, strong. I ran out of adjectives. I was moved. I found it hard to believe they were written by this fat man for this fat girl. Glenda said nothing. She told me later that she hadn't liked them.

'They're the best things he's ever done.'

'I know. I know. Why does he say it's got to end?'

'Well, death – you can't deny it. But now is what counts. That's what he says.'

'Ray, I want another baby.'

'On the spot. Come here.'

'I'm serious. I want to start one soon. I feel it's time, you know, to turn a page. Things are coming back at me. I can't explain.'

'John Jolly? Ron O'Connor?'

'Not just them.'

I saw she meant her father, and her mother, and the divorce, and the suicide: all those things I described as 'rubbish' and had seen myself as sweeping out of her life. I had the glimpse she must have had of desolation, emptiness, and my response was hers: get out of there on the only path we had, which was forward – more love, more babies, more *us*, more of our marriage. She clung to me and cried.

'How long has this been worrying you?'

'It never worries me. It just comes. And then it goes. I don't remember. I know it isn't real. But I go into it like falling down a hole.'

'Listen –'

'Please Ray, don't worry. I can get out of it easily just by thinking of us.'

So Sharon was weaned – complaining – and after a month or two Glenda was pregnant. Everybody claimed it suited her.

One day Rose rang me at work. 'Ray,' she said, 'I've seen Helen Plumb.'

'When? Where?'

'It's fairly nasty. I don't know if I should tell you.'

'Now, Rose –'

'Yes, all right. You know behind the public library? Those seats where the winos drink?'

I knew them. I had done an article on alkies, winos, meths drinkers, sleepers-out; and drawn an affecting if inaccurate picture of Wellington's blue-haired matrons selecting their weekend romances while in the windy corner below whiskery old men in torn overcoats passed the bottle and sang, 'There's a long long trail a-winding . . .'

'I saw her there,' Rose said. 'I couldn't believe it. She had a patch on her eye. There was an old Maori man with her. She was drinking from a bottle.'

'When?'

'This morning.'

'You're absolutely sure?'

'I'm sure, Ray. Although she looked about sixty. I stopped and had a good look. She can't be more than thirty-five, you know. And filthy clothes. I smelt her. Like sour apple juice. And Ray, she said, "Have a drink, Miss Goodlad".'

'Did you?'

'It's no joking matter. And don't tell Glenda this. It would worry her.'

It worried me that she thought so. I wondered what it was she had seen in Glenda.

'Oh nothing, Ray. Pregnancy can be a difficult time.'

I found Helen Plumb the following morning. The sun burned down from the Terrace and glared off the concrete walls of the library. A smell, an essence, of vomit and wine and dog shit moved in the air. Helen was on a wooden seat with, as Rose had promised, an old Maori man. He seemed to be sleeping. She was wearing an overcoat with cloth half an inch thick. It was frayed on all its seams and burst at the elbows. She wore man's shoes and a man's felt hat with a nameless feather in the band. She looked, as Rose had said, about sixty. Her eye-patch was cardboard blacked with ink and held on by a chain of rubber bands.

I sat down on the lawn and looked at her.

'Hey senor, you want a good time?' Helen said.

'Can I talk to you?'

'Talking's free. No free drinks though. You want to come in this school you pay. She's a dead marine.'

I gave her half a crown and she prodded her companion up and sent him shuffling off for a new bottle.

'Senor. Amigo. Come and sit next to me.' She was not drunk so much as brain-fogged. She behaved and spoke by a kind of rote, responding to stimuli muzzily sensed in a world that moved around her like an ocean. She was aggressive, kittenish, afraid, and scarcely knew why. Now and then a moment of clarity startled her.

I sat on the ribbed seat, at a distance. 'Are you Helen Plumb?'

This threatened her. Something black, with teeth, had swum up close. Her eye seemed to darken and contract. 'Helen Rewiti, that's me. Dunno other Helens.'

'You're Helen Plumb. Oliver Plumb's daughter. Beatrice Plumb's.'

'Who're you? Bugger off.'

'I'm Ray Sole. I'm your cousin.'

'If you're my cousin you got some money for me.'

I gave her another half crown. 'Listen, Helen. Your mother's dying. She wants to see you.'

Helen drank the dregs of wine from her bottle. She started to sing. The words had no edge but the tune came clearly: *I dreamt I dwelt in marble halls* . . . My mother had played it on our piano. She had learned it from her mother. Oliver had learned it. The leap from this burning corner and this woman to a drawing-room in a manse fifty years ago was too much for me. I got up and walked around the flower beds. When I came back Helen looked at me. 'Senor. Amigo. How'd you like a good time?'

'Helen, listen.' I sat down. 'Your mother is Beatrice Plumb.

Trixie. She's dying. She'd like to see you.' But I wondered about that. Would Beatrice want to see this woman? 'If you'll clean yourself up and stay sober, one afternoon I'll take you up.'

She moved her head like a boxer. 'You're one of those gangsters.'

'No, Helen.'

'They threw my girlfriend overboard. Don't let them throw me overboard.' Her hand slid into my pocket, cold and damp. I pulled mine out but she gripped me by the hip-bone. 'Take me away, amigo.'

'Let me take you to your mother. I'll give you some money.'

'My father gives me money. In my bank book.'

'How much, Helen?'

'A pound a week. He won't pay me if I go up there.'

'He'll never know. We won't tell him.'

The old man came back with a bottle of sherry. He opened it with a corkscrew from his pocket and gave it to Helen. She hugged it on her chest and seemed to sleep.

'Mr Rewiti?'

'No son, I'm John Peihana. Rewiti was the one who knocked her eye out.'

'Mr Peihana –'

'I don't touch that stuff, son. I've never been a drinking man.'

'Helen's mother wants to see her. Is there any way I can talk her into it?'

He shook his head. 'Her father doesn't want to see her.'

'He doesn't need to know.'

'He's a big man, her father. Big pakeha. He's a judge.'

'He's Chief Justice. But look –'

'He'll put the kibosh on her money.'

'Not if he doesn't find out. If we can get her sober –'

'You'll never do that, son. Stop Helen's sherry, she'll konk out. I'll look after her. You trust me. She doesn't need her mother.'

'I'd like to see my mother,' Helen said. She began to rock back and forth. Wine spilled down her coat. 'I'd like to see my mother.'

It took two more meetings to arrange. Helen kept forgetting who I was. I picked them up from their back-yard bach in Upper Cuba Street. John Peihana had Helen in a blue dress spotted with daisies. She had on a knitted cardigan and shoes that were a woman's, although broken. Her eye-patch was cut from purple felt.

We drove into the green suburb of Wadestown, where a scent of gorse and roses filled the air. John Peihana rocked his head. He did not seem impressed with what he saw. At Oliver's house he sat down on the steps and folded his hands on the knob of his stick. I led Helen to the door. Her eye was darting about, she trembled like a child – this woman of thirty-five who was so badly damaged there was no recognizable part of her left.

I had warned Mrs Barrett what to expect but her professional cheeriness became a little jerky at the sight of Helen Plumb.

'Ah, oh, come in. Wipe your tootsies.' (Although it was summer.) 'I'll just get Plumduff ready. She's not quite with it yet. She's been snoozing.'

We waited in the room with the French windows. Helen made unhappy sounds like a dog. 'It's all right, Helen. Nothing's going to happen.' I patted her arm.

'Don't let him get me.'

'He's at work.'

'I need a drink. Where's my drink?'

'As soon as this is over. I promise.'

'Senor?'

'I'm Ray, Helen.'

'I've got to spend a penny. Quick, quick.'

'Mrs Barrett,' I called. Helen's smell was making me desperate. I thought that she might squat and pee on the floor. 'Mrs Barrett, she needs the toilet.'

'Ah,' Mrs Barrett said, 'ah, the wee house. This way, dear.' She put out her hand but stopped it short and led Helen without touching down the hall. I went to Aunt Beatrice's door and peered through the crack. Her yellowness had turned to sepia. Hollows deep as spoons lay on her temples. I creaked as I leaned on the doorpost and she cried, 'Who's that? Is that you, Helen?'

'No, Auntie, it's me,' I showed my face.

'I don't know you.'

'Raymond Sole, Aunt Trixie.'

'Go away, young man. I'm expecting my daughter.'

I waited out of sight. After what seemed a long time, and bumps and grunts and scratching on a wall, Mrs Barrett led Helen back. This time she had her by the elbow. 'She tried to lock herself in. I soon fixed that.'

'Amigo,' Helen cried, grabbing my jacket. Mrs Barrett squeezed her elbow and made her yelp. She pulled her into the bedroom. 'Plumduff dear, here's your very own daughter come to visit. What a wonderful day.'

Beatrice held her arms out. She was like a jointed puppet, moving stiffly. I seemed to hear her bones click and hear an oily whirring as she turned. Her body, I thought, was barely alive; and the rest of her existed for this moment and would go out when Helen left. Tears made a crooked trickling on her cheeks.

'Helen, let me kiss you. We must put all the wrongs we have done behind.'

Helen made nothing of this. She was looking about in a panic. Beatrice was no one she recognized.

'Come closer dear so I can see you.'

Mrs Barrett gave Helen a nudge. Helen was throwing wild looks at me and making little steps in my direction. Mrs Barrett moved in time with her as though dancing. She jerked her head at me to get up the hall, then made a dab and closed the door.

I waited by Oliver's study. It was locked; and I glimpsed the attractions of being moral. But I had no time to think about it, or gain any clear sight of a seductiveness that made me dizzy, for Beatrice's door sprang open, cries came out, and Mrs Barrett dragged Helen into the hall like a pile of bedding and dumped her there. 'Oh!' she cried, 'oh! I knew you didn't do it in the lav. You filthy thing.'

I ran to them. 'What is it? What's happened?'

'She peed on the floor. All down her legs.'

I saw Aunt Beatrice struggling from her bed. 'You couldn't help it. I'll wipe it up.'

'Get back in, Plumduff,' Mrs Barrett shouted. She ran at Beatrice and threw her legs on the bed. Then she came back at me. 'Take that woman away. Don't ever bring her back.' She slammed the door.

Helen lay where Mrs Barrett had dropped her. She was curled into a ball and making little dog whimpers at the carpet. I tried to lift her but she flopped like a corpse, so I ran down the hall and called John Peihana. He came in slowly, leaning on his stick.

'Helen. Get up, girl.'

Together we helped her up. Her patch had ridden up her forehead and her eye socket had the same spoon-hollow as her mother's temples. Through it ran the glued joint of her lids, with eyelashes criss-crossed like stitching. John Peihana lifted the patch and made it straight.

'She wet herself.'

'Get me a towel, son.'

I fetched one from the bathroom and watched while John Peihana helped Helen get her pants off and went down on his knees and dried her legs. He took a clean pair from his pocket and helped her put them on.

Mrs Barrett came rushing from the bedroom. 'Haven't you got her out yet? It smells like tomcat in there.'

I took Helen out and down the path. John Peihana followed with her wet pants on the end of his walking stick. He pushed them into a hydrangea bush. In the car he gave her a medicine bottle of sherry.

'You leave us alone now, eh?'

'Yes, all right.'

I dropped them in Cuba Street and watched them walk away, Helen holding his hand like a child, John Peihana tapping with his stick. Then I drove to Rose's and had a bath. I did not want Glenda knowing this.

13

I wondered where the money had come from for his glossy handbill. Not from Fred Meggett, I was sure. Duggie had cut that connection. *Career: Financial consultant, Meggett Enterprises, 1954–57* . . .

Financial consultant sounded grand. Surely he had been no more than second or third in the accountant's office. One-line speeches. He would make up for that tonight. I watched him as the mayor plugged on through one of those introductions that wobble away from neutrality and wobble jokily back. He was a National man and had run Duggie close for the nomination.

Duggie kept an interested face. He practised looking mild, then looking sharp. Honest, thoughtful, resolute, amused. He impressed as quick among the half-dead. The mayor, globbing out phrases, was his zombie. I scribbled that in my pad, then scratched it out. I was not here to glob out phrases myself – or let my special knowledge lead me off on side-tracks from my job; which was to report this meeting of Douglas Plumb, National Party candidate for Loomis, held in the Loomis Town Hall, November 17, 1960. My paper would not thank me for clever phrases, or cynicism about this coming man.

Financial consultant, Meggett Enterprises, 1954–57. B. Com. 1955. Currently Director, Thornley and Plumb, Consultants, Property Developers: Thornley and Webb, Estate Agents; Thomas Tax Consultants. Age, I added, twenty-eight. Young man in a hurry. He had the credentials and the cash, now he was after the real thing. I made a mental scratching out of that. Duggie was never simple. What he'd come to here was a stage in his growth. I had a knowledge of it better than his, but I could not untangle it from will and ambition. Organic Duggie. Duggie as Superman. I was going to have to worry at them alone and present him to our readers simply as Douglas Plumb, one of the party's bright new men, who just might snatch the Loomis seat from Labour. He was running a campaign that had his opponent flapping around like a headless rooster.

'Duggie,' I had said, 'what's your philosophy in politics?'

'I don't have one of those. I leave the airy-fairy stuff to Latham. He's got a philosophy. Ask him. It's about all he has got. And it comes from Russia. With love. Lift Jack Latham up you'll find Made in Moscow stamped on his bum.'

'You don't want me to print that?'

'Say behind.'

'Right. Good stuff. It's a dirty fight.'

'He started it.'

'He says you did.'

'You've talked to him, eh?'

'This morning. You've got him hopping. But he's no mug.'

'He's got a lot of bloody words. You take out the bloodies, Ray.'

'Sure.'

'I'll do you if you make me look bad.'

'Take it easy. My paper doesn't print bloodies anyway. Tell me more about Latham.'

'University egghead. Nothing in there but a kind of yolk. He belongs to a party that gives us all this shit – nonsense, Ray – about the common man but he wouldn't know one if he tripped over him. Talks about people in multiples. "The masses." What the hell's masses? That's not kiwi talk. That's from Moscow.'

I quoted from Duggie's handbill: '"The class war has no place in New Zealand." "The individual does not exist for the State." He says you didn't write that. Says it came out of the sausage machine.'

'I wrote it.'

'It's word for word Muldoon's.'

'We think alike.'

'This playboy label he's pinned on you. Any comment?'

'I live a moral and an honest life.'

'Come on, Duggie.'

'I live a moral and an honest life. I hope Mr Latham can say the same.'

'He makes bachelor sound like a dirty word.'

'That's his problem.'

'How do you feel about the outcome of this?'

'Loomis? I'll win it. No question.'

'Mr Plumb exudes confidence.'

'Sounds like shitting. That's enough, Ray. I'm switching you off.' He reached out and flicked a switch on my temple. 'Have a drink.'

'The Playboy Bachelor. You've probably got inflatable girls in there.'

'I'll tell you, Ray –' Duggie came back with a bottle and two glasses. '– I'm going to get Latham one day. I'll wait for him. Nobody's saying that stuff about me.'

'You'll get him on election day.'

'No. He'll win. He'd better win.'

I blinked at him. He pushed a drink at me. 'You're a bloody innocent. You think I want to spend the rest of my life in a marginal seat?'

'Does the party know this?'

'They know I can't win it. What they don't know is how close I'll get. They'll know I'm here.'

'And next time round . . . ?'

'A safe seat.' He drank. 'I'm not the only one. Silly bloody Brierly's doing it in Avondale. He doesn't think I know.'

'So what you want is to lose by one vote.'

'One hundred. That'd do nicely. Brierly won't get close to that.'

'You'll look sick if you win. You might, you know. People seem to like you for some reason. You should have kept your Kings College voice and your yellow waistcoat.'

'You'd better forget that, Ray.'

'It's a good voice now. Just right of centre. You've got your clothes right too. You might win.'

'I won't.'

'I know a few people who won't be voting for you.'

He did not like that. 'Who?'

'My mother.'

'Your old man will.'

'I wouldn't be too sure. Beak might. Myra won't.'

'She won't vote for Latham either.'

'Why not?'

'She's dead. Cancer. In here.' He dug his thumb at his crotch. 'Probably used the bloody thing too much.'

'When did she die?'

'Week or two back. She'd had it for years. Probably had it when she married Beak. She should've had cancer of the mouth.'

'You're unbelievable, Duggie.'

'Why? Here I am.'

'She was your girlfriend.'

'You want me to cry some tears? Myra was a big girl. She knew what she was into. And she liked it. You couldn't stop her, you'd have needed a football team. As for the cancer, it's like a car accident. It could get you any time. It could get me.'

'Cancer won't get you.'

'Meaning what?'

I did not know. I had the sense of something looming over Duggie but it would not take shape.

'Meaning you? Listen Ray, I talk to you. I don't talk to anyone else. But if you ever say anything . . . if you print anything in your paper . . .'

'I want you to carry on. I want to watch.'

'So watch. But keep your mouth shut. You coming to my meeting?'

'I'll be there. God knows why. I should be watching Muldoon. He's getting a start on you, Duggie. He'll get in.'

'So? He's ten years older. He's not going anywhere. He's too damn pushy. This party doesn't like it when you push – not when they notice. Now piss off, Ray. I need some sleep. Big night tomorrow.'

He came with me as far as the door of his flat. I stood on the porch a moment looking across the slope of Mt Hobson at One Tree Hill. 'This is the one you want. Epsom. Holyoake country. Old Snyder's bound to retire next time round.'

'You're saying it, not me.'

'I'm right, aren't I?'

'Don't make me fight two elections at once.' He closed the door.

I drove home to Loomis, where I was staying. 'I talk to you. I don't talk to anyone else.' There was something pathetic in it. I wondered if I was all that kept Duggie human. Was that the reason he took the appalling risk for a politician of standing naked before a journalist? There was more to it than self-display. Perhaps he did not know the reason himself: just grabbed me instinctively. But I laughed at that – gave it Duggie's laugh. 'All this bullshit about the mind. I've got better things to think about, Ray.'

Mum said, 'How's Duggie?'

'Sparking on all six. I told him you weren't going to vote for him.'

'Good. What did he say?'

'He didn't like it. He reckoned he might get your vote, Dad.'

'I'm not saying. I don't go much on this Latham joker though. He's too high-falutin.'

'There's nothing wrong with intelligence,' Mum said.

'I don't like the stuff he's saying about Meggett Enterprises.'

'It's aimed at Duggie,' I said.

'I don't like it.'

'Fred's getting a bit too big too fast.'

'You think so?'

'I know. I'd get out if I was you.'

The next day I was round the campaign headquarters, talking with candidates and managers. My paper – the *Evening Post* – had me in Auckland for a look at three or four key marginals. It seemed to me this was going to be National's election. Labour, with its majority of one, had no ground it could lose, but bits were crumbling away all along the line. I predicted a National landslide, a majority for them of twenty or so. There were going to be plenty of new faces in Wellington. New careers. Clever grabbing. I admired Duggie's patience in waiting for next time.

Back in Loomis, late in the afternoon, I called on Beak Wyatt. He lived in a house on Dean Street, a blind road running along the creek opposite Millbrook Road.

'Hello, Beak.' I offered him my hand. He held it for a moment without pressure. His bony head seemed dented on one side, shaped like a sickle. He did not smile or make any movement of his face, but gave the impression of being set a short way back in time and of having to bring himself forward to see and understand.

'I thought that was your car. I didn't reckon you'd come in here.'

'Can I talk to you a minute?'

Again that pause while he understood. Then he walked ahead of me into the kitchen and went on peeling carrots at the sink.

'I heard about your wife. I'm sorry.'

He rinsed a carrot under the tap. 'Thanks.'

'I brought a couple of bottles. Maybe we can have a drink?'

'The opener's in the drawer. I don't drink much.'

I filled two glasses and took him one. He was peeling a potato and the skin curled away from his knife and bobbed like a ringlet. He nodded at me to put his drink beside him.

'Sit down, Ray.'

I pulled out a chair and sat at the table. A woman had run this kitchen once. It had floral curtains and pretty crockery and pot-mitts run up on a sewing machine. Beak had let it go. Dust balls stirred on the lino and long-legged spiders hung on the walls. A Mighty Meatery calendar, torn off at July, lay where it had fallen on the sideboard. The ceiling, tongue and groove, greasy with cooking moisture and furred with dust, sloped towards the stove, where Beak's head almost touched it as he put on the pot of vegetables. He was six foot four, skinny as a high jumper.

He brought his glass to the table. 'What are you doing in Auckland?'

I told him. 'Duggie thinks he might get your vote.'

'Does he?'

'How'd you like him for your MP?'

Beak drank some beer. His Adam's apple went up and down. 'No,' he said.

I finished my glass and poured another one. 'How are you getting on, Beak? Are you all right here?'

'I'm all right.'

'What do you do? All alone?'

He turned his eyes slowly on to me. 'I think about things.'

'What things?'

'Remember the Yank who broke his neck at the Pool?'

'Munro Gussey?'

'I think about him. I didn't yell out. I could have saved his life. But I was scared of what Duggie would say.' He swallowed more beer. 'Duggie knew he was going to dive.'

'I don't think so –'

'I told Myra about it. She said he would know.' He got up and poured the rest of his beer down the sink. 'I don't like this stuff.' He put a pan on the stove and laid in a chop. 'Myra had cancer of the cervix. She was in hospital six times. The last time was July. It took four months.'

'I'm sorry, Beak.'

'She wanted to die properly. Die well. She read it in a book.'

'And did she?'

'No.' He turned from the stove and looked at me. 'She wanted me to kill her. Pills or something. Smother her with her pillow. I couldn't do it.'

'Beak, it's like getting hit by a car. No sense.'

'Myra didn't love me.'

'I don't know –'

'She told me. It didn't matter. She's the only one who ever talked to me.' The lid of the potato pot started jumping. He turned down the element.

I said, 'I knew Myra. I liked her.'

Beak came back and sat at the table. 'She said you and Duggie raped her in a van.'

I wondered if he was going to attack me. But he gave a smile, took out his handkerchief and wiped his nose – his famous nose. His Adam's apple bobbed as he swallowed. That was famous too.

I said, 'It was rape. In a way. I think about it the way you think about the Yank.'

'Do you?'

'Now and then.' The pause he made, that lag in time, forced the truth from me. 'Not very often.'

'It wasn't you she blamed. She reckoned he was raping you too.' The chop was burning. He got up and turned it with a knife. 'I think about it. I wonder why any of us are alive when Myra's dead.'

'Beak –'

'I'm not going to kill anyone . . . My tea's about ready, Ray.'

'All right.'

'Take the beer. I don't like it.'

I took the unopened bottle and went to the door. But I could not leave him like that: turning his chop, eating at the bare table.

'Does anyone come and see you?'

He looked surprised. 'I don't need anybody.'

'What about Myra's friends? Do they keep in touch?'

'She didn't have friends. We were friends to each other.'

'You can't stay here alone, Beak.'

He prodded his potatoes with a fork. Steam broke past his face and curled on the ceiling. He carried a plate to the table and put it down. 'Duggie came once. After we got married.'

'What happened?'

'We saw his car so we hid in the bedroom. He went around the house yelling out. He knew we were there. Myra – she hid her face in the pillow so he wouldn't hear her laughing.'

'What did he do?'

'Yelled out some name.' He gave a little smile in my direction. 'That name you used to call her. Then he went away.'

'I never called her that.'

'It doesn't matter.' He took his potatoes to the sink and poured off the water.

While he was busy I let myself out and drove away. That evening I sat in the Loomis Town Hall reading Duggie's career and his credo yet again. Watching Duggie. I could not see him either as simple or complicated. From time to time I lost sight of him altogether, he seemed to float away in a fog like Merlin. He changed all the time for me, the way Grandpa Plumb had changed. I worried at him but he would not come clear. As for Beak, he stood unmoving, rather like Ted Sole.

The mayor finished and sat down, settling his chin on his chest. Duggie walked to the microphone and lifted it aside. He took a little bundle of cards from his pocket, slipped them out of their rubber band and laid them on the lectern. So far he had looked at no one. He watched the cards a moment and scratched his jaw. It was a good attempt at 'presence' for a beginner but he kept it up just a shade too long. A couple of feet shuffled, a cough broke out. He raised his eyes and made them flash down the hall. 'Friends,' he cried. 'Ladies and gentlemen. People of Loomis. My friendly rival, my colleague, your mayor, has been generous to me in his introduction . . .'

It was a big meeting for Loomis. I made a rough count of two hundred and fifty people. Dad was there. Roger Sutton was there; chalky face, red mouth, scowling in an aisle seat near the back. A dozen old Dalmatians and their sons were in the front row. Duggie was going to have to say something on government aid for the wine industry. And Father Pearce, in an open shirt, would no doubt have a question on state aid for church schools. That was going to be a hard one for Duggie. 'Religion is shit,' he had told me; and when he had to say, as on radio earlier in the week, 'We live in a Christian society,' or some such thing, he sounded as if he did not quite know what he meant. The words came out too quickly. Latham hadn't got on to it. Possibly Latham didn't want to. Was he a Christian himself? I thought there might be an article in the religious beliefs of candidates.

'I,' Duggie said, 'am a Loomis boy. I grew up here. This place is in my blood. I went through Loomis school. I sailed tin canoes on Loomis creek. I had a paper run up Millbrook Road. I raided orchards there. Yes, my friends, Matty Barbarich, Tony Sumich, your orchards. And you put a couple of pellets in my behind. My father was an orchardist – still is. When I was a schoolboy I helped in the grape harvest. I washed bottles for you, Waddy Corban. And I came down to this hall – Loomis Town Hall – on Saturday afternoons, with sixpence in my pocket, to watch the Buck Rogers serial and cheer Johnny Weismuller playing Tarzan – and whistle at Jane. This is my ground, this is my home –'

'Why do you live in Epsom, then?'

'– and over in Epsom I feel like an alien, I'm cut off from my roots, and I can tell you this my friends, if I'm elected in Loomis, *when* I'm elected in Loomis, the first thing I'll do, the very first thing, is go out hunting for a house to buy. Vote for me in Loomis and I'll come home to Loomis.'

He did that well. He got them. I had to swallow and pretend there was no prickling in my eye.

'Now,' Duggie said, 'let's get down to brass tacks – and I don't mean Walter Nash.' He spent half an hour on National's policies; they were 'solid and sensible'; and he too was solid and sensible. He had a long look at Nordmeyer's 'black budget', throwing in figures, prescriptions, with assurance. There was hardly an emotive word in it. 'Oh Duggie,' I thought, 'you're good. Don't try too hard or you'll win this seat.' He presented a surface hecklers could only chip at, and with his voice that was round and sharp he rolled right over them or cut straight through. A voice, I thought, like a beaten-copper shield, phoney but antique-looking, and when he wanted to he turned it edge on and chopped with it.

So far he had not mentioned Latham. But at the end he gave a sigh. 'A pity we can't stay on this level.' He took a sip of water and put the glass back on the table with a bang. 'But this after all is an election campaign. So I'm forced to muddy my hands. Excuse me for the word I'm about to say . . . Latham.'

That got a laugh. And some angry yells.

'He's got all his nephews and nieces here. He probably sent them out by bus because none of them live in Loomis. He doesn't live here himself. I've heard he drove through once and bought a pound of apples. On the strength of that he's set himself up as an expert on the fruit industry.

'Now, I've been the subject of some nasty attacks from this man. He seems to think if he can't win your votes through reason he can win them with a sort of vaudeville act – a mixture of muck throwing and cheap wisecracks. He makes a great song and dance over the fact that he wears an RSA badge and I haven't got one. Well, I haven't got one because I was only thirteen when the war ended. He wasn't much older. He's not much older now. But he got into uniform just at the end. They sent him away to guard a few bombed-out buildings when all the shooting was over. On the strength of that he got his badge. Well, I want to announce tonight that I fought in a war too. I'm still fighting in it. And that war, my friends, is the war against communism. I'm even going to pin a badge on my own lapel. I made it myself. Now . . .' He took something silver out of his pocket and fixed it on his jacket. 'You can't see it so I'll tell you what it is. It's a kiwi. It means I was made in this country, not in Russia. And I've even got some battle honours. Do you know what this says, here? It says, *C-Force, 1951*. Yes, my friends, I was one of the thousands of New Zealanders who enrolled in the Civil Emergency Organization back in those days when the communists tried to wreck our country. I fought in the war of fifty-one. And where was Mr Latham then? I'll tell you. He was giving comfort to the enemy. He was scribbling pamphlets. He was taking part in illegal marches. As I said to a journalist friend last night, turn Jack Latham over, you'll find Made in Moscow stamped on his behind.

'And I see we have some of his friends here tonight. Listen to them yapping their commie slogans. There's a few card carriers in this hall. Well I've got news for you, you don't scare me . . .'

He kept on like that for some time and had the hall in an uproar. The constable at the door moved uneasily. I thought if Duggie was trying to lose a few votes he had done it. His performance with the badge would have gone down well in Epsom but the ground in Loomis had a way of shifting. Duggie knew it. He drank some water while the shouts fell away. He smiled and dabbed his brow with a handkerchief.

'Now, let's get on to something less unpleasant. Let's have a bit of comedy. We'll look at some of the Labour Party promises.' He had a small gift for ridicule; he made one or two clever phrases. Nothing was new at this stage of the election, but Duggie worked hard and gave his performance some freshness.

Towards the end he said, 'Let me tell you a story. It's a sad story, and a foolish story, but then Labour's policies are sad and foolish. This took place in Loomis, when I was a boy. Most of you will know the Pool, down on the creek just above Moa Park. When we were kids that was our swimming hole. It had a diving board and changing sheds. They're probably gone today. They are? That's progress although it makes me a little sad. Anyway, the war was on. And one day two American marines arrived at the Pool with their girlfriends. Pretty girls. I know. I was there. I saw it all. The Yanks got away with the pretty ones. Not that these Yanks were much to look at. The one I want to tell you about was a skinny little bloke. His cobber went out on the end of the board and bounced around a bit – you know, impressing his girlfriend. And then the skinny bloke got up and he ran out on the board – and he did a swallow dive. Beautiful! But my friends, let me remind you – the tide goes out down at the Pool. There wasn't any water there. He broke his neck. He died. Yes, one dead American. Oh, I'm not making fun of him. It was tragic. But that's not the point of my story – although doing a swallow dive into shallow water reminds me of the Labour Party too. No, the point is this: the next day, Monday morning, the Council had workmen down at the Pool putting in a post by the diving board marking off in feet just how deep the water was. So everyone could read it. Even Yanks. And that's the point of my story – that's what reminds me of the Labour Party – putting up their post after someone has dived in and broken his neck . . .'

It went down well. This was real life, and this was Loomis. Maybe politics was real as well. The *Herald* and the *Star* men wrote it down. I wrote: The Pool – Munro Gussey – Danger post – LP policy. But I felt that Duggie had told my secrets.

He got tough at question time – 'That's a stupid question and I'm not going to answer it. Has anybody got a sensible question?' Sutton asked about pensions and Father Pearce about state aid. Both seemed satisfied with what Duggie told them, though Sutton snarled and left the hall. Duggie wound himself up about the future for the wine industry – 'I see the day when we, when Loomis, will be making table wines to rival those of France and Germany.' The old Dalmatians did not look sure about that but the young ones nodded their heads. Nobody asked about Meggett Enterprises.

Dad and I drove back to Peacehaven. On Millbrook Road we picked up Roger Sutton. Bluey had died but Sutton was still in the cottage, an ogre or a joke to a new generation of Millbrook children. 'He lives in there,' Mum said, 'like a crab in a mud hole.'

'What did you think of Duggie, Mr Sutton?'

'He's not going to win this seat.'

'Why not?'

'He's too clever.'

I explained to Dad, 'Some people reckon Duggie really wants a safe seat next time.'

'Will he get one?'

'He'll get what he wants,' Sutton said.

'Are you going to vote for him, Mr Sutton?'

'I'm voting for Latham. I like a parliament that's full of fools.'

'Is that what he is?'

'I went to one of his meetings. He talked about fair shares for everyone.'

Dad went to bed and I sat scratching out my articles. When I heard a car in the drive I guessed it was Duggie and I had a drink ready when he came in.

'What I need now is a woman.'

'What you need is for me to tell you how great you were.'

'All right. Tell me.'

'You were great. You belong in politics.'

'Seriously . . .'

'I'm serious.' I had power over him. 'You speak well, you're quick on your feet, you can make a joke, and wring a tear. You don't believe a word of it. And you love it. It's meat and drink to you. You're a politician. And I nearly forgot, you're not too bright.'

'You're a cheeky bugger.'

'I tell you what you've got to know.'

'So I was OK?'

I loved this. 'You were OK. Your party bosses are going to hear about you. Sutton thought you were good.'

'Sutton, eh?'

'He's not going to vote for you. He reckons you don't want to win.'

'It didn't show?'

'Only to people like Sutton. Duggie, leave out the fall of the Roman Empire. It didn't happen like that.'

'Who cares how it happened? It happened any way I like to say.'

'Suit yourself. I wouldn't do too much red-bashing with those old Dallies though. They don't like Khrushchev any but most of them have got a photo of Tito in the kitchen.'

'Yeah. You're right. Those eyes.'

'Stick to Munro Gussey.'

'Who's Munro Gussey?'

'The Yank who broke his neck.'

'Was that his name?'

'I was round at Beak's today. He talked about him.'

'What did you go there for?'

'To say I was sorry about his wife.'

'Ha! How is Beak?'

'He remembers things. Like Munro Gussey. He says he knew he was going to dive. He didn't yell out because he was scared of what you'd say.'

'Silly bugger.'

'He told Myra about it. She said you would have known.'

'Did she? It beats me why you people get so worked up about the past.'

'You used it in your speech.'

He shrugged. 'I don't let it screw me up.'

'Was she right?'

He drank his whisky, put out his glass for more. When I had filled it and he had sipped again, he lay back in his chair and sighed. 'I'll tell you something, Ray. I can't remember. Sometimes I think I knew. And I didn't care. I wanted to see what would happen. But mostly I'm not interested. It was what? Twenty years ago?'

'Seventeen.'

'So? It's the bloody dark ages. What else did Beak have to say for himself?'

'He told me how you walked round his house yelling out Miss Gobbloffski.'

'Shit!' He pushed his glass away. 'What do you think you are, my bloody conscience?'

'I have a hard enough time being my own.'

'What's your game then?'

'No game. I'm interested in how you feel about things.'

'I don't feel about them. Not Myra. Or Beak. That's finished. I don't see what it's got to do with me now.'

'You re-invent yourself every morning? Handy in politics. But you'll have to be careful. Things have got a way of coming back.'

He gave a petulant lift of his hands. 'I was feeling good when I came round here.' I had a moment's pity and could find no basis for it but affection. It troubled me that Duggie and I were bound.

When I let him out I said, 'Duggie, you were great up there tonight. No bullshit, Duggie.'

14

Peacehaven at new year was scented, lovely. I walked on the lawns and through the gardens with Sharon's hand in mine and Gregory on my shoulders. We played hide-and-seek up and down the terraces and in the summerhouse. Memories pricked at me, I laughed loudly with my children, and had to turn my face away from adults so they should not see my eyes were wet. I was wounded and renewed, and welcomed it, and hated it at times, seeing it as a kind of self-abuse. I was the Wellington journalist not the weepy boy. But if I had wanted to avoid descents I should not have had children, and not have brought them home.

'Why do you call this place home?' Glenda said.

'Do I? I didn't know. That just shows . . .'

'What?'

'The way it hangs on. Wadestown is home.'

'Don't you forget it. I wish your mother wouldn't call you Raymie.'

'So do I.'

Things were easier when Becky came. Her loudness invaded me and left little space for memories. 'Quit that moping about,' she yelled. 'Come and have a beer. Come and talk to Tom. He wants to know who's putting the boot in down in Wellington.' Tom was her husband, a 'young executive' with a tobacco company. It was the first time I had heard that term. Becky used it without irony, though it brought a flush on her husband's cheeks.

Tom and I got on well as long as we talked about sport. On everything else we disagreed; and settled into grinning at each other shiftily. We thought each other bloody idiots and left it at that. Becky, thick as a tractor tyre, called us 'great old buddies'.

She had three sons, the youngest Sharon's age. When Bobby and his wife came up from Pukekohe there were eight children on the lawn. They surrounded Mum, grizzling for biscuits. She enjoyed them – and taught them please and thank you – but wanted to get away after a time. Her own children concerned her more and she tested our happiness with looks and questions.

'Lay off, Mum.'

'I'm not prying, Ray. I do like Glenda.'

'She keeps to herself. She's not used to this.'

'I wish she'd talk to me.'

'What about?'

'Oh, things. You.'

'No chance. Glenda keeps it here –' I tapped my head. 'It won't come out for you or anyone.'

'But you are happy?'

'Sure. We're happy.'

She took me to visit her brother Robert. We drove north to the Kaipara harbour and found him in his shack on a half-acre section out beyond Helensville. Robert's history is a curious one. He lived at Peacehaven until the war – never a friend, never a girl – then spent four years in conshie camps. When he came out he turned away from his family for some reason – Mum hints at some unspoken disagreement with his father – and lived on a farm with a bunch of religious cranks who practised free love and communal sharing. He had a 'wife' – not wives. They turned him out finally for sins against the ethic of the place: his father had left him the cottage and instead of selling it and giving the money to the commune he let Bluey and Sutton stay on there. When they expelled him he wandered north and found his shack on the Kaipara harbour. He had been there ten years but seemed unchanged to me from the Robert who had worked in the gardens at Peacehaven. Slow and adenoidal. Shirt tucked in his underpants. It astonished me that Mum had romanticized him. She set him up as a kind of saint.

It was a frustrating day. I never managed to match my pace with it. We sat on the jetty in the tidal creek and watched the yellow water creep in the mangroves. We talked in sentences that would not have been out of place in an infant reader. 'See the crab on the mud.' 'Listen to the blackbird.' 'I like to hear the blackbird singing.'

After lunch Robert took me out to look at his set lines. We rowed down the creek on to the harbour. I told him about Duggie – 'Ah.' – and my wife and children. 'You're lucky, Ray.' There were snapper on his lines and flounder in his net. I got quite excited hauling them in. Robert scaled and gutted them and threw the entrails to the screaming gulls. Rowing back, and making a hash of it, I asked him about his days in the camps. I told him I wanted to do two articles, one about the first war – Archibald Baxter, the crucifixion posts, all that stuff – and one about the second.

'Ah,' he said.

'So how about it? I'd only need an hour. We could do it this afternoon.'

'No.'

'Why not?'

'I don't talk about it. There's plenty of blokes who'll tell you.'

'Well, how about that place you went to live in? Parminter's? *Truth* did a job on it but it might be worth a look.'

'I don't talk about that either.'

'What do you talk about?' He didn't answer. 'Why did you go there? Why didn't you come back to Peacehaven?'

'You ask a lot of questions, Ray. I suppose –' I noticed his breathing; bronchitic I thought, but I found out later he had emphysema. '– I suppose it's hard for a newspaperman to learn there aren't any answers.'

Cleverness? I looked at him with a new interest. But he said no more and the work of rowing silenced me – it blistered me – and I watched with a sour admiration the ease with which he sent the dinghy along when he took my place.

Mum and I quarrelled about him on the drive home. I told her his way of life was a cop-out. Goodness, I said, was an active thing. Had she heard of the tree crashing down in the forest? If no one was in earshot then there was no sound. And goodness only exists where people are. Nonsense, Mum said. What about saints and hermits, living by themselves in caves and deserts? Was I telling her they were wasting their time? Too right, I said. The only good they did was feeding the lice with their beards. She told me that I disappointed her.

I disappointed my brother and sister too. Like Tom they wanted tales from Wellington but it wasn't power struggles that interested them – I had embroidered a few for Tom, before I found my virtue was his vice – it was what Becky called 'the bedroom stuff'. 'Who's up who?' Bobby said. 'Come on, Ray. You newspaper blokes are supposed to know everything.' I'd heard a rumour or two but I wasn't saying. And if I had, Bobby and Becky would still have been disappointed. Both had an eager belief in orgies involving diplomats and cabinet ministers' wives. It seemed that our mother's lessons in purity had left them unaffected – or had they gone through struggles like my own and come out dirty-minded as a pair of gossip-column journalists?

'If you could see cabinet ministers' wives . . .'

'Well, what about those parliamentary typists? You can't tell me' etc. etc.

Glenda gave little smiles, trying to join my family. Becky bossed her like the netball captain she had been, and patted her condescendingly, and made remarks about people who went around head in the clouds. Bobby winked at her, making sure she got his double meanings, and joked about 'a certain party's' prowess in the sack. 'For a while there he thought all you could poke with it was the fire.'

I extricated Glenda and we walked about the section. 'I'm sorry. They're pretty horrible.'

'It's not your fault. I like your father.'

'Dad's OK. So's Mum.'

'The children like her. Who's that man over the creek? In the garden?'

'Roger Sutton.'

'He's the hunchback? I thought he looked odd.' She shifted to get a clear look through the trees. 'Poor man.'

'We've tried to help him, but he won't take help.'

'I see why not.'

I showed her the eel pools, dirty now with rubbish from the houses. I shifted rocks but could find no lobsters. A smell of rot came from the water. Glenda took my hand. 'You shouldn't have come.'

'I knew how it would be. Let's look at the culvert.' Its barrel pointed at us. We looked through the shrinking tube at a world impossibly green; the magic world children in books step through mirrors to, through waterfalls and doors in the trunks of trees. 'Let's go there,' Glenda said.

'The water's dirty.'

'We can have a bath.'

We took our sandals off and waded in. Slime and silt came over our ankles. It had a creamy thickness not unpleasant if you forgot the smell. 'Vichyssoise,' I joked, but Glenda did not laugh. I made her face out dimly, glimmering at the faery world ahead. Then I found she saw it differently. 'It's like floating up from under water.'

We came out to a little waterfall, a moss-green pool, stones patched with silver lichen. Ferns grew in crevices round the sides of the basin. The trees bent down from the banks as though watching something in the pool but all we saw there was the shape of them and a lightening from the summer sky. Looking up, we saw it flat and pure. To reach the day we would need to rise again from under water.

'This is more spooky than I remember.'

'I like it here.' She leaned on the culvert, looking happy. Behind her dusty blackberry vines rose in frothing waves to Millbrook Road. A car went by. She did not seem to hear.

'Look back where we came from.' I pointed at the same magic world. 'They're interchangeable.'

'So where do we belong?'

'Not with Bobby and Becky. Still, we'd better get back to the kids.'

'You go. Let me stay a while.'

'You OK?'

'I'm fine. I just want to be by myself for a bit. I'm not very good at families.'

So I went back and endured more of my brother and sister. I told them Glenda was resting and Bobby made jokes about nipping in to see if she wanted anything. He was impressed with her good looks. I got him away from that by opening the *Star*. 'Any news of Beak Wyatt?'

'He's run away with some sheila if you ask me.'

'Who'd have Beak?' Becky said.

'He had a wife. She was a pretty girl.'

'If it isn't a woman someone's done him in,' Bobby said. 'His house is locked up. Car in the garage. He wouldn't leave his car.'

'I think he's wandered off,' I said. 'His wife's death hit him pretty hard.' But I believed Beak had killed himself. I remembered him asking why we should be alive when Myra was dead.

The next day we had a party at Peacehaven. The food and drink were in the summer-house and we helped ourselves through the afternoon. Glenda had the chance to meet some more of my family. She met Mirth and Willis, and Willis too liked the look of her. She met my uncle Emerson, the tomato grower, the Sundowner of the Skies. He was a shy man, but crazy in an aeroplane. She met Esther and Fred Meggett and their younger son Adrian. They rolled up late in Fred's royal-blue Mercedes with the custom-built upholstery and the built-in cocktail bar. Esther stepped out holding her flagon of port in its brown-paper bag. Duggie came late too. I hadn't expected to see him but his new girl, Tania, wanted to meet his parents. He found that amusing. 'She wants to marry me.'

'What are her chances?'

'Doesn't hurt to let them keep on hoping. Makes them willing.'

'And she is?' We were standing on the brick bridge looking at the party. As usual Duggie had me: I felt all my boyish sexual unease. He made a tweaking motion in the air. 'Give them a quarter turn they poke out like sticks of chalk.'

I watched Tania – black-haired, sun-tanned, in a linen skirt and schoolgirl blouse – sitting on the lawn with Glenda, while Duggie told me what he did to her. She was an art teacher at a girls' high school and had made his C-force badge for him. 'Bloody good painter. So they tell me. Hey, you know those things they paint on the edge of books? You spread the pages and you get a picture?'

Yes, I knew. I knew what was coming as well.

'She painted one of those on my cock. We had it going on and off like TV all afternoon. You don't believe me? I'll make her come and tell you.'

'No, no. I believe you.'

'Yeah . . . Your little lady's quite a looker. Goodlad's daughter. How does that affect her?'

'She's over it.' He had no memory of her and that made me easier and marked a victory I made more complete by keeping from him. I told him I believed Beak had killed himself.

'He wouldn't have the guts,' Duggie said. 'Myra broke him in I reckon and he's gone looking for more. He's shacked up somewhere with his boss's wife. Well, someone's wife. Beak's a bloody dull subject. How'd you like the result?'

'I said National would win. I can't say I like it.'

'In Loomis, I mean. Two hundred and ninety votes. I've made it look like a marginal. Some poor sod's going to get a shock.'

'Are they pleased with you?'

'Like I said, they know I'm here.'

We strolled back down the lawn and Duggie gave me a nudge. 'Who does Adrian remind you of?'

'Only his mother. He goes after food like her.'

'Scrape off a couple of layers of fat.' I looked and shook my head. 'Remember that Yank called Errol?'

'I thought you weren't interested in the past.'

'Maybe not. But I wouldn't mind something on old Esther. On Fred either. He's going too bloody fast. Too damn greedy. I want to put a lot of ground between him and me.'

'You shouldn't have said you worked for him in your glossy.'

'No, I shouldn't. Tell your old man to get away from him. Easy though. I want old Fred to stand up as long as he can.'

We sat down with Glenda and Tania and I saw how the girl lit up when Duggie came close. He was good-looking all right, with his auburn hair and pale-lashed eyes and the comic-strip jut of his chin. His bottom and short legs spoiled the effect. It was better when he sat down. Tania put her hand on his. She laid her head for a moment on his shoulder, then shook back her hair and smiled at him. I saw nothing ahead for her but bad times with Duggie – apart from good times in bed and, as he had told me, in the bath, in the lounge, on the kitchen table. I looked at her breasts and thighs and hips shaped like an apple, and with my wife's fingers twined in mine and my children playing on the lawn, I wanted to be with Tania, I wanted her fore-edge painting me. She felt my lust and gave a startled look and gripped Duggie by his knee.

'Douglas and I went to a party last week and I met Mr Holyoake. I liked him. I really did. I mean, I'm Labour. I'm not changing that for anyone.'

'I like it,' Duggie said. 'It gives her something. Like having a girlfriend who's Chinese or cross-eyed.'

Tania blushed. She gave Glenda a look of apology.

'You paint?' I said.

'Yes. I do.'

'What sort of things?'

'Landscapes mostly.'

Duggie was grinning. She looked at him; and I saw her understand. Her face went white and her eyes seemed to darken and turn in. In a tiny voice, from far away: 'Hills. I like hills.'

Duggie patted her. 'You should show Ray and Glenda. They'll buy one.'

'Have you had an exhibition?' Glenda said.

Bobby and Becky arrived, bringing Esther.

'That's what we need. An exhibition,' Bobby said.

'You boys did all right for yourselves,' Esther said. 'Pretty girl for a wife, Ray. I didn't think you were going to make it.'

'He followed my example,' Bobby said. 'You can learn all sorts of things from your big brother.'

Esther put her wine down next to Glenda and lowered herself heavily on to the grass. She pulled her dress back from her pudgy thighs, 'Top me up, Ray.' She thrust her glass at me and I filled it from her flagon. 'Nice looking kids you've got. Glenda, that's your name. I'll tell you something Glenda, your old man gave me the best tips I've ever had. He was my bible. *Goodlad's Hot Tips*. I stopped winning when he died.'

'Yes?' Glenda said. Her face took a marbled appearance, pink and white.

'I wish he was still alive,' Esther said. 'I need some luck. He should have married Josie Mottram instead of killing himself.'

'She went to England,' Glenda said.

'She lost a good man. I always felt sorry for Graham Goodlad. It's no crime to go to bed with a woman. Not that dumb old Oliver would know.'

'My father loved Mrs Mottram,' Glenda said.

'That stuck out a mile.'

'But the trial was really too much for both of them.'

'Oliver was too much. I always said it was Oliver who killed him.'

'No. It wasn't.'

'Maybe. Well, he knew his horses. Here's to *Goodlad's Hot Tips*.' She drank some wine.

I pulled Glenda up. 'Come on. Let's talk to Emerson.' I led her over to the summer-house. Her face had pink blotches on the cheeks. I could not tell whether she was trembling with anger or distress. 'Why did you do that?'

'I thought it had gone on long enough.'

'No, no, no. That's the first time anyone's ever said his name.' She freed her hand and ran to Sharon and Gregory and knelt on the lawn with them. I saw Duggie and Tania watching us so I went on and talked with Emerson. He told me about his days in the flying circus and on the mail run from London to Paris in the thirties. I stayed half an hour with him and when I came round the summerhouse Glenda was gone. Duggie strolled over.

'She seems to be a jumpy lady, your wife.'

'Did you see where she went?'

'Down by the creek somewhere.'

I found her sandals by the mouth of the culvert, and looking in saw the dish-flat world at the end of the tunnel. I waded through and found her by the pool.

'Come back to the party, Glenda.'

'I just wanted a few minutes by myself.'

'I'm sorry I made a mistake.'

'It's not your fault.'

I led her back and kept close to her while we talked with Fred and Adrian. Fred was paunchy, triple-jowled, he had a blue boiled eye and had still his red rough butcher hands. Jovial, his voice like wooden clappers, he praised my wife's good looks and me for getting her, while Adrian ate mince pies, a little greedy for the neutered Tom, but sleek and fat and shiny, with hair thoroughly oiled and eyes that had an inward look of boredom. A description that, as they say, tells more about the writer than the subject. It comes from a mental twitch there's no getting rid of. I could, with a little effort, have written: Fred, successful, jolly, bending from his affairs just a trace absently, made friendly attempts at flattery, while Adrian ate mince pies, turning his mind on a boy's concerns. But I don't know. I'll never know. It's all approximations and all choices. I do not know what Glenda meant when she said, 'What a creepy boy.' *Creepy* sets me hunting but I rarely catch anything. She said nothing about Fred. I suspect he reminded her of her father.

As for Mirth and Willis – these were their happiest days. They had sailed home to port and were cosily moored. They groaned and creaked with devotion, rubbing flanks. If you liked that sort of thing they were fun to be with. Tania – had she forgiven Duggie? did his betrayals only make his women love him more? – Tania was enchanted, fascinated. A little of it was enough for me, I don't disapprove; but as much as Grandpa Plumb and Oliver these two locked out the world. I remembered Mirth, with inhuman face, with hair like Strewelpeter, running through the grapefruit trees clutching her butcher's knife while Willis, with grotty crotch and popping eyes, peg-legged madly for the orchard shed. And Duggie howled. They did no damage these days. They were charming in a slightly gruesome way. Our comic turn. Duggie stayed on the other side of the summer-house.

'Everyone has foreign names today,' Mirth said. 'Willis probably knew a Tania somewhere, didn't you Willie? In one of your ports.'

'They let you call them any name you liked if you had the money.'

'Now Willie, don't be naughty. Tania goes very nicely with Plumb.'

Tania blushed and looked to see if Duggie had heard.

'My dear, I'll give you some advice. Duggie's like his father. He has strong passions. You can't say no to Duggie for very long. So let him, you know, let him . . . You modern girls do, I know. And Duggie is not a man you can keep waiting. Nor was his father. Were you, Willie? It's bad for a man if he has to wait. They should teach that in the schools. Then there wouldn't be so many of these boys standing on street corners only thinking. Really, we should have summer camps where young people could go and just make love. Like those health camps we sent Melva and Irene to, Willie.'

'I could be headmaster.'

'Now Willie. Ray could have done with something like that when he was a boy.'

I went round the summer-house and found Duggie grinning. 'Now you see why I don't go home.'

Merle and Graydon Butters also came. She pushed him along Millbrook Road in his wheelchair, rolled him on to the lawn, and I put them here for the effect they had on Glenda. It was this: when Merle bullied Graydon to talk, and he unloaded words from his tongue with an agony that made us sweat; and she pretended they came beautifully and told him that we all, his dear old friends, understood him, and held his face in her hands and looked in his eyes, 'I know you're in there'; and we laughed; then Glenda took the handles of his chair and said, cool and English as her mother, 'Do you mind Mrs Butters, I'll just take your husband for a walk,' and pushed him across the lawn and up the drive and vanished with him in the guava trees.

'Well . . .' Merle said. 'Who is that woman?'

'She's my wife. I think I'll have a word if you'll excuse me . . .'

'What are you playing at, Glenda?'

Graydon was in the shade of a tree, with his head slumped on his chest. I could not tell whether he was resting, weeping, dead. Glenda stood behind him. She came at me and pulled me along to the back of the house.

'Couldn't any of you hear what he was saying?'

'No one can understand him. He'll never speak again. Merle just tries to keep him going.'

'I understood. It was plain as day.'

'All right. What then?'

'He said, Make her stop.'

'Yes – even so –'

'And you all just laughed. You let her go on treating him like a baby.'

'Glenda, she's his wife. They've been married for fifty years.'

'He said, Make her stop.'

'So you made her. Here she comes. Are you going to make her again?'

Merle wheeled Graydon away.

'I want,' Glenda said, 'I want you to take me to the station. I'm going home.'

'Glenda, we can't go.'

'By myself. You stay here. It's your family.'

'Glenda –'

'I'm not used to it. I can't handle families. I don't know who they all are. I don't know who you are any more.'

'We've only got three days. Please, Glenda.'

'If you won't drive me I'll take a taxi.'

'What about the children?'

'They've got to learn. You bring them back.'

'If they've got to . . .'

'It's too late for me.'

I borrowed Dad's car and drove her to the station. She was in time for the Express. I put her on, rented pillows for her, said goodbye. She was clear-eyed, pink and pretty. She laughed and kissed my cheek. I did not know who she was.

15

I worried about my maturity and quickly seemed to come to the end of myself. My spasm of lust for Tania seems comic now, but I took it to mean there was little to me. I chased after substance recklessly. I became as headlong as a boy. My fantasies took a weird simplicity. No fore-edge painting, no kitchen tables. I wanted to unbutton my wife and lie my hand on her breast. No more than that.

But it had not been simple for some time. Complications broke from us in tangles, like the innards from a broken clock. I look at our conversations and see blind forays, retreats. The words we used had no common meaning. We looked at each other from distances and found no way of coming close – though we tried, with chat about Sharon and Gregory, with buying things for the house and holding hands in the pictures.

I did not know what was wrong with her. I asked her to see a doctor and tried to send her off on holidays. But no – no doctors; they would only give her tranquillizers or advise her to find a hobby or a job. She did not need things to do. The problem was of a different sort. That was as far as she would define it. As for holidays – Wellington and Wadestown were her places. She was happy there. She asked me please not to send her away.

I still found toothpaste on my brush. When I went to bed Glenda was lying awake. She took cat-naps in the day she said, so I was not to worry. But what did she think about, I asked, lying in bed in the darkened room? Please tell me, Glenda. Oh, she said, things. Everything. We made love. That was still all right, she enjoyed it; though she made few movements and was quiet. Our old house shuddered in the wind. A drizzle of dust fell from the silver sprats.

Out in the world I was busy. I had turned myself into a political journalist and my editor had promised me the job in the Press Gallery when Morrie Horne grew tired of it. Morrie said he would be tired of it soon. He liked a quieter life and had his eye on Special Features. Meanwhile, I thought about my Uncle Emerson. Talking with him had given me ideas. *The Sundowner of the Skies. Emerson Plumb's story, as told to Raymond Sole.* First a chapter on his boyhood and youth – his motorbikes not his father. Nobody would want to know about the Reverend Plumb. Then learning to fly in England; and the crazy flight, Croydon to Australia in the same year as Kingsford Smith and Amy Johnson. Then the flying circus, the wing walking. And mail-run flying in Europe. And the Solent flying boats, seven hours chugging over the Tasman Sea, with landings on the two beautiful harbours. I saw it all, I had it written in my mind. In the last chapter I would tell how he tracked down his old Gypsy Moth and spent a year rebuilding it and made it fly again. I roughed out the plan. I made a summary. Then I rang Emerson and told him the favour I meant to do him. When could I come up with my tape recorder?

Five minutes later the whole thing was gone. I put the phone down shaking. I was hollow with disbelief, and grieving for my book, and blind with anger at these idiot Plumbs, these bloody drongos. What right had Emerson to kill my book?

In revenge I wrote an article on him. What I did not know I invented. Nobody took me up on anything. But it was not enough. I still had my notion of a book, and my torments were not so different from those of a real writer. My problem was I had lost my subject and could not find another. I never saw a book as other than someone's account of his life – and the process I imagined never varied: the famous person talking, Ray Sole taking it down. I asked Alan Webster what I should do. He seemed to think ghosting respectable and he told me to see a publisher: most of them had lists of people anxious to have someone put them on paper. So I went to Reeds and within a week was talking with Albie Marsick. Not the sort of famous person I'd wanted, but a start. His memory was good; he told me what he'd eaten for breakfast at every hotel on tour. He remembered every line-out jump he'd made. So *Play the Man* was born, *The Albie Marsick Story, as told to Raymond Sole.* It seemed to me as rich in incident as *War and Peace.* And Albie himself was a tragic hero. That match where he was ordered off at Cardiff Arms Park . . .

(Let me get my career in literature out of the way. I did another rugby book, *Boom! Boom!* I did *Sweet Millie*, the story of Millicent Bean, the musical comedy star. I did Frank Murphy's story (the union boss): *Nor Shall My Sword* (his title). I helped Jim Horrocks with *Touch Cop*. Horrocks made my footballers seem like marshmallows. 'Just off the record Ray, I'll tell you what we did to that cunt . . .' Stomp! Thud! Aargh! I hated Horrocks. Sitting with him, listening to his hatreds, I felt stirrings of nausea; but I got the book finished. And that was enough. I made plans for a different sort of book, *M. J. Savage*: started research, did some interviews. I've still got the stuff in an old suitcase. One day I'll give it to the Turnbull Library.)

Glenda was kind about *Play the Man*. She said it was well done and agreed it was a good way of making extra money. Diana had a lot of fun with it but I told her we'd sold thirty thousand copies. Alan sold five hundred of his books. 'Oh well,' she said, 'if it's money you're after. But Ray, I'm worried about Glenda. What's gone wrong with her?'

Everyone was worried about Glenda. 'What's the matter with Mummy?' 'She's all right, dear. She's just having a think.' 'Why does she have to think all the time?' Cute? Not at the time. Not now. I told Gregory that she would stop thinking before long and he was not to worry because Daddy was here; and always to remember that Mummy loved him very much. I told him how special Mummy was; but I was beginning to think of her in terms like those she had used of her mother: pale, cold, lost, sad. Sad was the word I used most. I did not know exactly what it meant. It banged around in my skull, setting up reverberations, then it started wailing like bagpipes.

'Glenda. Glenda.'

'Hallo, Ray.'

'Have you looked at the children, Glenda?'

'I've given them a kiss.'

'Sharon's got earache.'

'I know. I took her to the doctor.' She did those things. She played with them and read to them and smiled and listened; but it was as if she had learned how from a book. At times I saw her stop as though seeing it, and her hands gave a little jerk and she looked at the children with desperation as though she had remembered there was something she must do, some way to save them.

'Glenda, do you have to go to bed?'

'I'll be awake when you come.'
'I want to talk to you, Glenda.'
'What about?'
I know you're in there somewhere. Please come out.

I was not always gentle. After a while I found it hard to be even interested. I looked for easy cures. Her father was the trouble, I believed – the bastard who had shot himself and left her to carry on. She had been angry with me for pulling her away from talk of him. OK, I would talk. She wanted to hear his name? I would say it. I'd drag him from his hiding place and hold him in an armbar for her to see.

'You've got to get him out of your head. He's like a bloody maggot, eating away. Now tell me, you're grown up now, you're not a girl, tell me how you really feel about him. How do you feel about a man who can't face a bit of pain and shoots himself and leaves his daughter to face it for him and carry on?'

That was the way it went. I believed it was practical. Shock tactics.

She looked at me with her turned-in look, eyes out of line; and went out of the room and closed the door.

'Glenda,' I yelled, 'Glenda,' ripping it open, 'don't you see he's ruining all our lives. He might just as well have shot us all.'

But I was alone in the hall – children behind their doors, Glenda behind her door. I heard her clothing rustle as she changed and heard the bed creak as she got in. She gave a little sigh, neither happy nor sad, expressing something – contentment? dissatisfaction? – whose referents were unknown to me. It was like a sound from outside the house, out in the night. I turned away in fear, as though from a door into nothing; and went back to the lounge and flicked the play button on my recorder and heard a slurp of beer and a voice say, 'First tackle of the match Ray, he tries this pansy side-step, thinks he's goin' past me, and I hit that little bugger under his ribs, bowled him arse over kite, heard the air come fartin' out both ends, and I swear to you Ray, no bullshit, he lies on the ground and he says "Mam", like a lamb bleatin'. Talk about laugh. After that he drops every ball he gets. I had him shittin' himself.' That was Boom Casey, hero of *Boom! Boom!* I thanked God for him.

When I went to bed after midnight she was awake. And yes, we made love. That happened almost nightly. It was the way we touched. But it seemed to me she felt pleasure on her skin and underneath was not open to me. I penetrated into emptiness.

Meanwhile – I like that word – Duggie prospered. I don't mean he made money, though he made it. Jack Latham called Muldoon 'the monstrous fart of a flatulent party'. Duggie's arrival had that quality. From '60 to '63 he was into everything. And when he came forward in his duck waddle with some 'grassroots' remit – some plan for hanging or birching or for the outlawing of the communist party – there was a buzz in the conference hall that in political terms was a shout of welcome. But Duggie was too smart to be just the 'backwoodsman' party liberals called him. Being a character had its dangers too. He learned how to be quiet, he learned to give the appearance of following. That was not an easy thing for him. But he made it serve, he used endorsement as a substitute for thought. He took things over and made them his. 'Other men laboured and he entered into their labours.' That was his way – the classic way for a politician.

He put his name forward for Epsom in 1963. Snyder had retired and sixteen people joined the chase for that blue-ribbon seat. Mark Brierly was one. While Duggie had been splashing around Brierly had crept in. Duggie was noticed, Duggie gave an impression of strength – but Brierly, ah, he was a gentleman. That counted for a great deal in Epsom. He and Duggie and a bank economist and the regional division vice-chairman were the ones with a chance. They nudged each other about in a civilized way. Duggie learned to give a little smile. And he made a lot of ground when he began to escort Sally Carpenter about. Sally was the daughter of a Cabinet Minister; a beautiful girl in her enamelled way; a kind of princess in the social world of the National Party. 'Professional virgin,' Duggie winked at me. 'She's for the duration.'

My paper sent me up for a look at Epsom. That was an unusual expense but interest was high. If Brierly or Duggie won the nomination he was safe in parliament for thirty years. It was, my editor said, the perfect springboard for a career – take that line, have a look at them in depth.

I had no time for that. The day I arrived in Auckland Cyril Butts came on the scene. I had rung Duggie and arranged to see him in the morning. Then I sat by the fire talking with Mum and Dad; listening to Dad's worries about M.E., and Mum's about Robert, who was dying. She wanted to bring him down to live in the cottage but Roger Sutton would not get out and Robert, who owned the place, would not evict him. I told them about Glenda, not too much, and saw Mum puzzle for answers, and complain inwardly about the unfairness of things. She knew as well as I there could be no happy ending.

When they had gone to bed I wandered about the house, looked in the study, looked at Grandpa's books – Ovid, Wordsworth, *The History of Pantheism*. Patted the Buddha, gross and spiritual; played some golf shots with a walking stick. Then I walked in the wet grass down to the bridge and heard the water running. Well, I thought, this is where I came in. Time's gone by, the rest of it is atoms knocking about. But I saw the thought as marking my limitations. I did not believe it, but had nothing else. So where was I? Other people got further than that; what was the matter with me that all I had after thirty years was a set of Pavlovian mental tics? Where in them was I? Raymond Sole? There was no answer. Was it possible there was no Raymond Sole? I – or something called I – made my doggy way from feed to feed. I kept my belly full and a number of mental appetites satisfied. I read books – a bit. I listened to music – a bit. I did my best for my wife and children. But if there was no more than that – I might as well join Duggie Plumb in the National Party.

I laughed. That was the answer: wisecrack your way out of trouble. Then I went up to the garage and looked at Grandma Sole's glory box, her china cabinet, her 'sweet' etc, left to me when she died. They were piled against the back wall. I should have to tell Dad what to do with them. I shifted the fire set and opened the box. There were the towels and embroidered cloths, the slabs of linen and antimacassars. The sight of them was – moving? – touching? – sad? I felt threatened with speculations about 'meaning', and I closed the lid and shrugged and said, 'What am I going to do with the bloody things?' The sensible thing was sell them to a junk shop – choose the odd bit for Glenda though, so Dad would not be hurt. I would get on to it.

I locked the garage and was caught against the door by car lights in the drive. They came at me, blinded me, and I thought I was going to be crushed. But Duggie braked, skidded, left his lights glaring, his door wide. He punched the hood and kicked the garage door. Rage frothed out of him.

'Shut up, Duggie.' I jerked him, pulled him after me, got him into the house and put a glass of Dad's whisky in his hand. 'Now, what's the matter? And keep your voice down. You'll wake Mum.'

His face was white and his eyes had a thickening in their blue that made them seem to plunge down and down.

'Ray,' he said, 'they reopened nominations tonight.'

'So, who are they letting in?'

'Cyril Butts.'

'Ah, Sir Cyril. Someone to carry on the Snyder tradition.'

'The old bastard's been dithering. Last week he said no. He'd made his decision. Tonight he's reconsidered. He wants in. He's had people coming to him – "people whose opinion I respect". The old cunt. He wants it on a plate. I'm not going to give it to him.'

'What are the others doing?'

'They've pulled out.'

'Brierly?'

'Him too. He's coming out to make a grab for Loomis. Latham'll eat him.'

'But you're staying in?'

'I told them straight off. Hignett was the one who came and told us. Said Sir Cyril had changed his mind and the electorate committee was reopening nominations. I told him he couldn't do that but he said they already had. And they wanted us all out – Sir Cyril didn't want all the hurly-burly and so on. I asked him how he'd get on in parliament if he couldn't take a nominations fight. Hignett didn't like that. But the bastards all pulled out. Graceful, you know. Wouldn't dream of standing in Sir Cyril's way. Even Brierly. He went green though. Stupid cunt. I stayed in.'

'They won't like that.'

'They'll have to like it. Hignett took me off for a little talk. Told me to wait – "Sir Cyril only wants one term, well maybe two. In six years you can have it." Thinks I'm buying that. They'll have another Sir Cyril by that time. And I'm not waiting six years for anyone. That's my seat. I've worked for it. They think I'm standing down for some old cunt who's so pickled in gin he can't stand up straight. I told Hignett. I'll tell bloody Holyoake too. There are people in Epsom who want me. They nominated me. You want a story Ray, I'll give you one.'

'You want me to say Butts is pickled in gin?'

He said quickly, 'I'm not saying that. Here's what I'm giving you.' He could not even hint that Butts drank too much. He could not say that at sixty he was too old. Keith Holyoake was fifty-nine. He simply said how much he admired Sir Cyril's career – an MP at thirty-one (a good touch: Duggie was thirty-two), a minister in Sid Holland's government; his courage and dignity when he lost his seat (another good touch – Butts should never have lost that seat); the skill with which he'd handled his new job as High Commissioner in London, a job calling for talents of quite a different order from those he had exercised in his parliamentary career. And the scandal of his recall by Nash's Labour government; the honourable retirement, the knighthood putting a seal on his career. No man had done more etc, etc. Duggie organized it beautifully, he turned Butts into a dodo and two-time loser. And those 'talents of quite a different order' – that meant boozing if you were in the know.

'Nice work, Duggie. Now what about you?'

'I'm carrying on because I believe in myself and the National Party. Much as I respect Sir Cyril I believe the voters of Epsom want a new face. An energetic member. We're in the sixties now . . .' and so on. At the end of it he'd got his colour back.

I said, 'He's still going to beat you. You'd stand a better chance out here in Loomis.'

'That's what Hignett said. Brierly wouldn't have a look in. But it's no deal. I'm having Epsom.'

'What do you know that I don't know? Have you got some dirt on Butts?'

'He drinks himself paralytic every night. I'll make sure one or two people know that.'

'They know already. It's one of the things that makes him a character. You're allowed to be a boozer when you've made it.'

'Ray, I'm having Epsom. OK? It's mine.' He laid the words down like coins on a counter. I saw he had nothing left but belief in himself. He had lost belief in the orderly sequence of events. That was the night on which his life in politics really started. Chance became his principle of action.

I interviewed Cyril Butts the following day. He quivered his plum-red jowls at me, boomed his famous laugh, sprayed me with spit that was pure gin, and told me how much he looked forward to the hurly-burly of the house again – how he'd missed it – and serving with his old colleagues Keith and Jack and Ralph, and serving this great little nation once more. I asked him if he hoped for a cabinet appointment. He got cagey and talked about what he had to offer in terms of sheer experience – did I realize he'd been in parliament with Gordon Coates before the National Party took that name? This could surely not be overlooked. But basically, well, he was happy to play whatever role was asked of him.

'How do you feel about keeping younger men out?'

'Ah, Mark Brierly you mean? He's a fine young man. A credit to the party. What a future we've got when young men like that are coming along. And the other chap – what's his name? – Douglas Plumb. I understand their disappointment. But they will have their day. And politics is a battlefield after all.'

He had a coughing fit and his face turned purple. I went round the desk to pat his back but he knocked me aside with his tree-trunk arm and grabbed his drink. A swallow put him right. His colour remained alarming and I wondered if somewhere more blood vessels had broken. Duggie might have his hopes on a by-election.

Sir Cyril Butts was chosen as candidate. People who were at the selection meeting say Duggie smiled. He stood up and said that he wished Sir Cyril well, naturally, but more than that, he gave him his whole-hearted support, and what he would like to do now was make himself useful, he would like to turn his knowledge of the electorate to account. People had told him he should try for Loomis. But no, no, he'd made his home in Epsom and that was where his heart was. So . . . he offered to serve on Sir Cyril's campaign committee. With this Duggie won back the ground he'd lost in opposing Butts. He showed himself a man of 'moderation' and 'good judgement'.

Sir Cyril could only respond by being delighted. Someone told me that although he smiled he was afraid. I don't think that can be true. There's a photograph of him shaking hands with Duggie on that night. He's leaning back a little, the pupils of his eyes seem dilated. He was noticing Duggie for the first time. Duggie looks like a little boy.

He ran Sir Cyril's campaign. Sir Cyril of course did nothing. He burbled. He went through the motions. Duggie shuffled him about. Drove him here, drove him there, held doors open for him. He called for the cheers and led the singing of *For he's* etc. I wondered what it was all about. Duggie as puppet master? That was not what he wanted. Was he just demonstrating the mistake the Nats had made? There he was pouring out energy while Sir Cyril got slower and slower, forgot his speeches, burped on radio.

'What's your game, Duggie?'

'I've got no game.'

'You think they might replace him?'

'He's knocking back a quart of gin a day.'

'Is that it? You're feeding him the stuff?'

'No, Ray. I'm the one who tries to stop him drinking.'

Duggie was first to Sir Cyril when he had his stroke. It happened at a meeting in the Teachers College hall. I was there. I should have been somewhere else but Duggie and Sir Cyril fascinated me. I was at a press table set up at the side of the stage almost in the curtains. I could watch them both: Sir Cyril ripe and dewed with sweat; pumped up, bulging here and there as though he were a bladder with weak places; and Duggie on the other side, in folds of curtains like the trunks of trees. He watched Sir Cyril Butts with the openness of a child. Face white against the curtain, eyes deep black. Where did he keep his rage when he was good-fellowing through the day?

'Look at Plumb,' the reporter by me whispered. 'Look at his face.'

We looked at him. He looked at Cyril Butts. And Butts lost his place; he lost himself; half turned, eyes mad and blind, and shuffled round in a three-quarter circle, facing Duggie. He dragged the podium down. His notes went looping, diving, off the stage. He sat down with a slap on his behind, lay down hard, with a wooden thumping of his head. Air came out of him horribly and spread across the stage.

Duggie was first there. He pulled Sir Cyril's bow-tie off and ripped his collar open. Then he tried to give him mouth to mouth resuscitation. There must have been six doctors in the hall. They lifted Duggie away. They got busy: poked Sir Cyril, thumped his chest, rearranged and listened. Then they squatted on their haunches like boys around a dog that's been run over.

We waited in the auditorium. Hignett came through the curtains, dabbing his eyes and mouth with a handkerchief. 'Friends, I have a very painful duty . . .'

Duggie, I said to myself, how did you do it?

We found him at the back of the stage with tears in his eyes. 'Mr Plumb. A statement, Mr Plumb.'

'The loss – the loss to the National Party. It's immeasurable. I can't say any more.'

'Mr Plumb?'

'I had only known Sir Cyril for a few weeks. But in that time . . . I take this as a personal loss. I can't say any more.'

'What will your plans be now?'

'Please. Please. Give me some time. I can't have any plans. I've got to come to terms with what's happened tonight. The loss . . .'

Later on I rang his flat. There was no answer. I drove around and waited outside for an hour. I tried the electorate office. He wasn't there. I tried Sally Carpenter. What a tinkling voice she had. No, Douglas hadn't called tonight. She really couldn't say where he might be. This dreadful news must be a shock to him. My next guess, my best guess, was Tania, or some other. That was a way he might celebrate. But I couldn't remember any second names. So I gave up.

He announced his candidacy after Sir Cyril's funeral. Brierly had already been chosen for Loomis. Duggie had no difficulty in beating the economist and the vice-chairman. On election night he took Epsom by more than three thousand votes. Brierly went down by fifteen hundred.

So Duggie Plumb came to Wellington. He was thirty-two. Already the road behind him was strewn with beaten foes. 'Watch him,' I said. 'He's going to be boss.' No one took me seriously. McIntyre and Gordon, Talboys, Muldoon, Walker, were up ahead. 'Well,' I said, 'at least he's going to make them know he's there.'

He came up to see me after the post-election caucus meeting. 'How did it go?'

'I'm the new boy. I kept quiet.'

'There's a lot to learn.'

'Sure. I'll learn it. Where's your little lady?'

'Gone to bed. It's time you got married, Duggie. Latham's going to trot out this playboy stuff.'

'Let him. You got anything to drink?'

I gave him beer, which was all I had. He drank it thirstily. Being new boy had him edgy. He showed no signs of being satisfied, but

158

was looking ahead, looking for ways of shortening the steps he had to take. They made him angry. He was ready *now*.

'Tell me Duggie, how did you know Butts was going to die?'

'I didn't. I saw there was a chance he'd crack up though.'

'So you stayed close?'

'I made sure every time he looked over his shoulder he saw me. It got so he was looking all the time. The poor old sod thought I was putting poison in his booze.'

'What did you do?'

'How do you mean, Ray?'

'The night he died. You looked as if you were sticking pins in him.'

'Did I?'

'I was watching you, Duggie.'

'Well,' he said; he drank more beer, 'like I told you, Epsom was mine. I couldn't listen to the old bugger snuffling on any more.'

'So?'

'I stuck my hand in the back of his head and gave his brain a squeeze.'

16

For a second or two I took him literally. When Bobby's wrestling holds had made me cry I was terrified he would open me up and put his hands inside to work a cure. I saw Duggie's hatred as giving him the power to open Butts. It held me blind, in an unnatural light; then he laughed.

'You know what I mean.'

I shrank still. He had willed Butts dead. I could only see it as a physical act.

So it brought things back into a natural light when his career went suddenly wrong. The cartoonist Sharples drew him climbing a rope and leaning down with scissors to snip it off beneath him. That was Duggie repudiating his past. But the piece of severed rope turned into a snake and fixed its teeth in his behind. It was labelled Meggett Enterprises.

The M.E. collapse and Fred Meggett's imprisonment for fraud were heavy blows for Duggie. He issued statements defending himself, spoke on radio and TV, but it did no good. He had been with Meggett once and Meggett was a crook. It's a toyshop world in politics. Mistakes are not measured by right and wrong.

Latham called for Duggie to resign. There was never any chance of that; but Duggie found himself locked in a cupboard. He had hoped to move the Address in Reply when the session opened. Muldoon had made his maiden speech that way. *Here I am*. Now Duggie was going to say it. But he never even got to second the motion. Up there at the back, alongside the dimmest Labour men, he was in a corner like the dunce. I lounged in the Gallery and watched him – felt for him, but also wanted to laugh. *Hubris, nemesis*. I wanted to fly down paper darts explaining what had happened. He kept his face still. He never smiled. He never blinked. And watching him, I began to be frightened. I understood

Duggie was at work, he was making himself. When he got through this he would be Man.

It is time for me to say where I stood in politics. Easy. I stood nowhere. I rationalized it by saying that I followed my sense of right whichever way it led me. It was, I said, the honest thing to do. My socialism was gone – it had never had any real existence. I grew up breathing haunted air. But Grandpa Plumb's socialism was sentimental; and mine was insubstantial as a shadow. I read nothing, thought nothing, but did a lot of 'feeling'. I joined no organization or party. What I managed was to idealize a class. Joe the wharfie, yelling slogans, made no dent in my idea of him. When I thought of working men I saw myself. What a lot of people there were with my face and my sensibilities.

As for journalism, one reason I chose it was my belief that the press stood for enlightenment. The old machine in Charlie's shed was a sacred object, even though Charlie had been on the wrong side himself. When I left Gerriston I still believed journalism might be truth-telling. And I worked for the *Dominion* and later the *Evening Post*. It would be easy to make fun of myself, but that would be to overlook the waste. My stupidities are not the point. The point is that I withered and grew old. I was old at thirty. I passed through no cleansing fire; no fire of thought, experience, language. Daily I rubbed against the mediocre; the clever; the vain. And soon I could not discern, I had no idea of, things that were hard and bright and clean. Nevertheless, I told myself I followed my sense of right. That was how I justified the dislike of everyone that showed in my writing. I was thought of as 'hard-hitting'. Politicians started hitting back. I enjoyed that.

I treated Duggie just like all the others. When I moved to the *Sunday Post* and started my column he became a regular in it: Duggie Prune. He was in Keith Holysmoke's gang, with Jack Marshmallow and Rob Mudloon. Norman Berk and You What? led the other gang. That was the level. But it helped make Jolly John's the best-selling Sunday yellow in the country.

This takes me ahead, and I must come back. There's no getting away from the private life. All the rest is only clothes we wear. I went to a party. Glenda did not come but stayed at home in our double bed. A girl watched me. I drank a few more drinks and ambled over. 'Do we know each other?' She had crinkly hair that looked electric. I thought if you pushed in your fingers you'd get a shock.

'You're Raymond Sole, aren't you?' She gave me a close look, measured me. 'I wondered if I'd meet you down here.'

'Down here?'

'I'm from Auckland. I used to know your father.' She gave a little smile, mocking, sour.

'Ah,' I said, 'Beth Neeley. Well, well, well.' My father's 'mistress'. She had been his office girl and he had run away with her, leaving Mum at Peacehaven nursing Robert. Their cohabitation had lasted a week.

'Thanks for what you did for him. It should happen to every man at sixty.' I had never been able to imagine them together – my picture had been of Dad holding her hand and grinning shyly. Once or twice I sat him on her knee.

'He went back to your mother, didn't he?'

'Yep. And lost his money. How would you have handled that?'

'I'd have stayed with him. I just couldn't stand his guilt.'

'So it wasn't only his false teeth and his baggy underpants?'

'Are you always so nasty?'

'I'm a journalist. We tell the truth.'

All this was moody, edged, and during it we passed into a kind of erotomania. It was as impure as anything I've known – and I mean impure in no moral way. Desire came mixed up with idea.

'I'll drive you home.'

'I've got my own car.'

'OK. I'll follow.'

Her pubic hair was electric as her head hair. It prickled through her slip like copper wire. And when I hooked my fingers in her crotch a grey flash in the dark part of my brain illuminated caves where inhuman eyes looked out. There was no affection in our coupling. There was more excitement than I had ever known, and through the night an interest that was frantic and hostile. We had a good deal more than Duggie's sex-book fucking.

'I suppose you'll think I'm lying if I say I've never done it that way before.'

'Does it matter what I think?'

'Not really.'

'Were you pretending I was Dad?'

'No. Oh no. You're you. Not that I'm very sure what that is.'

'Are you going to want to know?'

'I don't think so.'

I did not want to know either. But that was not in my control. At the end a sleepy fondness grew on us. Our bodies seemed to want to know, and warm down the length of us, casually twined, we found ourselves able to talk in an ordinary way.

We did not spend very long with Dad. Revenge had been a part of her motive, but it seemed a small thing now, she wondered that resentment had troubled her so much. But she had had a sense of being wasted, she had seemed to take no part of herself away. Now it was over, she was back. Not exactly thanks to me, but thanks anyway.

My revenge had been more complicated. It was an act of violence to restore my balance. (To bring a bit of justice back was what I wanted to say; but that would have had the sound of complaint and I thought she might accuse me of self-pity.) Now, like her, I could carry on. Even, I said, if I didn't see her again.

'I'd like to see you. I don't want to hurt your marriage though.'

'You won't.'

'I'd forgotten how good it was. Just sex.'

'You want more?'

'Yes, I do.'

'There must have been other men since Dad.'

'One or two. Like little dogs. With their tongues hanging out. Telling me how nice I am. "I love you, Beth." You won't do that, will you?'

'Not me.'

'I might need it one day but I sure don't need it now.'

I went home in the dawn. Glenda was sleeping. She stirred and opened her eyes and smiled at me. 'Is that the dawn?'

'The party went on late.'

'I was lonely. Mm, you feel warm. You've been with a woman, haven't you?'

'No . . .'

'She smells nice. Please don't pretend, Ray. I've been waiting for it to happen. I don't mind.' She put her hand on my chest. 'Bumpity bump. It gives you away.'

'I'm sorry, Glenda.'

'No. It's my fault. Was she nice?'

'She was all right.'

'I hope it was better than that. Oh, you want to have me too. I think you should wash first.'

So I washed and I had my wife. Again desire was mixed up with idea. Afterwards she stroked my chest. 'It's bursting out of there. Who was she, Ray?'

'A girl. That's all.'

'Are you going to see her again?'

'I don't know.'

'I think you should. I'm no good to you any more.'

I denied that, of course. But she told me it was not for me to say; and she told me not to worry, she didn't worry, not any more, she had a place to go and nothing could touch her when she was there.

'Do the children touch you?'

'I'm no good to them either.'

We slept a while, my front cupped round her back, and were woken by Sharon bringing us cups of tea. She was used to seeing us naked and she weighed Glenda's breasts in her hands. 'I wish mine would get a move on.'

'They're doing very nicely.' Glenda put her top on. 'Mm, good tea, love.' But she was an illusion. Bed, warmth, family; she was no part of it. And I saw her as a kind of perfect robot. She had no life as we had life. Sharon felt it too. She went to the living-room and practised on her flute.

I stayed away from Beth for half a week. When I called on her again we came at each other greedily. That was her mouth on me, a human mouth. I licked her sweat and that was human sweat. Glenda was no good to me any more – now that she had said it I said it too, feeling no guilt. I hungered after all Beth's imperfections, everything she offered I could taste, it nourished me. Yet Glenda, back in Wadestown, immeasurably distant, kept one human attribute that made everything I took from Beth illusory in the end. That was her grave acceptance of her death. I saw clearly where she was, but could not keep my eyes on it and, turning away, quickly forgot. I could not bear to look; but the residual memory – no more than a fleeting image, Glenda's face – troubled me through the day, through my work, in the office, out of the office, when I was with Beth.

Glenda, I said, for God's sake, whatever you're going to do, do it soon.

At night she played the piano, music that was watery and pure. 'I must play more often.' She stood and looked at the harbour. Then she smiled and kissed me. She kissed Sharon. 'Don't stay up too late, love.' She sat on Gregory's bed a moment; and Sharon and I lolled and watched TV or read our books. Then Sharon went and I was alone in the room, looking at what was happening and wondering what to do. When I went to bed she was still awake. But I did not touch her and she made no sign she missed me in that way. One of us, and both of us, drifted off to sleep.

What was she? How can I answer? I had no way, and have no way of getting close to her. Her death was *her* death. I fight not to cheapen it with my emotions.

Her note read: *Dear Ray, I've taken the car. I'm not sure whether I'll be back tonight. I kissed the children. They look beautiful. Love, G.*

She had put toothpaste on my brush.

The wind howled round the house and rattled the windows. On the garage roof iron squealed. I ran out to check that the doors were locked. My dressing gown flapped about my ears and wind gusts had me lurching like a drunk. I saw my neighbour's greenhouse burst. Slates from his roof came looping down at me. I ran inside and slammed the door. What a day for her to take the car. How was I going to get the kids to school and myself to work? Trees would be coming down all over Wadestown.

'Sharon,' I yelled, and she came out in her pyjamas. 'Get the breakfast will you. Your mother's gone out.'

'Where?'

'How would I know? Get Gregory up. On second thoughts, leave him. The pair of you better stay home. There'll be wires coming down.'

'Will Mum be all right?'

'I hope so. She shouldn't have gone out.'

Sharp little draughts played through the hall and bedroom. Puffs of dust sprang out of the wainscots. Over the bed the sprats turned with more animation than they had shown since the day Glenda had hung them up. I dressed, shivering, and pulled the blankets straight. I thought about Beth and worried about Glenda. She was not a good driver. Then the phone rang and I forgot about her until night.

Morrie Horne, chief reporter now: 'Ray, I've sent a car for you. The *Wahine*'s on Barretts Reef. She's taking a hell of a pounding. You team up with Colin. He's out at Palmer Head. Stay on this side. I'll send someone else round the harbour.'

I heard a horn blowing at my gate, and yelled at Sharon and Gregory not to go out. Then I was at Breaker Bay, watching the black ship, free of the reef, drifting up harbour, with waves bursting on her and spray like hands reaching over her decks. There is nothing so helpless as a sinking ship. She lumbers, sighs, and seems to want her death.

At midday she was off Steeple Rock. Passengers swarmed on the decks. They wore orange life jackets and moved in clumps, like bees. The ship had too much black on her, she showed her hidden parts. The sea was more alive, all broken points and angled planes – and the *Wahine* was dead. People came sliding down her decks. Some climbed into boats, which started lazily, like fish, and slipped down into troughs. They seemed to stay and stay, it did not seem there could be valleys deep enough to keep them there so long. When they came up they were heavy as logs of wood.

I stayed at Seatoun wharf till late afternoon, watching boats and life rafts ride through the surf and people stagger on the beach. I found survivors to interview. I watched the ship go down under the waves. In the evening I was back at my desk. I rang Sharon and told her I would be late. She and Gregory had been watching the news. More than thirty people were missing, she said, and others had been washed ashore dead. 'Yes, I know.' It seemed impossible that in the slow sinking I had seen people had died.

When I got home the children were asleep. Sharon had left a note on the table. *I'm sorry about the* Wahine. *I've put some dinner in the oven. I'm a lousy cook. I hope Mum gets home soon. Sharon.*

By that time Glenda was dead. No one saw her die and I can only guess at the details. In fourteen years I have played many versions over but they do not differ in their essential facts. She was at Makara in the morning, watching the sea smashing itself on the shingle beach. She bought a bread roll and ate it in the car. Then she drove back down the road towards Wellington. At Makara South she turned out to Oteranga Bay and drove along the hilltops in a wind that must have threatened to lift the car off the road. She stopped and opened farm gates and drove through, and shut the gates again, while the gale whipped her face and legs and sent her hair streaming out. When the road dropped down to the bay she saw the white wave-broken strait, and Terawhiti Hill, dragon-backed, immense, in all that wild water and wild air. She drove down to the stream and left the car and waded over. In her yellow parka and corduroy skirt she followed the path down to the cliffs at the west side of the bay and started round towards the cape. The air boomed. Spray rattled on her. But I suppose in her a stillness and a cold weight. She felt a gravitational pull towards death. But it was *her* death, *her* death. I must not suppose.

Along towards the cape, an hour's walk, she stopped. There was nothing left of the island. It ran out in the sea. Over the strait South Island hills made a blur on the air. Glenda took off her shoes, her parka, took off all her clothes; she took off her rings and took the wooden hair clip from her hair, and she walked into the sea and was drowned. Or perhaps she died smashing on the rocks. Nobody knows. Her body was never found.

The police drove me out to see the car. I walked along the coast with them and saw where she had left her shoes wedged under a rock with her wedding ring and engagement ring and hair clip in one of them. They showed me the half mile of shore where the wind had blown her clothes.

Yes, I told them, she had been depressed. I offered them the word because they had to have something. It was the word I offered the children too. And once I tried to persuade them it might have been an accident. She had gone there to be free, had taken off her clothes to feel the rain. People did that. Then a wave had come . . . I told them about the seventh wave.

Sharon smiled and patted me. 'Thanks, Dad. But we can take it. Don't try that.'

17

This part of Golden Bay has one of the highest rainfalls in New Zealand. Water comes off my roof in curved sheets. I look at the world through water. It presses on me, thunders. I cannot hear my dishes as I wash up. I cannot hear the flames in my iron stove.

In my parka and gumboots I slosh up and down the paths. The Aorere runs black, runs amber, then runs clear again. Ché and Carlo, in yellow slickers, walk down from the house with a thermos flask of soup for me. They flash their smiles but won't come in. They have built a lake in the garden and squelch off there to break a wall and let some water out. Ché belongs to Bella Ross. Sharon's new man turns out to be a lady.

Time passes in the trailer. How it passes. Mornings rush away, decades vanish. I eat cold breakfasts. I don't want fug until my work is done. I sit with my sleeping bag drawn up to my waist and wear two jerseys. At lunch-time I light the stove and eat beans on toast or a can of stew. The air gets thick and I part it with my hands. It fogs my brain, which is nice sometimes and other times nasty. I feel a part of me die: nice, nasty. So I go out walking, or drive into Collingwood and try to find out what the world has been up to. The usual things. I grin with admiration and disgust. And driving back, the pain in my chest starts up. I don't want to crash and kill anybody, but on these roads, in this weather, there are not many cars. I have looked in Sharon's *Pears Encyclopaedia* and diagnosed angina. Soon I'll go over to Nelson and see what can be done about it. In the meantime Sharon watches me – doesn't bully me to go. She walks round to the trailer to see if I'm OK. Bella doesn't like that. She wishes I would clear out, one way or the other. With heavy irony, she calls me 'the necessary male'. Sharon grins and doesn't stop calling me Dad. We're secure with each other. They too seem secure. They bicker fondly, at times they're openly carnal –

strokings and soft kisses and fingers intertwined. I don't mind. I can understand Sharon wanting Bella. She's a good-looking woman. I wouldn't mind her myself, which she's aware of, and narrow-eyed about.

But I don't need her, or any woman. I have Glenda and Beth. Glenda is dead, twice dead. I've read it over. And see that my life has made me adjectival. I don't like that. The truth is in nouns and pronouns. Adjectives blur things, adverbs too; and verbs can falsify. Glenda. That's the truth. Glenda died – less true. Glenda drowned herself. That can't be said in three words. I haven't enough words for it. Only Glenda.

This leaves aside the question of responsibility. I have, of course, blamed everybody involved, and absolved them. I do that daily. I absolve Graham Goodlad. I ask myself if I have the right, and don't care too much about the answer. It's the same when I absolve myself. I loved Glenda and she loved me. Love is said to be enough. It isn't. Perfect love? Another adjective. In fact, we're fallen. Let's keep that 'f' lower-case.

The rain makes the sound of a train in a tunnel. The sheet of water turns silver on its edge where the wind blows it. My chest is hurting me. I'll lie down.

Sharon has had a letter from Gregory.

'Hi Sis, Here we are in the North. Our Work goes well. Last week we brought the Good News to Helensville. Tonight it's Warkworth. The rain comes down but the joy of doing the Lord's work never ceases . . .'

That work has taught him full stops and capital letters. Happiness too. Reborn among the reborn, indelible LOVE and HATE etched on his hands, he travels about the country with the Good News; strums his guitar, sings in his creaky voice words simple enough to be true; and confesses that once he hated his Dad, confesses to drugs and drink and theft and to being second in line at the gang-bang. Tells how he heard the Word, how Christ saved him. Gregory Sole, great-grandson of a man who heard something similar in his youth.

'Thank you, Sharon. He seems all right.'

'Many are the pathways.'

'It was never his fault.'

'Or yours. Remember that.'

She absolves me. We're a presumptuous lot, but it's hard to carry on without some cheek.

'The curve of tragic action is a curve of self-discovery. On the other hand, the comic curve is one of self-exposure . . .' Where does that leave me? Is my life experience or spectacle?

After four years and seven months Beth showed me the door. She pointed to it and said, 'The door's right there.' She said, 'You and your wife are so bloody boring.' 'I never talk about her.' 'You don't have to talk. She's in there behind your eyes Ray, swimming like a fish. Anyway, I'm getting married.' 'Who to?' 'Are you really interested? No, I didn't think so.' She married a high school teacher and went to live in New Plymouth. 'You were always second best of the Soles.' There was no malice in that; she was putting her memories in order.

I was glad to see her go, although I loved her. She overlapped with Glenda; and when she went took Glenda too. She took the Glenda swimming like a fish, and left me Glenda of the student flat, and Ghuznee Street, and Wadestown. Not a person that I understand; but my wife, a girl I love. She escapes me continually and goes into her dark. But I'm no longer guilty, no longer obsessed, and because I don't wait for her to come out she comes before long.

I've had other women, but not to speak of. The ones I've had would not speak of me. The only fantasy I allow is that one day I'll meet Tania, whose second name I never knew. With her I'm unreserved. It's love that I imagine and not sex. It can't happen. I asked Duggie about her once and he told me she was married to a farmer and had turned herself into a breeding sow.

The sky was clear today. Lead Hills and Mount Olympus stood out pure and cold. I asked Sharon how they compared with the Himalayas and whether she found it possible to think of them as Cerebrum of the Earth.

'You don't remember that?' she cried.

'I do. I've got your letters.' It pleased me to see her blushing. I'm eager to find simplicities in her.

'Burn them.'

'I won't do that.'

When she was gone I took the letters from their old cigar box.

On the flap of the envelopes she had written: Sender: Archana, Himalayan Peaks, Cerebrum of the Earth.

Beloved Father (she wrote), I pray that you are well and in peace. Please do not write to me. I have left the ashram, at least for some months. I shall let you know my whereabouts in due course. There will be no post-box in the deep, secret, sacred regions I shall be roaming before the monsoons come . . .

And she wrote: I have been in an ashram at Uttarkashi, halfway to the source. The walls are lapped by Ganga. Her waters are thunderous, louder even than the ocean surf. It is hard to express what Ganga means to me. She has given me so much stillness, so much faith and understanding. Near her mighty flow I feel protected. There is no fear, even of death. One can be so open that prana can replace the need for food . . . Never do I need to think of returning to the world.

And: May you soon reach that Peace within. Love, Archana.

I had loved her toughness and her honesty. Flesh and bone had not been more real. Now it seemed she was floating away on a cloud. As I read her letters I made exclamations of distress. At the end I cried, 'Your name's Sharon, not Archana.' I took out the photo box and looked at her in her school uniform, with silly hat and duffel bag and cocky smile. In those days she had learned French not Hindi. Wisdom came from a best friend Jo and a boyfriend Selwyn. She quoted their opinions relentlessly, and that was in order. Late at night she often saw through them and would announce it with a shrug. She Jekyll-and-Hyded through her teens from silliness to good sense – all OK with me, and fascinating. I was spectator at the making of an adult: said as much to Rose when she nagged me about the freedom I allowed 'the child'.

'You didn't let her go away with them? Three boys and one girl?'

'Stop worrying, Rose. Sharon knows what she's doing.'

'But one tent. How are they going to sleep?'

'In sleeping bags.' I could not tell her I did not think Sharon was a virgin, even though for Rose virginity was a state of mind and morality less important than Self. I could have argued that Sharon's Self was intact; but left it with the opinion that she had more good sense than both of us.

And in three days Sharon was home. 'I didn't go to the Sounds to lie in a tent and smoke pot.' That was the last I heard of Selwyn. But late at night (Gregory still out and likely not to come home) she said, 'There was an old man in a house round the bay. He was like a little monkey in a chair. He had a male nurse who brought him drinks. And a big flash launch he never went out in. I watched him through the hedge. He sent his nurse to tell me to clear out.'

'Ha!' I thought this was a tale about privilege.

'He was K. D. Mottram, the brewer. The nurse told me he was eighty-four. And lived on Complan.'

'Mottram, eh?'

'I know who Mottram was, Dad. Mum told me that old stuff.'

'When?'

'Right through. It was instead of fairy tales. She sat on the bed and talked. I'd go to sleep and dream about her father – eyes like glass. And Mrs Mottram in a turban, like an oil sheik. When I saw Mr Mottram's launch and jetty it was like walking through a door into fairyland. I went swimming off the jetty the way she did. The water was so clear you could see your skin, all the pores and hairs, all golden, you know, magnified, transformed. There were little fish with transparent flesh, the light came through and you could see their backbones.'

'No,' I said.

'It's all right, Dad. I'm all right. Mum was mad but I'm not.'

'She wasn't mad.'

'In a way she was. I suppose Grandpa was just a sort of con-man. A lady-killer. But Mum got kind of fixated on him. She had a kind of vision. Peace, perfection, light. Purity. And nothing was any good after that. Not you or me, or Gregory. Even though she tried.'

'Sharon –'

'She had to die, Dad. But I won't, don't you worry. I did a poop on Mottram's jetty before I left. A real biggie. I suppose poor old Selwyn will get the blame.'

'Did she tell you about watching them?'

'Yes. Grandpa and Mrs Mottram making love. The whole bit. It was interesting. I found the place they did it. Somewhere there. There was no magic spring or anything. I'm glad I went. It's kind of finished.' She laughed. 'Pooping was juvenile. But it seemed the thing at the time. For K. D. Mottram. Underwater though, what Mum saw . . .' She had a little frown of interest, a Glenda inclination of her head, and I saw her suddenly as not reachable by love, not knowable by me, not to be saved or understood.

She said, 'We're so proud and selfish. Me. And you. And Greg. And Rose. And K. D. Mottram. Even though it's the same light shining through us all.'

'I don't know any light.' I was frightened.

She grinned at me. 'Maybe my language isn't right. But you know what I mean.'

'I don't.'

'You don't want to.'

'I want to know what *you* mean. I don't suppose I ever will.'

'No.' She patted me. 'Mum loved you, Dad. She kept on telling me. But I guess you were too human. You couldn't compete with old Graham Goodlad and his diamond eyes. I'm off to bed.'

She kissed me and was gone. And the next year went to Auckland to study in an ashram; and at nineteen to Holy Ganga, where she meant to conquer Self. Rose and Felicity, for their separate reasons, were appalled.

'Here,' I said, 'listen. "I feel a new, a Real birth. A wonderful change has occurred in my life. So much joy, so much unity. The cerebrum of the earth; so close to Heaven."'

'Oh!' they said, 'uh!' They grunted with pain. Listening to them, I felt almost cheerful about Sharon. They were not women you could laugh at though.

Felicity said, 'Those so-called holy men are charlatans. They feed off girls like Sharon.'

Rose said, 'What she'll end up with is hepatitis.'

I don't know that her holy man fed off Sharon, but he did some other nasty things. And she got hepatitis.

When she came home she was light as an elf. Her skin was golden white and dry as crêpe paper. Hollows lay on her face where her girl-fat had been. 'Sharon, is that you?'

'I think so, Dad.'

Her holy man had set out to destroy her – through overwork, humiliation, insult. 'The idea was to break me up in pieces until I really didn't exist any more. And then put me together in a way that, well, satisfied him. I had too much pride and selfishness. It's a technique he's got. I think he's mad.'

'You won't go back?'

'Not to that ashram. But I'll go back. I'm not finished yet.' She told me of a village in the Kumaon Hills, and a cave where she had lived in a temple complex: of gathering wood and washing clothes and learning Hindi songs . . . of temple bells and mantras and the conch shell sounded to drive out evil spirits and evil thoughts. That is what she was going back to – and the deodar trees and mountains and icy rivers.

'Sharon,' I said, 'if you get hepatitis again you'll die over there.' I told her about Alf's friend John Willis who had been killed by a second attack of hepatitis.

'I got it on purpose,' she said. 'That was how I escaped. I had just enough me left to get sick.'

She sat on the veranda playing her flute. Rose and Felicity came visiting and a war of doctrines raged. Every time I went out to break it up they started laughing. I felt superfluous and I went off and clipped the hedge. Although they could not agree, they shared a biology, and had a knowledge I could not have, and an ease together that made me aware of clumsy limbs and clumsy tongue and a lack of fineness like the lack of a sense. There are circuits in the female brain that astonish me. There are times when I know that men are rudimentary beings.

Gregory rode up on his motorbike. I heard his engine surging and fading in the hilly streets.

'Sharon's home?'

'She's round on the veranda with Felicity and Rose.'

He scowled and clomped his boots and kneaded his greasy leathers.

'You've got some more tattoos.'

'Yeah. Had 'em done.' A swastika on his left cheekbone and something like the star of David on his right.

'That swastika's the wrong way round.'

'Yeah?' He shrugged. 'S'pose I better go and see her.'

'Greg. Where are you living? What are you doing?'

'I shift around.'

'Any job?'

'Don't need a job.'

He had accused me of letting his mother die. 'No, Greg. I loved your mother. But she was gone somewhere else.'

'I would've saved her. You didn't try.'

'I did –'

'You were too busy fucking Beth.'

That was at fourteen. Now he did not seem to know who I was. Life among the *Skullmen* had blotted out his past. I took it as a good sign that he remembered Sharon. We walked around to the veranda and she ran at him and hugged him. 'Oh, Greg. Oh you look tremendous.' She patted his tattoos. 'Hey, they're wild.' Her peastick arms encircled him, her wrists crossed like crossbones under the skull emblem on his back. 'I thought you mightn't come.' She pulled him into the hall and closed the door.

'Well!' Rose said.

'Was that Gregory?'

'A swastika! If he comes out here I won't trust myself.'

'What a mess you've made of them, Ray. An unholy mess.'

'Maybe.'

'No maybes about it. They're drifting like bits of flotsam. You know what they've got inside their heads? Chaos. Temple bells and swastikas! It can only end in lunacy.'

'It's lunacy already. Your children, Glenda's children, are lost, Ray. If man is in any way a superior being it's through his mind. Through his power of thought. And Gregory comes in here with *Love* and *Hate* written on his hands. And a skull on his back. And Sharon! Sharon! Temple bells indeed! There's bats in her belfry.'

'I blame you, Ray.'

'And I blame you.'

I left them frothing and fizzing and clipped my hedge. They walked out past me – no goodbyes – and drove away in Rose's car. I did not blame them for their anger. Sharon and Gregory were nothing to please rationalist and Catholic. Yet I understood what Rose and Felicity could not: that they were at a beginning not an end. It struck me as an interesting start. The danger to their bodies troubled me more: hepatitis and dysentery and motorbike accidents.

Gregory said, 'So long, mate,' and rumbled away on his Norton. Sharon raked up my hedge clippings. 'Don't worry about the *Skullmen*, Dad. He's just passing through.'

'And you're just passing through Eastern religion.'

'Ah no. That's different.'

In six months she was off, not to mountains and deodar trees after all, but to Poona, to the ashram of a swami called Ragneesh. I helped with money. 'Don't get sick.'

Gregory was at the airport too. He had scars on his cheekbones in place of tattoos, and a van with donut tyres and paintings of Satan and his angels on its sides. It was called *Van Demon*. He had a girl in skin-tight leather and a see-through blouse. He introduced her to Sharon but not to me. The Boeing climbed over Evans Bay.

'So long, mate,' Greg said, and drove away.

18

At about that time I had the first of my letters from Alaric Gibbs. He started by telling me I didn't know him. In spite of its being obvious that seemed to carry a threat.

'I think we might meet to our mutual advantage. I have written a book . . .' I relaxed and yawned. Then said, 'Damn': the manuscript was on its way 'under separate cover'. That meant I should have the trouble of returning it. 'I have had an interesting life. Before the war I worked as an engineer in Malaya and East Africa, building roads and bridges. In the war I was attached to the New Zealand Engineers and saw service in the Middle East and Italy. When I returned to New Zealand I joined the Ministry of Works and worked on hydro installations. My life falls into three parts and so does my book. However, the publisher to whom I submitted it . . .'

The manuscript arrived the following day. I took it into the lounge with my coffee and started reading; and thought perhaps the publisher had been hasty. With pruning and livening up . . . The war parts were well done. But no, I wasn't going to be drawn in. *M. J. Savage* was my book. Late that night I pulled it from the drawer of my writing desk and spread it on the carpet. I felt a tingling in my fingers. It was seven years since I had done more than open the drawer and look in. Now I had Savage on the floor, all his parts. 'St Michael', 'the brewer's pimp from Sydney'. All I had to do was put him together.

I was up till dawn fiddling with tapes and letters. I shifted them about like a jigsaw puzzle. Gaps showed up but that didn't worry me. 'Now then. Now then.' Mickey – Joe – Savage belonged to me. Before I went to bed I put Alaric Gibbs' manuscript on the kitchen table so I wouldn't forget to post it in the morning.

As things turned out, I delivered it. John Jolly sent me to

Auckland to interview an American Country and Western singer who was on a secret visit to fish for trout. I finished with him early and sat in my hotel room while the city squealed and mumbled and the harbour bridge gleamed like a smile. Bridges made me think of Alaric Gibbs. I took his manuscript out and looked at part three. It had none of the life of the early parts. He mentioned his wife and daughter frequently. 'And so I came home from that mighty structure, that river tamed, to the cottage and garden that was my own "little bit of heaven", and found my ministering angels waiting for me. A man can know no greater joy than this: a job well done, and dear ones to welcome him back to his hearth.' The sentimentality was a new note. He had scarcely mentioned wife and daughter in the first two parts.

I walked up Parnell Rise in the summer twilight and found Gibbs' house at the back of the chocolate factory. He was watching television and I had to tap on a window to get his attention. He switched the set off with a dab of his finger. 'It's meant for imbeciles. Nevertheless I watch. Well Mr Sole I didn't expect a visit. Tell me what you thought. Wait though, we'll have a Scotch.'

I told him his book needed hard work. If he was interested I would give him the names of a couple of people who might take it on. I mentioned the cost and he said, 'I'm not surprised. I'm no writer.' The first two parts had been 'put down' with his wife's help after the war. She had curbed his flights of fancy – his references to her. Then he had left the thing for twenty-five years, and taken it up again recently, just for something to do. The best part had been typing it with two fingers: that filled up the days admirably.

His wife was dead? I asked.

'Yes. Oh yes. She passed on fifteen years ago. Your verdict doesn't surprise me, Mr Sole. Here, keep it as a souvenir. It might have some value one day.' He gave a smile that showed more gleam of teeth than I had expected; and when I demurred put the manuscript firmly in my lap. 'You're the only public it will have. Another drink?'

His room gave little of him away. It was neither this nor that: neat nor untidy, dark nor light. The book by his chair came from a library. It was one of Ross Macdonald's Lew Archer stories. The pictures on the walls were photographs of bridges and viaducts, all beautiful and, it seemed, defying nature. On a piano with empty candle arms and a closed lid studio portraits of Gibbs' wife and daughter faced the room and seemed to smile gravely at the point where their eyes would meet. That would be where Alaric Gibbs was placed, completing the figure. The girl was beautiful. In her eyes and brow she resembled Glenda. But the memory that stirred was of some other. Just as I'd missed knowing Graham Goodlad I missed the girl.

'I noticed you looking at my Ross Macdonald. Do you like him?'

'Very much. He's better than Chandler.'

'Do you think so? Chandler comes first. Do you know that essay of his on the art of murder? Where he says –'

'"Down these mean streets goes a man who is not himself mean."'

'Yes. "Who is neither tarnished nor afraid." Now that's superb. He gets nothing but his fee for which – remember? – "he will protect the innocent, guard the helpless and destroy the wicked".'

'It's a bit sentimental.'

'Nonsense. Nonsense. It's romantic, yes. It's valorous. Chivalric. My God, it's human in the only sense I care to give the word.' His nod of emphasis set his white hair stirring. He was a wispy man and almost seemed to rustle as he moved. Dehydrated face: it looked as if it would soak up water. Pointed cheekbones, pointed mouth, ears from which the lobe and curl had melted. Yellow wax. I wondered if disease had eaten him. But he was stiff, immovable as iron. There was a frame in him that would not bend. Some ideology possessed him; some belief or doctrine. I thought of his letter – 'you don't know me' – and the threat returned. Perhaps there was no doctrine. Perhaps just – just? – a bitter love or hatred. He looked as if a wind would blow him away; yet inside, his mass . . . The star that collapses on itself? White dwarf?

He said, 'I enjoy your column in the *Sunday Post*.'

'That? It's here today and gone tomorrow.'

'No, it's good. Of its kind. One mustn't be fair with politicians.'

'Definitely not.'

'Mudloon. I like that. And Duggie Prune.'

'Believe it or not, he's my cousin.'

'Yes, I know. There's not much I don't know about Plumb. You don't let him off lightly, cousins or not. I knew him once.'

'Oh?'

'Yes, my daughter . . .' He aimed his finger at the photographs.

'Miss Jennifer Gibbs,' I said. 'He took her to the National Party ball in '54. I saw the photo in the *Weekly News*. She looks like Kim Novak. An actress,' I explained. 'And my wife.'

'Jenny and Plumb were engaged. Not officially. I've followed his career. Let me show you.'

He left the room and came back with three scrapbooks bound in imitation leather. 'Jenny started this one. I've kept them going. Here.' He opened one of the books and showed me a newspaper photograph. 'That's her with Plumb.' It was the photo I remembered: Duggie and Miss Jennifer Gibbs dancing at the ball. The girl on the furry newsprint looked like a war bride. She looked like a piece of cloth Duggie was waving. With short-back-and-sides, he was as smooth as a bullet.

The next entry, dated four years later, was a piece about Duggie's joining Thomas Tax Consultants. Then the entries came thick and fast. Divisional conferences. Party conferences. The Loomis campaign. Epsom campaign. The Meggett affair. Duggie in Epsom again, '66. Duggie as Junior Whip, as Under Secretary for Trade and Industries. Minhinnick cartoons. Tom Scott articles. And Duggie married. Half a book on that.

'You've even got Duggie Prune.'

'I don't think there's anything I've missed.'

'But why?'

'He interests me. That's a good one.' He tapped an entry damp with paste. It showed Duggie yesterday, facing the Hell's Angels and Black Power. Their leaders had sleeves ripped off at the shoulder and arms that bulged and shone like Christmas hams. They hung over Duggie, who had his chest out and finger up. 'The Minister of Police, Douglas Plumb, at his meeting this morning with leaders of' etc. He looked valiant and decent. He looked clean.

'The sort of photo that makes Prime Ministers.'

'Is that where he's going?'

'It's where he wants to go. Why have you really got this stuff, Mr Gibbs?'

'It's a hobby.' But he could not keep his smile. He was obsessed. 'What I need to know is what goes on underneath.'

'So you sent me your book?'

'I hoped it might be a way of meeting. I have to give him a chance.

You know all the things that are not in here.' He laid his hand on the books. 'He was a child. What happened then? You see, I'm fair.'

'What did he do to your daughter?'

'Ah no –'

'Something bad?'

'No, Mr Sole. That's what I've got already. You tell me the rest. You defend him.'

His eyes were dry and small, like the rest of him. They held no power that I could see. Perhaps he compelled me with his obsession, fished memories out of me on the hook of it. I talked for hours. I told Alaric Gibbs things I had not told Glenda, or Beth, or Rose, or my children or parents. Before that night Duggie had had no shape, and there were parts of me unknown. I have a shifting memory of the night, it's never still; but we – Duggie and I – were flesh and bone at the end of it, and our workings clear. It was Duggie who mattered. I was a by-product.

I've already 'put down' a part of his life. If I've done it at all clearly it's because of Alaric Gibbs. If it's true then I found the truth that night. I saw a lightening in the sky and heard birds singing in his garden. I was dry and spent; lethargic, happy, dull; as though I had been all night with a woman.

Gibbs asked what Duggie had taken from his childhood. I was not sure. That was the darkest part. A knowledge of how people feed on each other? A sense of the viciousness in life? I did not know. Wasn't it just another case of innocence betrayed? We all went through that. But Duggie, somehow, was rounded off by it, made neat and clean. He never developed a sense of other people.

'Gave his brain a squeeze,' Gibbs said. 'What did he mean by that?'

'Exactly what he said. He'd set the conditions up. I won't say it was out in the open like that. But somehow he knew the time was right, if he pressed, if he went in there and let Butts feel him Butts was dead.'

I did not betray Duggie exactly. At times I exaggerated my delinquencies, my viciousness, to make his less: but Alaric Gibbs only smiled at that. There was a Grand Guignol quality to him and I was close to laughing at the melodrama of this trial in absentia; but could not bring that croak of amusement out. I drank a lot of whisky. He drank none.

'Latham?'

'Ah. He had ways of getting under Duggie's skin. But Duggie waited and he got him. It wasn't so long ago.'

'Tell me.'

'Well . . . Latham found out Duggie's first name was Sebastian. Sebastian Douglas. And he never let it alone. He made it seem as if he was only evening things up for Muldoon calling Bill Rowling Wallace. Every time Muldoon said Wallace Rowling, Latham would come back with Sebastian Plumb. He made it sound effeminate. It used to twist Duggie inside. It made him homicidal. Anything else he could take, but not that.'

And Latham called Duggie 'the crocodile', and though the Speaker made him apologize Latham played endless variations: 'tears' and so on, 'the Honourable member with the friendly grin'.

Latham was one of the few politicians who stood up for Ron O'Connor when Duggie as minister forced him out of Broadcasting. After years of silence O'Connor published a little volume openly homosexual – his first real poetry, Alan Webster said. O'Connor was controller of children's programmes. He knew what he risked but told me he had hidden long enough. 'Plumb'll get me fired, Ray. I won't quit. I'll make him do it.'

Because Duggie did not care he was forced to act. He was, he said, concerned for the safety of our children – 'our most valuable investment in the future' – and he let himself be photographed with a delegation of 'parents' and 'morals campaigners'. Then Latham jumped in, identifying a witch-hunt, and calling Duggie Sebastian, with that intonation, and a lisp added. He made it seem Duggie had something to hide. And Duggie lost his temper. It was hard to tell who he was after, O'Connor or Latham. He got O'Connor fired without much trouble; but he seemed to be a little tack-spitting man, vindictive, hypocritical. He frothed against permissiveness and liberalism and 'long-haired trendies' and 'so-called artists'; and knew at the end that Latham had made him perform. 'Ray,' he said, 'I'm going to get that prick. If I wait twenty years I'm going to get him.'

He waited five. Labour had come and gone. Norman Kirk was dead. Rowling seemed unlikely to lead the party for long. To most of us in the Gallery Latham seemed likeliest to take over. In

Muldoon's National government Douglas Plumb was Minister of Police.

I was in the house that night. The debate was on the gangs and what should be done to stop them terrorizing folk and fighting their battles in the streets. A government bill, Duggie's bill, would give the police wider powers of arrest. It would set up squads of what Duggie called 'shock troops' and give a specially appointed government tribunal the power to order unemployed gang members into work camps. All over the country people cried 'fascist'. I cried it myself. But Labour's attack was tired. They still seemed dazed by what had happened to them in November. Latham was tired, half-hearted in his argument. The problem, he said, was a social one, not 'law and order'. The government should address itself to that. Then his habit of attack overcame him.

'Mr Speaker.' His face turned cruel. He pumped with his arms like a distance runner. 'Mr Speaker, let me tell the House some simple scientific facts about the human brain. I'll keep it simple, not to tax the understanding of my friends over there. The brain. The human brain. That miraculous organ, that wonderful machine. Did you know, my friends,' he swung to the government benches, 'that it's in two parts? We have the cerebral cortex, the part that makes us human, the part that differentiates us from the beasts. We all have that, though sometimes it's hard to believe. And then we have the other part – the medulla oblongata, also known as the reptile brain. It's the part we share with the beasts. It's the seat of all those emotions we've been hearing so much about – hatred, anger – the violent emotions that we are led to believe exist only in Black Power and Headhunters and Hell's Angels and Skullmen. What rubbish, Mr Speaker, what rubbish! The reptile brain has much wider dominion than that. I've only to look opposite at all those friendly grins, and one in particular –'

The house was boiling over by that time: a dozen government members on their feet, the Speaker rapping with his gavel, Duggie standing, making pushing movements with his hand for a chance to speak.

Latham stabbed with his finger. 'If the Minister, if the Minister would only come out of those swamps and jungles where he spends his time –'

'I do not,' Duggie shouted – and his voice climbed over Latham's, it rasped and bit like a saw – 'I do not spend my time in motel bedrooms with schoolgirls only fourteen years of age.'

I felt as if the blow had been made at me. I felt hollowed out, as if half my being was ripped away. I think everyone in the room felt that, even the government members. In the silence Latham curled slowly over, he brought his hands up to cover his face and sank into his chair. Duggie sat down too, with a jerky movement, like a bad actor.

An isolated shout came from someone on the Labour benches. It was a sound of grief. Latham sat hiding in his chair. That was enough. At last he took his hands down and looked at Duggie. He was like someone waiting to die. Duggie, casual, arm jacked on his seat, legs crossed, watched him with an interested expression. Duggie, I thought, you got him with the solar plexus punch.

In the end, in a silence that was never going to end, Latham stood up and walked out of the chamber like an old man. We ran from the Gallery and met him in the corridors and followed, yapping questions, to his office, where he nodded to us once and closed the door. He wrote out his resignation and pushed it out a moment before a Labour squad arrived to guard him from us.

When we got back to the chamber Duggie was gone. I hunted round town for him half the night. He told me later he had driven to Mt Victoria and had sat there watching the city, enjoying himself.

That was Latham.

'But I don't know. Duggie's got a hole in him. His triumphs leak away.' It was past three o'clock. Gibbs poured whisky in my glass. 'He doesn't believe in the past. So none of his enjoyments stay alive. What he really gets is that he can't be guilty of anything.'

'Convenient,' Gibbs said.

'Oh yes. But he's a cripple. When we were boys we knew a cripple called Sutton. Club foot. Hump back. He and Duggie recognized each other.'

At some other time I said, 'My grandfather knew the powers of evil. They were demonic. You could front up to them like a wrestler. And you fought them with reason and right behaviour. In the cause of Man. It isn't like that with Duggie. Evil's nihilistic. A vast emptiness. You fight that with a raging in the ego.'

Gibbs drove me to my hotel. 'There's no pity in consequences. He can't get away,' I said. 'Can he?'

Gibbs gave a shrug. He was casual, almost contemptuous, and he stopped my babble of words by leaning across and opening my door. 'There you are. I think you can make it to bed all right.'

I stood swaying on the footpath. 'Don't blame him too much. He's thirsty. He's empty. He can never find what he wants.'

'I don't think I can take that view. Here.' He put his manuscript in my hands. 'You keep it. I know you haven't read it all. Don't bother.' He drove away. That was an end. The detail of it all floated away. I found myself in a state of happy collapse. But sleeping in what was left of the night, with Alaric Gibbs' story on my chest, I dreamed of a page and cried out at the meaning held in it.

When I woke I looked but could not find it. It had been only a line or two in the second part. It told how Gibbs had bought an automatic pistol, a Walther P38, from a Canadian sergeant in Ravenna. 'A lovely gun,' Gibbs wrote, 'beautifully balanced, and because of its double action very safe.' He had brought it home with him, but kept it in his strong-box because his wife told him it made her nervous.

I could not remember why I had cried out. The night receded and Gibbs became squeaky and eccentric. I was sick from whisky and lack of sleep, and angry at the wasted time. I threw the manuscript into my bag and forgot it.

19

Becky picked me up from the hotel and drove me to Loomis. We went down the back way, past Moa Park and the Meggett house. An old man was chipping weeds in the drive.

'That looked like Fred.'

'It was. Adrian brought him here when Esther died. He works in the garden. Potters round. Talks about how big he was. Ha! He runs a book. Tries to, anyway. Adrian gets his cobbers to ring up with bets. He keeps the old man like a sort of pet. You've heard what they say about Adrian?'

'It's probably true.'

'Mr Big. About what you'd expect with his old man a Yank.'

'You know that?'

'It's no secret. Fred seems to think it's a hell of a joke. I'll tell you this, if one of my kids goes on drugs I'll come out here with a gun and shoot Adrian.'

We drove through the Loomis Fred had built – all supermarkets and boutiques – and along by the scummy ditch of Loomis creek.

'All the best murders happen in Loomis.'

'They've never found old Beak.'

'Never will. It's time they pulled this down and built a new one.' The bridge gave its machine-gun rattle. It was only then I felt I was back in Loomis. Millbrook Road was sealed but had no footpaths. The pines stood on the bank with scarred roots leaking gum. A hedge of feijoa trees cut the cottage off from the road. *Journey's End*, the name said on the gate. Mum could never resist that sort of thing. The cottage itself was glossy with paint and hatched with trellises and the lawn was as perfect as a putting green.

We found Mum and Dad walking in the garden. 'Ray,' Mum said, 'look at this,' pointing at a leaf breaking through the soil. 'Convolvulus. I thought I'd got rid of it but still it comes.'

'You'll never get rid of it,' Dad said. 'It's like . . .'

'Dandruff,' Becky said.

'Maybe. You're looking well, Ray.'

'He's looking tired.'

'Boozing all night,' Becky said. 'Serves him right.' She stayed for a cup of tea, then kissed Mum and Dad and drove away.

'She's a loud girl,' Mum complained.

'Her heart's in the right place,' Dad said. He had aged in the year since I'd seen him. His face was puffy and badly shaved. When he put his fingers on his cheeks they left grey dents.

'I thought you'd be down at bowls, Dad.'

'I don't play any more. Do you see that girl –?' he fluttered his hand by his temple, waiting for the name.

'Beth Neeley.'

'I know, Meg. I'm not senile.'

'She's married,' I said. 'Lives in New Plymouth. Got three kids.'

'I'm glad. I've been off colour, Ray. I'm going to lie down.' He went to the bedroom and I heard his heavy sigh as he lowered himself on the bed.

'What's the matter with him?'

'You won't tell the others? He had a heart attack. Just a little one. But it's more than that. I think he's had a stroke. He can't remember. He can't find the words he wants.'

She told me how it had happened. 'He was in town and he went into one of those underground lavatories. You know the way he dreams. It wasn't till he was down there that he realized it was a Women's.'

'Ha!'

'Don't laugh. He's so conventional. He should have raised his hat. But he panicked. He started to run. And that made some silly woman scream.'

I could see it: Dad running up the stairs, through the streets, and the woman screaming; and the eager clerk from the menswear store charging like Boom Casey and bringing him down with a flying tackle.

'They put him in a doorway and kept on holding him and calling him names and it wasn't until a policeman came they realized he was having a heart attack. It wasn't a bad one. They let him come home

187

next day. But he has to take pills now. The doctor says he should be all right.'

'What about the stroke?'

'I don't know whether it's a stroke or he's lost his grip somehow and he can't get it back.'

She told me that he'd gone to the opening of the bowls season and played in a four and when it was his turn – 'What is it when the balls go crooked, Ray?'

'Bias.'

'He chose the wrong bias. The ball –'

'Bowl.'

'– bowl went curving in the wrong direction and ended up in another game. So they brought it back and gave it to him, and he did it again. The third time – everyone was embarrassed, Ray, they just put it in his hand and looked away, and he said for a million pounds he couldn't tell which was the proper side. So he put it down and he came home and I don't think he'll ever go back again.'

In the afternoon I went with them to have a look at Peacehaven. The drive had narrowed to a foot-track in the weeds and the terraces were overgrown with biddy-bid and foxglove and Scotch thistle. On a patch of lawn the summer-house, never more than a frame of manuka boughs, had fallen into a mouldering pile, held in a net of roses.

'Fergus used to mow the lawns but he can't now. And she can't afford a man. We always thought Wendy was rich, but with inflation . . . Merle's wealthy of course, but she doesn't help.'

'Merle?'

'Wendy took her in. Didn't you know? To save her going into a home. They can't stand each other.'

'Merle's leaving all her money to . . .'

'The Spiritualist Church. It drives poor Wendy wild.'

The two ladies were on the back veranda in seagrass chairs ravelled like old knitting. Wendy had grown huge; blubber-armed, tyres on her throat. Merle was a scrawny hen. She hopped down the steps to welcome us. 'I told you he was coming.'

'Meg told you,' Wendy said.

'Raymond. Ah, dear boy.' She pricked me with her nails.

I went up the steps and kissed Wendy on her cheek, which was cold, dry-cold, and soft. My nose sank in.

'She thinks she got a message you were coming. She's a noodle.' She put her finger by her head and drew a spiral.

'The Reverend told me,' Merle cried.

'The Reverend is far beyond your reach. Meg, do you want to show him over the house? Call me when you get as far as the study. I'll put the kettle on.'

The house was tumbling down. 'It wants thousands spent on it,' Dad said. 'Look at that. That's your piles. Watch.' He took a tumbler from the bench and laid it on the floor. It rolled in a half circle into a corner.

'It'll see me out,' Wendy said, wheezing across to the kettle.

'Roof's rusted through,' Dad said. 'Gutters are gone. Borer the size of huhu grubs, Ray. You can hear 'em chewing.'

'Spiders. Mice. I don't draw the line,' Wendy said.

'Spiders can pass through,' Merle said. 'They are messengers.'

In the bathroom Dad showed me a bar screwed on the wall. 'That's so Wendy can get out. She was in the bath all night once.'

'She couldn't lift herself up,' Mum said, 'and she wouldn't let Merle telephone for help. I don't think any man's ever seen her naked. She kept on running hot water in so she wouldn't freeze. But then she had to – you know. So she let Merle ring. Fergus had to do it. She was too heavy for me.'

'She made me tie a . . .'

'Scarf.'

'– over my face. It was like . . .'

'Blind man's buff.'

'Slippery,' Dad said. 'I couldn't hold her.'

When we reached the study Mum called Wendy, who came with a key. 'It's out of bounds for Merle. She thinks I keep George here in a bottle.' She locked the door behind her. For a moment we were in a cave, then she crossed to the window and pulled the curtains back and the desk and chairs and ghostly ranks of books took on substance. Some things coming out of the past make one shake apart and reassemble. But in that room, where I had not been in fourteen years, I was curious, no more. Walking sticks. Desk that would have seated ten for dinner. I remembered. *Ars Amatoria*. I found the book and pulled it out and Wendy, sharp in the study, with, it seemed, most of her bulk melted off, grinned at me. I grinned back, but was uneasy. The present not the past made me shiver: this woman, now, guarding what was dead; happy and cruel, circling the artefact of her life; with Merle Butters scratching at the door. Later, on the veranda, drinking tea, I managed a view that troubled me less: listened to Merle and Wendy squabbling over George Plumb, and agreed with Mum that they were like two seagulls having a tug-of-war with a scrap of bread.

Merle beckoned me and led me away. She took me to her bedroom, flitting ahead, and showed me her electric blanket.

'Wendy doesn't know. She'd put my rent up. Raymond, why I brought you here – I saw your wife last night. Glenda, isn't it? She was beautiful. And she's so happy. She was floating like a fish. Like Ophelia. I asked her if she had a message for you but she just smiled and swam away. I must say that was disappointing. What's the use of coming through if you've got no message?'

This was the past that broke me into pieces; and when I came together I had Glenda. And that part, the Glenda part, of myself. I do not mean I understood it, or that I don't puzzle at it still. But it was in me, she was whole. I no longer knew the fear of not having her.

'Raymond, are you all right?'

'Thank you for telling me.'

'Your grandfather had some messages. He doesn't come for nothing. But they're for Wendy. He wants her to let me in the study. And he wants her to burn that book she wrote about his life. He says it's idolatry. It's going to burn anyway. She's going to have it cremated with her when she dies. It's in her will. She doesn't know I know that.'

'Come on, Merle.'

'You were naughty spying on me. And that Duggie. You won't tell her about my electric blanket?'

In the night I walked along Millbrook Road to the boundary post where the seal ended. A dust road ran into the hills, and far away, over the valley, I saw lights shining in the house where Willis and Mirth had lived. Coming back, I listened to the fall of water from the culvert. I walked up the drive at Peacehaven, looked in the windows, and saw Merle in bed, reading through steel spectacles a Mills and Boon romance; and Wendy at her study desk, sorting papers. She stretched her huge arms and yawned on her breast, looking for a moment crucified, then scratched her ribs. I went round the back and climbed on to the veranda. I sat in a seagrass chair and watched the Sole houses beyond the fallen bridge. Trees had grown up round them. They looked as if they belonged there.

On Sunday we drove to Bobby's for lunch. He lived in Epsom and had just been appointed headmaster of a school in Otahuhu. He had wanted something in a better district, but at least he had his house among 'the nobs'. He lived there with Melody his wife and their daughter Jilly.

He welcomed me by rattling the *Sunday Post*. 'What's all this garbage about the gangs? You're soft in the head, Ray. Duggie's on the right track. Except he doesn't go far enough. I'd flog 'em. I'd volunteer myself. And enjoy it. And chop their hands off if they beat up people. Hang the skeletons round their necks.' He mimed it.

'Bobby!' Mum said.

'And castrate the buggers if they rape girls. If one of them touched Jilly here, I'd do it. With hedge clippers.'

'Bobby!'

He grinned at her. 'There's too many bleeding hearts, Mum.'

Jilly was no more complimentary about my Country and Western singer. His poor lined face offended her. But I thought she was old herself, older than Bobby. He played at being hard, but she was hard, a tough little dame, and she was smart. It was written on her face that she wouldn't be around this dump much longer.

Melody served the lunch I had forgotten – Sunday dinner. Lamb and roasted pumpkin with peas and new potatoes; mint sauce and gravy; and a trifle with so much sherry in it I drank it from my spoon. Then Jilly went out. 'Out,' she answered Bobby from the door.

'What a kid, eh?'

'Shouldn't she tell you where? She's only thirteen.'

'Modern times, Mum. They've got to have their freedom.'

'Is that what you say at school?' I asked.

'There's no Jillys there. Otahuhu kids need discipline. She's got it –' he tapped his skull '– up here.'

Dad slept in a chair and the rest of us played Monopoly. 'This is like Peacehaven, eh?' said Bobby, sentimental. But we had never played Monopoly there. I didn't tell him, Mum told him.

At three o'clock Jilly came in with a boy. They went to her room and played records. That woke Dad and he drank a glass of beer and was more lively. Driving home he said, 'Let's call in and see Duggie Plumb.'

'Why not?' Mum said. 'Before he's too puffed up to recognize.'

They had not seen him since Willis died, and then, Mum said, he'd been 'too busy' to go back to the orchard with his brothers and sisters and uncles and aunts for a drink. They had remembered 'dear old Willie' without him, and Melva sang *Danny Boy* while Cliff played the comb.

'He might have been too upset,' I said.

'Nonsense. He's a Tory.'

We walked up his path of crazy-paving and rang a bell that chimed four happy notes. Sally answered the door. I had to remind her who I was.

'Oh, Ray. You're a Wellington face. I have these faces, Auckland and Wellington. It's the only way I keep track. Douglas is busy.'

'We won't keep him. Mum and Dad would like to say hallo.'

She showed us into the lounge and went to fetch him. He came in stretching himself, flexing his shoulders. 'Gets you, sitting. Hello, Meg. Gidday, Fergus. Long time no see.' He shook hands with them.

Mum had decided to play the visit as a comedy. That saved her from moral outrage. She gave a little curtsey as she took his hand.

'Now, Meg,' Dad said.

Duggie grinned. 'You're like my old man. He used to play *The Donkey's Serenade* on his mouth organ.'

'I would have played *The Green-eyed Dragon*.' She smiled at Sally. 'He feeds with greed on little boys and puppy dogs and big fat snails.'

'I've never gone for little boys,' Duggie said. 'Can I get you a drink, Fergus?'

'I wouldn't say no to a whisky.'

Duggie made us drinks.

'We won't keep you if you're busy,' Dad said.

'Just finished. I try not to work on Sunday but sometimes . . .' He shrugged.

'You're planning your concentration camps,' Mum said.

'Meg.'

'Let her go, Fergus. The lunatic left interests me.'

Sally laughed. The sound had a disembodied beauty, a clarity that startled. She used it as a command and we fell silent.

'Politics just won't leave us alone.'

Mum said, 'I'm sorry.' She gave the artificial smile that was her expression of dislike. She had met Sally once, years before, and found her 'quite empty', 'a kewpie doll'. 'It must be hard being married to a Cabinet Minister.'

'My father was one and now my husband's one. I should have known better. It's like being married to a chameleon.'

'Duggie would always be royal blue.'

'Sally's making a point,' I said. It was the first real thing I had heard her say. Duggie married her shortly after he went into parliament. I had not been able to decide whether he had extended 'the duration' to his career or whether her indifference challenged him. Sally was indifferent to most things; but that, by a paradox in her nature, made her lively. She played her smallest actions to impress. Lightly once, 'Oh,' she said, 'marrying him was a calculated risk.' There was calculation but no risk. I used to feel that if you picked her up she'd be as light as balsa. Unsinkable. She bobbed around, gay and sweet and perfect, surviving through an indifference that lifted her out of the way of all shocks. Once when drunk I said to her, 'I suppose when Duggie gets you home he stands you in a corner and switches you off.'

'You funny man. I won't tell Douglas you said that.'

Now: 'They don't know they're changing. They do it just like breathing.'

'Dry up,' Duggie said in a pleasant way. 'She does it too. Look at her. A little bit of feeling because we're family. Come on Sal, sit on my knee.'

But she took a chair beside him, put her hand on his. She bent her mouth in a perfect smile, and was quiet.

Duggie said, 'More garbage in your column, Ray.'

'That's what Bobby said.'

'When are you going to give up this smart-arse stuff?'

'I can go on as long as you can.'

'You're starting to repeat yourself. You need some new jokes.'

'Tell your boss to shuffle his cabinet.'

He smiled at Mum. 'What do you think of him, Meg?'

'He'll do better work one day.'

'See?' Duggie grinned at me.

'He's writing a biography of Michael Joseph Savage.'

'If that isn't an admission of failure I don't know what is.'

Duggie had worn no better or worse than me. We had both put on weight. We had padded cheeks and incipient jowls: the steak-fed look. His colour was high, mine low. I wasn't sure which was healthier but wondered if the broken veins in his cheeks were a sign he was starting on Cyril Butts' way. A politician had only to limp or hesitate over a word for rumours to begin about his health. There had been none about Duggie's. He worked hard, and relaxed too hard (so we heard), and liked his drop; but played squash when he had the time; and once in a get-fit week he had put on shorts and jogged on the beach at Worser Bay. The photo showed him comically short in the leg.

He went out to the kitchen for some ice. I followed him. 'Do you remember a man called Alaric Gibbs?'

'Alaric?'

'The Fall of Rome. He was king of the Visigoths.'

'I don't know any Alarics.'

'This one's an expert on Douglas Plumb. He keeps a scrapbook.'

'There's quite a few people do that. Mostly female.'

'Sally's right. You do change colour.'

'I give you what you want from me, R. Sole. Who's this Alaric?'

'A retired engineer. He told me you were engaged to his daughter once.'

'He'd be lying then.' But he turned on me suddenly, with an almost frightened grin. It was not from memory so much as from the shock of going back. There must have been a rushing in his mind, a flashing past of things he had no time to focus on. 'Jenny Gibbs.'

'Were you engaged?'

'She thought so. Why did you have to spring this on me, Ray?'

I had not seen him so off balance since the night Cyril Butts had put his name up for Epsom. 'What happened to her?'

'I don't know.' He looked at the tray of ice cubes in his hand and did not seem to know what to do with it. Then he put it on the bench and broke some out. 'Give me that jug.' When he had it full he grinned at me. The pink was back in his cheeks. 'Jenny, eh? That's a lot of girls ago. Can't say I remember her old man.'

'Go and see him. He'll give you her address.'

'I don't play around in the past.'

'You could play around now.'

'With some old bag of forty-five. I've got something better in the next room.'

'And the rest.'

'And all the rest. What do you want, Ray? Some dirty stories? Why don't you go in the dunny and toss yourself off?'

Mum put her head in. 'What are you two talking about?'

'He's playing Jiminy Cricket. Take him home, Meg.'

'Still quarrelling? When you were boys you never stopped.'

'We've stopped now. I don't need him any more.'

In the car, I said, 'Duggie's tired.'

'His wife's under a strain,' Mum said. 'I felt quite sorry for her.'

'She'll be around when Duggie's gone.'

'I wouldn't like to see him Prime Minister,' Dad said. 'Whatsisname . . . ?'

'Muldoon?'

'He's bad enough. But I think Douglas Plumb would be dangerous.'

20

My father died in the winter. He felt a bitter impatience with mind and body and his contempt for them hastened his end. He died without tranquillity or acceptance, with an inner jerkiness and a disgust with death. Sour recollections cast shadows on his life, making it seem of small account. All this surprised me. I had looked for him to make an end having lessons for µs. I had not expected him to be impatient. The fear that I should do no better complicated my grief.

Merle Butters was dead too and Wendy proposed that Mum should join her at Peacehaven. 'Never,' Mum said. 'I can't think of a worse fate than being locked up with Wendy. You haven't heard how poor old Merle went have you?'

She had been unwell and, it seems, died peacefully in the night. When she did not come for breakfast Wendy 'peeped in' and saw her 'sleeping like a baby'. It was the same at lunchtime and late in the afternoon. 'It must be doing her the world of good.' On the second night Wendy began to worry, but she felt in the blankets and Merle was cosy and warm. 'It was her electric blanket,' Mum said. 'Merle had been dead two days before Wendy woke up.' She gave a little laugh, then started to cry. She was crying for Dad. 'Don't worry about me, Ray. I'll be happy here till my turn comes.'

A third death that winter was Helen Plumb's. I had not seen her since her visit to her mother. I went round to her bach after several months and found two old men living there. The woman in the house told me John Peihana had started falling over all the time. Some Maoris came and took him away. She wasn't sure about Helen but someone said the Sallys came for her. 'Maybe they put her on the island.' That seemed likely. I paid the rent owing and forgot her.

Now I saw Helen dead on Oliver's lawn. It had rained all night, with storms of hail. The clouds had blown away when I came off the zig-zag and saw three men guarding something in the hydrangea bushes. Their breath made grey speech balloons on the air. I walked over and saw Helen's shoes crossed like an X. 'Everything's under control.' 'Press.' I went across the lawn and looked at her: the same sort of coat with broken buttons, the same empty bottle on her chest.

'The woman in the house gave us a tea-towel.'

I lifted it and looked at Helen's face. Her patch had slid into her hair and a pool of water filled her eye socket. Lashes made their stitching on the bottom. Her other eye, unhuman and alone, seemed like a specimen on a plate. I covered her face and turning saw Mrs Barrett watching me from the door. She closed it when I approached but I knocked softly and said, 'Mrs Barrett, it's Ray Sole. Sir Oliver's nephew.'

She pulled me in. 'This is dreadful.'

'You know who that is out there?'

'I know. She came last night. She wanted to see Sir Oliver. I wouldn't let her in.'

'So she lay down on the lawn and died.'

'That's not my fault. I didn't know.'

I asked if I could see Oliver. She made me promise not to mention 'that thing', and led me to the room where I had visited Beatrice.

'Here we are Ollie, here's Ray come to pay a little call.'

'Ray who? Who is he, Barry?'

'I'm Raymond Sole. Meg's son.'

Oliver sat in a bed with polished knobs. He gave the impression of having long dry bones that might be used one day for blowing tunes on. 'You're my nephew?'

'I called to see you once a long time ago.'

'You married that girl. Goodlad's daughter.'

'Against your advice.'

'Young men seldom take advice. What do you want this time?'

I thought, To hell with 'Barry'. 'Your daughter Helen died last night on your lawn. She came to see you but she couldn't get in.'

Mrs Barrett came at me hissing but I put out my arm and kept her off.

'What's this? What is this, Barry?'

'I told him not to tell you.'

'People don't die on lawns.'

'Helen did. You'd better think of something to tell the police.'

'I'll tell them it's none of my concern. On my lawn! You should have got rid of her, Barry.'

'I sent her away. Vamoos, I said. She must have come back.'

'I paid money into that woman's account for forty years. I've done my duty.'

'You have, Ollie. He has. She came up here and peed on the floor.'

'What? What's that?'

'She peed on the floor. In this very room.'

'Watch your language, Barry.'

'With a Maori.'

'I loved that child. And my Trixie loved her. We gave her a home. And look how she thanked us. Running round with black men. Dying on my lawn. All my life, all my life, I've tried to live according to some standards. But people, people . . .'

'There there, Ollie.' She sat by him and held him in her arms.

'I've done my best.'

'He has. You have.' She dried his face with the sheet. 'Go away, please.'

I let myself out and waited till the police came. The soles of Helen's shoes stared at me.

In the afternoon I caught a unit out to Simla Crescent. I sat by a fire of pine logs and talked with Felicity while Nicola her daughter-in-law brought us cups of tea and plates of cake.

'I live off cake,' Felicity said. 'I'm sure it's bad for me. But I'm eighty-four. This is only made of rags and sticks.'

'Oliver must be . . . ?'

'Eighty-five. He'll be a hundred. First in, last out. He'll leave all his money to Mrs Barrett.'

'I think she loves him.'

'She loves the idea of him. I'd go and see poor Ollie but the only thing he knows about me now is that I'm Catholic. He quivers when he sees me.'

Our talk of Helen was mainly anecdotal. There was little to say. Her life was impenetrable and every time I worked a little way in, back I was sent reeling by a sense of waste and pain. There must be more, I thought – *some* other thing. Felicity?

'Of course.'

'Don't give me that.'

Impenetrable too. She told me how she had come to her church. Through waste and pain. Then had come a time when, safe inside, she had sought out danger. 'I had Him here,' she said, touching her breast, 'now I had to have Him here.' She tapped her brow. 'I had to know Him in my mind. That kept me busy for forty years. It wasn't exactly a waste of time. I was always in good company, you see.'

I asked about now.

'Now? I sit here drinking tea. And waiting for Him. It's all so plain, and yet at the heart of it it's mystery. A loving God and Jesus Christ, His Son. *Mysterium tremendum et fascinans*. Go on, pull a face. You're like Max, Ray. Always wanting to know.'

'So did you.'

'Yes. Forty years. That was my life's work. Hard work too. But, *laborare est orare*. Ha! I'm like my father, dropping bits of Latin everywhere.'

When I left she gave me some notes Max had been working on when he died.

'They're for your book. Max's father was a Fabian. Savage used to come to pick his brains. There's a lovely story there about Savage sitting on Max's glass slate and breaking it. A big one, eighteen inches. Savage said he'd buy a new one for him, but he didn't. Max had to remind him. Then Savage turned up with a little one, six by six.'

'That's pretty good for a political promise.'

'How is the book?'

I told her I had put it aside again. 'Everything's there. The work's all done. But I can't bring it together.' I could not make a whole round life. I lacked the stillness and the breadth; I lacked the measure. I had the energy for it but found that I needed tranquillity too. 'I guess it's just too hard for me. But I'll keep this. Thank you.'

'Don't stop trying, Ray.'

'No,' I said.

I went home and put Max's notes in my writing desk. Four years of my life went by. There's no way I can give them any measure. All I can do is put down notes. I stayed in my house in Wadestown. I repapered my bedroom and painted the window sills. One day I took Glenda's mobile down from over the bed. The fish were coated with dust, it grew on them like fur. I took them out and burned them in the garden incinerator.

At night I sat in my chair and watched TV. I became addicted to *Coronation Street* and *Close to Home*. I never missed any sporting event. I even watched grid-iron. My friends called me a hermit or a slob. On the other hand, women seemed to find me mysterious. That was in the beginning. As our affairs went on they began to find that what they had thought deep was only empty. Several of them said as much, and more. Clever girls. They complained that I wasn't there, or that only part of me was there, and part was fun for a while, but they started feeling used and feeling dirty. Our terminations were noisy. Once I joined a girl – it's not their fault I can't think of them as women – joined her in crying, and that gave us a couple of extra weeks. When she left she called me creepy.

I looked after myself. Ate well. Drank expensive booze. My clothes were sharp. I wore a leather coat and Italian shoes. But my friends were not friends, they were people I drank with. And my girls were not women. In spite of that, I was not unhappy; only not happy.

Towards the end of that time I heard a voice. Softly in my ear it said, 'R. Sole.' It came from narrow windows, thin as a bat call. It came in the noise of traffic, and wagons crashing in the railway yards. In trees, in lifts, in doors that closed with a well-bred huff. Sometimes it came shouting from high scaffolds, where men in hard-hats perched against the sky, 'Gidday, Arsehole.' I thought at first someone was out to get me – Duggie Plumb? Then I thought I was going mad. There was no one I could talk to. I talked to my doctor. He told me I needed a holiday, a Pacific cruise, or maybe something harder, a walk on the Milford Track. 'Ha!' I said. Going out, I thought a man in his waiting room said, 'R. Sole.'

So I talked to John Jolly. I sat in a quiet bar with him and told it like a joke. He was a bitter man who lived with cats. Ash and cat hair drifted from his clothes. Nicotine stained a sore patch on his mouth. He started rolling cigarettes to hide his disbelief at the gift of power I made him.

'R. Sole? It could be me.'

'Come on, John.'

'Head noises?'

'No.'

'What would you be hearing if your parents had called you John?'
'You tell me.'
He lit a cigarette. 'It's a judgement, maybe?'
'Why?'
'You know what you've done, I don't. Or what you haven't.' He gave me a quick half-angry grin. 'She's a life problem, boy. See a shrink. Join a church. Jump off a bridge. In that order.'
'I'm serious, John.'
'I thought you were. You want me to say you've got tangles in there. Then you can take a pill or hire a doc to unpick it all. Nice and easy.' He shook his head. 'Sorry.'
'Is that all? That's a big help.'
'Like I said, she's a life problem.'
'What's that mean?'
'You got it handed to you. Gift from God. OK, leave that out. But you got handed this nice shiny thing and look at it now.'
'Look at yours.'
'Sure. No touché though.'
'When did you get religion?'
'I haven't got it, Ray. I can look but I can't touch.'
I left him there, dropping ash in his lap, and walked up the hill to Wadestown. I was so contemptuous of him that I did not hear my voice for several days. When it came it had a tone of sadness. It seemed to suggest I had failed again. I found I was afraid of John Jolly. He remained sour and dirty, his usual self, but I had surprised him into speech, he was changed for me.

In 1981 I went to Canberra to cover the Commonwealth Heads of Government Meeting. When it was over I visited Sharon in Sydney. She was living with Desi, a Scot who had 'rescued' her in Poona. I was not surprised to find her with a man. Carlo was a surprise.
'Who's his father?'
'You don't need to know.'
'An Indian?'
'That's obvious. You're shocked, Dad.'
'I'm not. I'm not. I like all this mixing up.'
'What do you think of him?'
'He's beautiful.'
Sharon wanted to come back to New Zealand. She wanted a little

house, a bit of land in the Coromandel or Golden Bay where she could mind her own business.

'Will Desi come?'

'If he wants to.'

'Are you going to get married?'

'Good God, no. Do I have to get married before I get your help?'

I could not imagine any future for her. Desi and she did not approach each other. They had no words, they had no looks or glances. He loved her, that was plain, but usefulness was all he had to offer. He had been useful in Poona, and was useful here. Would be, for a while, in Golden Bay. For all his muscles and beard and male smell he had no gender. In the bathroom I found contraceptive pills in a cupboard. But sex, I knew, was another thing.

'How will you live?'

'I'll grow stuff. I'll share. Desi can work.'

'Aye,' Desi said, and held up his arm for me to admire.

I walked through Kings Cross to my hotel, trying to discover where Sharon was. The 'peace' she had found by Holy Ganga? That was gone. She had sniffed when I mentioned it, and had laughed at 'understanding'. Nothing I could admire was in their place. She worked too hard at toughness and honesty.

But that night I had no time to sort Sharon out – and have never done it – for a message under my door asked me to telephone my brother urgently. He was gulping and sniffing and his sounds hollowed me out. 'Where have you been? I've been trying all night.'

'What is it, Bobby?'

'Bad news. Are you ready?'

'Yes. Tell me.'

'It's Mum. I'm sorry, Ray. She's dead. She's burned. The house caught fire. Becky pulled her out. She's got some burns too. But Mum – she died of shock. She didn't feel anything. Ray. Ray, come home. As quick as you can.'

I managed to get a seat on a plane that left in the morning. Sharon came with me to the airport, carrying my bag as though I had grown old. 'She was in her seventies. She had to die.'

'For God's sake don't tell me things I know. She didn't have to burn.'

'No. I'm sorry. I hardly knew her.'

'Then just keep quiet.'

'Kiss Carlo goodbye.'

I kissed them both and left them. Over the Tasman I tried to think of my mother but could not hold her. She vanished behind a figure in a burning shroud. Felicity had told me, 'There are so many ways of dying, but only one death.' I had felt wise in agreeing, but I could not make the statement fit my mother. I could not get past the horror of her dying.

Bobby met me at the airport and drove me to visit Becky. We sat by her bed and looked at her burns. She would have scars on her arms and face. She spoke in a thick whisper, painfully.

'She would light that bloody stove. I tried to talk her out of it. But no, it warmed the house.' And Mum loved wood fires, and loved her range. She had painted it every summer with aluminium paint; reminding herself of her mother, she said.

'The kettle wouldn't boil. The wood was green.'

Mum fetched a bottle from the shed. 'What's that?' 'Kerosene. Your father's trick.' She poured into the stove; and fire ran like a weasel up her arm; exploded in the bottle, wrapped her round.

'It was petrol,' Becky said. 'There was no label on the bottle. All I could see is it was pink. But I didn't have time . . .'

She threw a mat over Mum and put out the flames. Then she pulled her outside and laid her on the lawn and ran to Peacehaven to telephone for help, while the cottage burned. When she came back the flames were spinning like a whirlpool. She felt them sucking at her. Mum was unconscious by the hedge. Becky ran water on her from the hose. 'She never woke up. I don't think it hurt her, Ray. It was so quick. She just sort of gave a gasp and died.'

Bobby and I drove out to Loomis to look at the cottage. Only the chimney was standing. The stove had collapsed in an even heap. The totara piles had burned and the dirt in between was brown as cocoa. Bed springs and iron frames, Mum's bicycle with the tyres burned off, lay in mounds of charcoal. Pink and blue tears of melted glass gleamed in the ashes.

I turned Grandpa's Buddha with my toe. His smiling cheek lay in a puddle of brass. 'Bronze,' Bobby said. 'The old man had it wrong. Do you want to see Wendy? She's got the Rev. all to herself at last.'

'No,' I said. I left the Buddha lying. Wendy would fossick here and come on it as a treasure. But Mum was dead. The Plumbs were dead. And Peacehaven, Wendy Philson, had no meaning.

After the funeral I rented a car and drove to Wellington. I did not want to be in my house so I crept back. South of the Bombay hills I turned off the main highway and drove across the plains to Gerriston. I drove up and down the main street but saw no one I knew. Sausage flats with frosted doors and wrought-iron fences stood in the place of Primrose Hall. The stumps of the Phoenix palms were carved into garden seats. I stood on the stop-banks by the bridge and found them unconvincing. They looked as if children had patted them into shape.

The stationer's shop was still called *Kittredges* although Charlie was dead. I walked through to the *Independent*, knocked on the editor's door, and found Iris. We shook hands and said, 'Well, Ray,' 'Well, Iris,' 'You haven't changed.' She poured us drinks from a bottle she kept in a bottom drawer. She was thin and quick and stringy, with shaped and lacquered hair and diamante glasses. (I was square-built, with weak eyes and thinning hair.) We chatted amiably, and now and then caught each other in glances. Here we were. But once we had been a boy and a girl, eyes gleaming in the dark, amazed by what we were doing to each other. I told her about my slogan-writing.

'I knew. You had paint in your fingernails. Come with me.' She led me into the yard behind the building. The water tower stood behind the trees, with a swastika and a dollar sign ghostly on its side.

'The only lasting piece of work I've done.'

'It's coming down. We've got a new one.'

'Well, . . .'

'You've done all right. You're a name. Why don't you publish a book of those profiles you do?'

'Because,' I said, 'they're jokes. That's all they are. Funny for as long as it takes you to read them. Do you know,' I said, seeing what to do, 'I'm leaving the *Post*. I've been making a fool of myself. I'm irrelevant.'

'What to?'

'I don't know. I wish I knew.'

She gave me another drink and I took her to lunch. Then I kissed her cheek, she patted me, and I drove south. I was looking for Greg. Sharon had told me his itinerary.

I tried Cambridge and Putaruru but nobody had heard of him. In Tokoroa I found a minister who said a group of evangelists had been in town yesterday. As far as he knew they were heading down the island. Frankly he'd been pleased to see them go. One of them had tattoos on his hands.

In Taupo I strolled out from my motel and down by the lake I heard a voice singing. It was as creaky as an unoiled door. Greg had wanted to be a pop star once and I had told him sourly that he had the voice for it. I walked down and watched him from the dark.

> 'Come to Jesus.
> He won't let you down.
> Come to Jesus.
> He never wears a frown.'

I guessed he had written the words himself. He strummed his guitar while a girl at his side played a squeeze box and a middle-aged couple whose daughter she plainly was hummed the tune. When it was over Greg put down his guitar. 'Friends,' he said to the seven listeners, 'Jesus is real. He is here now. He is waiting to enter your hearts just as surely as he entered mine.' Religion had rounded his vowels. His clothes were clean, his hair was neat, and his eyes held a burning innocence. I was not going to question the quality of his happiness. I was pleased to see him happy and travelling a road.

'Once,' he said, 'I belonged to Satan. I served him.' He told his tale of drugs and theft and sex, while the girl made gasping sounds on her concertina. 'I hated my father once but I don't hate him now. Jesus won't let me hate. He makes me love. I hated everybody. Now I love. Friends, I pray to you, learn to love. Open up your hearts . . .'

I knew if I stayed I should begin to be disappointed in him. I moved back in the dark and walked along the lake shore, wondering if Greg and the girl were in love. She had a look of contentment but there might be other reasons for that.

When I went back they were packing up.

'Hallo, Greg.'

'Gidday, Dad. I thought I saw you there.'

The others sat politely in the van while we talked. He told me how he had stood at the back of a crowd and a hand had pushed him forward and when he looked round no one was there. He got to the front and tears were streaming down his face. I was shocked by the banality of it, but saw he was moved in remembering.

'That girl?' I said. 'The one with the concertina. Is she . . . ?'

'We share the Lord's work, Dad. We're both happy. Are you happy?'

'Me? Sure. Well . . .' I told him about his grandmother. He said the same as Sharon – 'I never knew her.'

'Is that all you can say?'

'Jesus has her, Dad. She's all right now.'

'She was all right alive. Let's not quarrel. It's good to see you looking so well, Greg.' I gave him news of Sharon and asked where he was heading. Then we shook hands and I went back to my motel and to bed. I had hoped that Greg would be a scientist – or one of many things, all distinguished. Sharon too. But that seemed impudent now, imperialistic; and hope itself a magnet to danger. I dreamed of them happy, but found their faces simple, out of focus.

Wellington. I told John Jolly I would stay with the *Post* until the election, then finish up. I put my house on the market, sold it well, but kept possession till December. Sharon and Carlo and Desi came over from Sydney and stayed with me a week before moving on to a property I had found in Golden Bay. Sharon was pleased I'd sold the house. She claimed it gave her morbid thoughts.

I wrote my column, packed up lazily. I looked at the fracture in my life and was pleased with it although I could not understand exactly how it had happened. More quickly than I liked I came to accept my mother's death. I even came to think it suited her and once or twice I wished Dad could have had something similar.

The election had me running. I was in Nelson and Palmerston North and Invercargill. But I was home in Wellington one night when Duggie called. We sat among cartons of books and vases wrapped in paper.

'Sorry about your old lady.'

'That's all right. You're looking tired.'

'I've been up in Kapiti. We're losing that. What I don't like is wasting time.'

'You're going to lose more than Kapiti.'

'Yeah.'

'It doesn't worry you, does it? That's the only way you'll get rid of your boss.'

'That's right.'

'What makes you think it'll be your turn? He's a confrontation specialist. They don't want another one.'

'Is that what you think I am? I can be anything you like.'

Expediency moved every thought he had, so nothing really was impossible. He could use the masonic grip while crossing himself and not be diminished. It was all in the service of Duggie Plumb. But lately he had reached a difficult place. The National Party had always been a party of fence menders. Now it was filling up with ideologues. Duggie, by design a populist, achieved the feat of having two styles. He moved carefully, making little signs, dropping hints; and slowly he moved out on to the right wing of the party. He was never the first to move, or second, or third; but he would be left standing when the others were knocked down.

Standing for what? I had watched him raking influence, people, power in front of him. He almost had more than anyone else, almost enough. What was he going to do with it? I filled his glass. He said, 'Parliament's for playing games in, Ray. The real thing happens somewhere else.'

'I know that.'

'Parliament is going to fall to bits. I don't know what happens then. But I'm going to be around.' He saw my nervousness and grinned at me. 'Nobody's doing it. It's inevitable. Then we'll be in the age of power. Manipulation.'

'And you'll be the man on top?'

'If I'm not, somebody will. There's no shortage.'

'What if I tell people?'

'Go ahead. Write your stuff. They'll only laugh.'

'That's right. There wouldn't be any point anyway. You're too soon, Duggie.'

'So what are you worried about?'

'The one who comes after you. And you right now.' He would destroy himself not us. 'You see it all out there. Outside yourself. You don't seem to have an idea of *you* and *other people*.'

He watched me; laughed at me.

'There's privacy. And relationships. You've got to go there, Duggie. You've got to find out what it's all about.'

'Do you know?'

'Not very well. But listen, what I'm talking about is being human. Knowing there are real people out there. And *back* there. *In* there.'

He was laughing again, but stopped as if I had struck him.

'Nobody owns any part of me. Not you. Or Beak. Or Sally. Nobody.' He came to his feet and held his hand up with the fingers spread. 'This is where I am. Here! Now!'

'Who's talking about Beak?'

His hand seemed to fascinate him. He closed his fingers, opened them, worked his wrist like a hinge. 'That's where I start and where I end.'

I took his glass from the chair and filled it with whisky. The sound made him blink and contract his face. With an old man's slowness he sat down. 'I always talk bullshit when I'm with you.'

'What about Beak?'

He wiped his hand down his cheeks. 'I'm tired. I need some sleep.'

'Sleep here if you like. There's a bed.'

'Can't disappear.'

'You came up here to tell me about Beak.'

'Yeah.'

'What about him?'

'They found him, Ray. All that was left of him. A pile of bones.'

'Where?'

'In the creek at Millbrook Road. They're putting a new bridge in. When they started excavating they found Beak wedged under the bank. What was left of him. Skull's gone somewhere. Washed away, I guess. Lot of bones gone.'

'How do they know it's Beak?'

'They don't. They're guessing. But I know. All the other stuff was there. Axle. Engine block. It's OK, Ray. I didn't kill him.'

He told me the story of that night. He had been out to visit Mirth and Willis – a rare event – and when he came back down Millbrook Road and saw the light in Beak's house over the creek he decided to call on him. He was half full of Dally wine and Beak made a danger signal, a light flashing. He had said that Duggie and I raped Myra. That was a story Duggie must stop.

He left his car at the end of Dean Street and walked along in the shadows. The street runs on a ledge with a row of houses above and one below. No one saw Duggie going along. He came to Beak's house and found it dark. The light he had seen was in a shed. 'I heard him in there, Ray. It sounded like a panel beater's shop. When I looked in, he was dressing himself up in bits of iron. He had an axle tied on his back. He had some of those counter weights from windows round his neck. And he had this engine block. God knows how he carried it. He had a rope round it and he tied it round his waist. There must have been a couple of hundredweight of iron on him.'

Duggie watched. He crept back from the door when Beak came out, and stood behind a corner of the house. Beak turned out the light and closed the door. That was a struggle. But he was leaving everything locked up. He walked down to the bottom of his section into a path leading to the creek. Duggie followed. There was no light. He heard Beak crashing around in the dark. 'He even tried to whistle,' Duggie said. 'It was that thing – you know, from *The Wizard of Oz*. We're off to see the Wizard. It sounded off key, as if he couldn't work his mouth properly . . . I didn't try to stop him, Ray. If he wanted to kill himself it was OK with me.'

Beak came to the pool above the bridge. Duggie saw it glimmering in the light of the street lamp. He squatted on the path and watched Beak wade into the water. He went in steadily, shaped like a hunchback. 'There wasn't any sound, just some splashing,' Duggie said. Beak stood still while a car passed on the bridge. Then he went on. His head seemed to float on the surface for a moment. That was all. It slid under. There was a bubbling in the water. It must have been, Duggie said, the air from Beak's lungs and from his clothes.

'What happened then?'

'I went home.'

'And forgot it?'

'After a while. I could have stopped him, Ray. But he wanted to die.'

'And it suited you.'

'It suited me. But it wasn't that bloody important.'

We drank some more and looked at each other. 'What do you want me to do?'

'I don't know . . . I'm used to trouble. I can handle it. Mostly I see it coming so I'm ready. But this – I'd forgotten it.'

'It's like the fall of Singapore. They had the guns pointing out to sea but the Japs came out of the jungle.'

'For Christ's sake!' He gave me a naked look. 'I'm scared.'

'They can never connect it with you.'

'That's not what I mean.'

'You're scared because it opens you up. You don't like that.'

'Why do you get at me? I came for help.'

I told him that I could not give him any. That was true. I could not think of anything to say that would be of use. All I could do was pour whisky in his glass. I tried to persuade him to stay the night. We talked about Beak. He told me the story several times and though he was drunker each time he was more in control of it.

I drove him home, out towards the strait. Sally was in Auckland. I took him into the house and put him on his bed and pulled his shoes off.

'Ray,' he said.

I stopped at the door.

'You forget all this. You wipe it out – this whole night.'

'I'll forget it.'

'I mean it, Ray. Else I'll do you. I did Latham.'

'Go to sleep, Duggie.'

'Yeah. Go to sleep. Ray! Ray!' He reared up, blind. He was like a seal looking round. He looked dark and slippery on the white expanse of his king-sized bed. 'Where are you, Ray?'

'I'm here.'

'We had some good times when we were kids.'

I turned out the light and went downstairs and did not see Duggie Plumb again.

21

The wild apple trees are in blossom by the roadsides. Sharon has cut the last of her winter cabbages and is planting leeks and celery and green peppers. Bella comes along behind and puts frost covers on the peppers. She made them out of plastic bags and slivers of bamboo. Bella is good with her hands. She is going to make sandals and belts in the trailer when I'm gone.

Although the sun spreads a watery light in the understoreys of the bush the cold stays on. The bottoms where I pad along will not warm up until high summer. The paths sink spongily and water drips and trickles in banks of moss. I increase the length of my walks gradually. The doctor said not to overdo things. I don't have angina but my blood pressure is up – nothing to worry about, 'You're not to worry.' I told him I was pretty relaxed these days. Out in the bush, in the huge silence, I hear no voice, no whisper, no R. Sole.

Yesterday I went up to the mine. The tailing mounds are grown with weeds and trees, but they had a roundness, a plumpness, that reminded me of thighs, and that of course made me see the shaft as a vagina. These images come unbidden and I can't see that they're ugly or that I'm to be condemned for them. But the darkness that surrounds sex in my mind would take some explaining. I remembered Hank and Jilly in the river – how they stood there in the light – and wondered if I was moved by them because they had no guilt. I went into the shaft a little way but the dripping walls and the darkness frightened me, so I came out.

A mile or so on I came to the forks. There was another chance for images but I kept them out. I climbed down to the water and hung my feet in it where it lay motionless in a little cove. I was not alone. What I took at first for a water-logged branch was a black eel lying half out from under a ledge. He was the biggest eel I had ever seen. He had scars on his body and a battered mouth. He took no notice of my feet above him. I left them there out of trust as much as bravado – but pulled them out soon because the cold made them ache.

Sharon had given me a Marmite jar of peanuts and sultanas. I ate them and drank from the river. On the other side the ridge was almost a cliff. Ferns and trees grew in clefts and hollows and supple jack hung like hair from ledge to ledge. I saw a goat picking his way down. He was tan and black and had a yellow beard and yellow eyes. His horns lay like plating on his skull. He came out neatly on the shingle bank. I heard his hooves clicking on the stones. He drank from the river, more easily than I, then stood in the sun, looking up the left fork and the right. Soon five more goats appeared. They climbed down, stopping and starting, and joined the old billy on the shingle. He watched them drink. Three were so fat I guessed they must be close to giving birth. When I moved they all jumped back and ran a dozen steps towards the bush. Then they stopped and looked at me. Their yellow eyes watched without curiosity. There seemed to be millions of years between us. They went up through the trees and clefts, jumping nimbly, stopping to look down, and when they were gone the bush went back another million years. It seemed to watch me with an uncaring eye and want all my memories and obsessions out of it. But I said no. I said no. I did not see why I should not stay. I belonged there as much as anything else.

I have given Sharon her Indian letters. She says they're hers and she has the right to burn them if she wants.

'Carlo will be interested one day.'

'Not if I can help it.' She promised to tear the stamps off the envelopes for him. 'When are you going, Dad?'

'Monday. I'll go through the Lewis Pass.'

'Are you sure you've got this job?'

'Morrie Horne thinks it will be all right.' Morrie is editor of the *Thorpe Evening Star*. He has offered me the job of assistant editor – subject to my 'not saying anything bloody stupid in the interview'. I'll have to pull my horns in, Morrie says. So I move south, against the population drift. Thorpe is the town where my grandfather fought his religious battles long ago. I don't think it's grown much since his day.

When Sharon had gone I looked in the cigar box to see what was left. Nothing much. Some letters from my mother, some from

Glenda, including her note on the morning of the storm, and two from Alaric Gibbs.

Gibbs' second letter came in a packet redirected from my Wadestown address. When I had read it I wondered what I should do. Duggie was a week dead, and Gibbs in hospital dying of his disease – and, I was sure, not saying a word. My duty was to hand the letter over to the police, but I knew at once I would not do that. I could keep it; or burn it and forget it. Once or twice I was tempted to sell it to Jolly John. In the end I decided to do what Gibbs had asked.

I'll put the letter here in the pages of this book, where it can stay until I need it.

Dear Mr Sole,

Further to our conversation, I have decided not to grant Douglas Plumb a reprieve. Nothing he has done since we spoke together has caused me to change my view of him. Once or twice in our talk I was swayed, I have to admit, and as a result I am leaving the completion of my task open to chance in one particular. But it's my belief he'll die. You must not blame yourself. You defended him most ably.

If you have read my memoirs with any care – I'm sorry to have given you that task – you will know that I own a pistol from the war. That is to be the execution weapon. Notice that I don't say murder weapon. Douglas Plumb is tried and found guilty and the penalty is death. I have studied him over a period of twenty-five years and my great achievement in that time is that I have put hatred aside. I will not claim that my act is impersonal. Somebody must pull the lever, pull the trigger, wield the axe. I am not without pride in being the one.

You will no doubt object that I should not be judge and executioner both. But there is no one else. Do you remember 'the man who is not himself mean', who is 'neither tarnished nor afraid'? I carry out the task he set himself. And nobody else knows the facts of the case. When I die – very soon – they will be lost. That is why I am writing to you. When my daughter passes on make this letter public in some way. Put the record straight. I know you are his cousin. I think you love him, and hate him too. It is more than likely you will hate me. But I ask you to carry out this task in the name of justice.

Let me tell you about my daughter, Jennifer Gibbs. She had no other name, just Jenny, Jennifer. My wife nearly lost her life giving birth and we had no more children after Jenny. She was six when I went to the war and eleven when I came home. The photograph enclosed shows her at fifteen. She was beautiful, you will agree. She was intelligent, she was happy – joyous is the word I often use. She drank up life. You will see there too a spiritual quality. She was pure. I used to think her incorruptible. I understand why Douglas Plumb would not let her be.

I could afford 'good' schools for Jenny. They did not spoil her. Such places often teach nasty lessons – they are chock-full of vulgarities and lies, I see that now. But Jenny came out unscathed. She had a simpleness that protected her. She believed in love and with her it was a practical thing. If I can put it so, love was as real to her as a bodily function. I do not mean man/woman love, I mean loving kindness.

I am not sentimentalizing her, Mr Sole. This was *her*. This was Jenny at nineteen, when she met Douglas Plumb. I don't remember how they met. Perhaps it was at the Shelly Beach baths, where she went swimming on Saturday afternoons. In that summer he was with us, suddenly there, about the house. It was Douglas this and Douglas that. He smiled a lot and deferred to me and I thought him a pleasant foolish boy. It was plain to both my wife and me that he was not good enough for Jenny. We admired her spirit in being 'in love' – everything that Jenny did was special – but soon it began to worry us. We began to wonder if she might be foolish.

That was the surface of things. In our worst nightmares we could not have seen what was going on. The business was carnal from the first – *the very first day*. I must believe he had watched her for some time, and she watched him, that he made a kind of poisoned air about them. Then he moved at her and she was gone. It must be that. In some way he turned her love against her. I see now she was pure but *corruptible*.

I watched her happiness, I saw in her a kind of nervous wonder. She was open in so many of her ways. I saw her doubts begin. Do you remember the ball? She was never happy again after that night.

Douglas Plumb grew tired of her. I've gone over this with the greatest of care. Perhaps she was tiresome. Perhaps her simplicities got on his nerves. I've weighed up these things – and much more – but I find them wanting in the balance. He destroyed her, either deliberately or out of boredom. Neither way seems worse than the other. It seems likely though that in the end he played a game with her.

I'll put it simply. Douglas Plumb made Jenny practise intimacies that twisted her life upon its base – worse than that – they twisted her in her soul. I won't say what they were. You will find them in all the modern books. It seems they're not horrifying now. He let her think she held him in this way. Pleasure and disgust were bound inextricably in her mind. Then, when he was thoroughly tired of her, Plumb told her that her appetites filled him with disgust. And, to keep it simple, Jenny went mad. He doesn't know that. I've thought I should tell him before he dies but I don't think I'll have time.

My daughter is in Carrington hospital. She was forty-six in January. I took her a bar of chocolate but she doesn't see out any more, she just sees in – we suppose she sees in – and I let another patient snatch it from me. She went inside in 1955 and she's never been out. They have given her all the treatments available. Nothing works. For some years she was aware of me and my wife but she did not seem to notice when Milly died. She doesn't see me any more, though I sit in front of her and say – this and that. I've tried saying Douglas Plumb but she doesn't hear. She's a woman with a smooth face and grey hair cut like a boy's. When they touch her on the shoulder she stands up. She walks when they give her a push. They turn her at the corners. *Where is she? Where has she gone?* I sometimes think that deep inside her head she's curled up tightly. She's warm in there, she's happy and smiles at herself. But perhaps she's screaming. That's a possibility, isn't it?

I don't believe I'll meet her when I die. Or my wife. It's not that I disbelieve in God. I have no belief one way or the other. It's possible He exists, but if He does then He's contemptible. He deserves Douglas Plumb.

There's not a great deal more I need to say. You need not worry about being implicated. I have destroyed everything that might lead the police to you. I've burned the scrapbooks. There is nothing to show I'm not a mad old man who hates the Minister of Police. I suppose someone will find out I had a daughter. They might even remember that she knew Douglas Plumb. But *she'll* say nothing. And I'll say nothing. All I have to say I've said in this letter. It's a matter of propriety not to have it known until Jenny dies – although she's dead. Please let no one see it till that time.

I will die in hospital not in prison, and die soon. I have cancer –

riddled with it, as they say. It's beside the point although it determines the time of Douglas Plumb's death. I have waited until the last moment so that I can keep on seeing Jenny. Now I can go no more. The doctors have given me up and put me on cortisone, which makes me eat like a horse and makes me fat. It will be effective for a short time, then the end will come. So I must go tomorrow. I telephoned his house a while ago – I have his unlisted number, I have everything. I heard him say Douglas Plumb before I put the phone down. With any luck he'll be home tomorrow.

I'll end this now and post it in the box on the corner. Then I'll have a good night's sleep and take a taxi round there in the morning.

I'm doing right. I hope that you'll agree. He deserves to die. There's just a chance I've overstepped the bounds. But if it's not my part to judge him then whose is it? I know the answer most people will give, and I don't believe it. I'm prepared to give him a chance though. I haven't fired the pistol since I bought it in Italy. The Canadian I got it from said it was in good condition. That was thirty-five years ago. I've kept the parts oiled but I haven't tested it. Tomorrow I'll point it at him and pull the trigger. I'm reasonably certain it will go off.

Yours sincerely,
Alaric Gibbs

He pulled the trigger and the gun went off. Those large bullets make a nasty hole. Duggie was thrown back into the umbrella stand in the hall. He lay there dying. Alaric Gibbs put the pistol on the doormat. He had not mentioned Sally in his letter and I think perhaps he had forgotten about her. She came running from the lounge and screamed when she saw Duggie, then tried to stop his bleeding with her hands. Gibbs walked down the path and sat on the garden wall waiting for the police. He said to one of the neighbours, 'I'm sorry about his wife.' He said nothing after that. Everything went much as he had expected.

22

The forks are the limit of my travels. Strictly speaking it's a confluence. Two rivers, creeks, rattle from their gorges and make one. I don't know which is the tributary and which the main river. After rain one may flow darker than the other. I have seen the left creek black with silt while the other runs clear as lemonade.

I sit on my rock munching peanuts. I have not seen the eel again but the old billy goat comes daily and looks at me. I wonder if he was tame once. Where are his wives drinking? Sometimes I think I smell him – a smell of age and nature – but it's probably my imagination. I smell the river: eels and scouring and decomposition. It smells clean.

There are mysteries. There are connections I cannot make. For half of Duggie's life Alaric Gibbs was ticking like a bomb. And Gibbs' life? Each was the centre of a universe.

Today I heard the rainbird – that urgent little song. It's beautifully exact. There's a knowledge there millions of years old. Before long rain hung in the gorges. The sun made a piece of rainbow in the curve of cliff down-river from me. Here is a place human will does not contaminate. I am gone from it but it's there, lying in the night. I can't imagine it. Imagination cannot touch it either.

I walked home in the rain – heavy rain rattling through the leaves and on my parka. I looked up and saw blue sky. And when I came out by the garden the clouds were black on the mountains and the sky was clear. The raked earth began to steam.

Sharon called me into the house and made me a cup of tea. She scolded me for getting wet. I must look after myself, she said, I'm not a boy any longer. I don't feel like a boy, but I don't feel like a man with high blood pressure either. I feel like a survivor. I feel like Ray, Ray Sole, Raymong, R. Sole. All of those. I've got some life in me. That's what I think. So I'll get to sleep, and in the morning put my things in the car and head for Thorpe.

Through the bush I hear Bella singing. Sharon plays her flute, an ancient sound, but a sound contrived. Carlo and Ché are yelling on the paths. Their mothers let them make their own bed-time. It's part of their programme in being free. I hope things work out for Sharon here.

Tomorrow I'll kiss her goodbye. And offer a man's handshake to her friend. And to Ché. And kiss my Indian grandson if he'll let me. Then I'll go. Get on with it.

MORE ABOUT PENGUINS, PELICANS AND PUFFINS

For further information about books available from Penguins please write to Dept EP, Penguin Books Ltd, Harmondsworth, Middlesex UB7 0DA.

In the U.S.A.: For a complete list of books available from Penguins in the United States write to Dept DG, Penguin Books, 299 Murray Hill Parkway, East Rutherford, New Jersey 07073.

In Canada: For a complete list of books available from Penguins in Canada write to Penguin Books Canada Ltd, 2801 John Street, Markham, Ontario L3R 1B4.

In Australia: For a complete list of books available from Penguins in Australia write to the Marketing Department, Penguin Books Australia Ltd, P.O. Box 257, Ringwood, Victoria 3134.

In New Zealand: For a complete list of books available from Penguins in New Zealand write to the Marketing Department, Penguin Books (N.Z.) Ltd, P.O. Box 4019, Auckland 10.

In India: For a complete list of books available from Penguins in India write to Penguin Overseas Ltd, 706 Eros Apartments, 56 Nehru Place, New Delhi 110019

Also by Maurice Gee in Penguins

MEG

The second volume in Maurice Gee's trilogy – 'A family chronicle of uncommon intimacy and strength' – *Guardian*

Meg is the youngest of the Plumb children. Emotionally dominated by her family – the terrifying George Plumb, a man driven to extremity by his wayward conscience; a loving, exhausted mother; her flawed and contradictory brothers and sisters – Meg is the one who cares best.

For fifty years she watches as they grow up into a New Zealand of the Depression and post-war boom, lovingly gathering up the harvest of their lives – and deaths – in this harshly tender, passionate quest to uncover the truth about them . . . and herself.

'Maurice Gee's trilogy is shaping towards the realization of as rich a tapestry as we have had so far of contemporary social life' – *Auckland Star*

A Selection of Penguins

AN ICE-CREAM WAR
William Boyd

As millions are slaughtered on the Western Front, a ridiculous and little remarked-on campaign is being waged in East Africa – a war that continued after the Armistice because no one told them to stop.

Primarily a gripping story of the men and women swept up by the passions of love and battle, William Boyd's magnificently entertaining novel also elicits the cruel futility and tragedy of it all.

'A towering achievement' – John Carey

'Quite outstanding' – *Sunday Times*

'If you can imagine John Buchan or Rider Haggard rewritten by Evelyn Waugh then you have something of the flavour of this book . . . Very funny' – Robert Nye in the *Guardian*

GINGER, YOU'RE BARMY
David Lodge

When it isn't prison, it's hell.

Or that's the heartfelt belief of conscripts Jonathan Browne and Mike 'Ginger' Brady. For this is the British Army in the days of National Service, a grimy deposit of post-war cynicism. It consists of one endless, shambling round of kit layout, square-bashing, shepherd's pie 'made from real shepherds', P.T. and drill relieved by the occasional lecture on firearms or V.D. The reckless, impulsive Mike and the more pragmatic Jonathan adopt radically different attitudes to this two-year confiscation of their freedom . . . and the consequences are dramatic.

A Selection of Penguins

VIDA
Marge Piercy

A dozen lovers, two hundred friends, thousands who had heard her speak at rallies . . .

In the sixties she was a symbol of passionate rebellion; now Vida Asch is forced to live as a fugitive. Years spent fleeing the FBI, travelling in disguise, and the experience of bitter sexual and political rivalries threaten to splinter her commitment. In her struggle to survive Vida has learned to trust no one, but when another outcast, Joel, enters her circle she finds herself reluctantly drawn to him . . .

THE BANQUET
Carolyn Slaughter

For months Harold watches and admires Blossom before he finds the courage to approach her . . .

Between them develops a rapport at first exquisite and fragile, then deepening to a consuming passion. Gradually Blossom realizes that this is forever – and that Harold has chosen her for something quite extraordinary. Propelled by an obsession both painful and terrifying, Blossom and Harold are swept towards the affair's horrifying climax.

A Selection of Penguins

WHITE MISCHIEF
James Fox

'A story which is as compelling and violent as a thriller, but which also happens to be one of the most dazzling feats of reportage in recent years' – *Time Out*

When the body of Josslyn Hay, 22nd Earl of Erroll, was discovered with a bullet through his handsome head just outside Nairobi in January 1941, the resulting scandal revealed a hornet's nest of upper-class decadence and misbehaviour . . .

'Marvellously entertaining' – Auberon Waugh

'Eccentric settlers and shady aristos, neurotic wives and sad drunks, *morphineuses* and lounge-lizards. The cast and setting are unique' – William Boyd

SCANDAL
A. N. Wilson

A rising star in the political firmament, Derek Blore has a reputation that is boringly impeccable. But is it? When Bernadette Wooley entertains every week the man she knows as Billy Bunter, she does not realize that her client is tipped as a future leader of his Party. Nor does she attach much importance to the hidden camera and tape recorder . . .

'Mr Wilson is a wonderfully funny writer in his wry, downbeat way' – Francis King in the *Spectator*

'Drily witty, deliciously nasty . . . rich entertainment' – *Sunday Telegraph*